Shadow Cell

A Novel

By

Joseph D'Antoni

Book 4 of the Wade Hanna Series

Copyright © 2015 Joseph D'Antoni
All rights reserved.

ISBN-13: 978-0-9830816-6-1

Library of Congress Control Number: 2015918246
ROYAL OAK PRESS*, PASADENA, CA
Printed in the United States of America

He soon changed his focus to the time period before the mission. During the four years of supervising his Intelligence training, Megan and Wade's relationship grew into something very special and personal. During his training time together the couple kept intimate emotions at bay because of the long physical distance between them, frequent college deadlines, training commitments and a professional respect for each other's professional relationship. After his graduation, their formal reporting relationship ended and there was nothing to stop their personal relationship from blossoming. Just as those personal feelings toward one another peaked, Megan vanished. Wade strained to recall details of what each had said to the other moments before departing on his mission, hoping it would lead to some small clue about her disappearance. The details were important but Wade found it difficult trying to recreate exactly what they had said to each other just before he left.

He was trying to remember exact words that might have given subtle signs he missed at the time. They always spoke over secure lines, but Wade had become increasingly suspicious about what Agency technology he could trust. It was not difficult remembering the plans they discussed on several long night calls. They would live together and share a foreign posting. Both were serious about taking the next step in their relationship as they eagerly awaited the right intelligence assignment to bring them together.

While Wade worked his way through the remaining final Agency courses, Megan advanced through the ranks of the Intelligence service to become assistant director for the CIA's Officer Training Unit (OTU) in Washington. He recalled how everything in their relationship seemed right, perhaps too ideal, before he departed on his Morocco mission. Something happened while he was gone and Wade now realized he may have missed clues Megan was trying to send on those calls. Wade was not a believer in coincidence when it came to intelligence matters so trying to convince himself their relationship and her disappearance was coincidental wasn't going to work.

Reflecting back in time, Wade remembered the only strain to their relationship had occurred when he became suspicious of Megan's questions about the sniper incident at the training session in Fort Benning, Georgia. Suspicions arose when Megan's questions contained information that she or the Agency could not have known. As her questions became more probing he reacted by withdrawing and making his answers vague and unresponsive. Suspicions caused his feelings toward Megan to cool. Megan and whoever might be listening in on their calls must have sensed his suspicions as she suddenly backed off. Although trying not to show his true inner feelings, Wade felt she or the Agency may have realized they were not going to get any more information out of him about that incident.

Cutting Megan off from his real feelings wasn't easy, but at the time he didn't know whom he could trust. Looking back, Wade wondered if Megan was trying to secretly communicate with him. Could it be that her questions were asked knowing that someone on the line was listening? Wade suddenly realized he was so preoccupied with his own investigation and suspicions that he may not have been listening to her closely enough. Wade now realized Megan may have understood exactly what she was doing. It was very possible that she was speaking to him in code because the Agency was recording their conversations.

Since most of their relationship occurred over long distance lines, there was little opportunity to express his suspicious feelings of her and the Agency even if no one was listening. Bringing back those forgotten old suspicions wasn't easy for Wade. With the passage of time even the murder of Special Forces soldier James Lockhart took on a separate life of its own. After the murder investigation settled down the shakiness in their relationship seem to also subside. They both had moved on and become closer in the months before his departure to Tangier.

With Megan gone, those suspicious times now took on more importance. Perhaps he had more insight into the Agency's wrongdoings. His mission to Belize had proven without question that at some level his Agency operated a death squad outside of official lines of authority. What Wade didn't know was if Megan knew anything about those activities. If she did was she trying to communicate or warn him just before her disappearance?

Wade racked his brain straining to remember fragments of those conversations with Megan about the Fort Benning incident. He remembered one incident they had discussed about Fort Benning like it happened yesterday. It was no accident that his team came under live sniper fire during a so-called normal night training exercise. The uncontrolled outburst of a psychologically impaired, professionally trained sniper was deadly and was never supposed to happen, especially on an Army base.

Two days after the incident the suspected sniper was found dead in a motel room just off the base, presumably a suicide. The homicide investigation that followed uncovered more clues about Lockhart's death. Led by a veteran homicide detective Gabe Morrison, the investigation at the very least pointed to a cover-up involving the base. Morrison's final conclusion was that the sniper's death was not suicide but a carefully staged professional murder.

Wade's suspicions over Megan's questions started right after the sniper incident. Her numerous awkward probing questions seemed to come from someone above her at the Agency. Megan denied that her questions were being asked or guided by anyone above her but Wade didn't trust that explanation and decided it was better to back off than push.

If the incident topic arose he just simply withdrew from revealing details. For a few questions he just made up bogus answers to see where they would resurface. Most of what Wade learned from the Morrison investigation he kept from Megan. At the time he felt Megan knew that he was giving only partial answers and sometimes misleading information. For some reason he couldn't explain why his feeling that Megan somehow knew that he was giving incomplete or bogus information bothered him more now than it did at the time.

Even when he heard his misinformation being repeated by the Army, in his heart Wade never believed Megan was knowingly part of a cover-up. Wade asked himself why she would have an interest in misdirecting the investigation of the Lockhart murder. He didn't have an answer now. He wondered at the time did he just tell himself if she was being manipulated by senior people above her? His later investigation revealed that staging of Lockhart's death came about from Agency people who desperately wanted this murder to appear in the records as a suicide.

Reflecting on how Megan's interest in the investigation changed, Wade remembered how quickly it diminished when the case turned from suicide to murder. He recalled at the time his coolness toward her came more as a result of cautious uncertainty rather than anything she did or said. At one point for some unknown reason, Megan's questions about the incident suddenly stopped as quickly as they started.

Wade remembered that several weeks after Megan stopped asking him questions another telling moment in their relationship emerged. Despite his instincts telling him not to, Wade shared his concerns with Megan about suspected Agency wrongdoing and he recalled Megan's response had been unexpected.

After initially brushing off his concerns Megan suddenly shared some of her own concerns about the Agency. At first they were things like protocol inconsistencies and people at different positions being treated unfairly. As she shared more of what she felt, her concerns expanded and took on greater importance. The more she shared the more she became invested in doing her own Agency investigation. At first Wade was suspicious of her quick change in attitude. Sharing similar Agency concerns seemed to become an increasing part of their discussions. The more they both investigated, the more sinister their concerns became. As they shared more new information about the Agency their fractured relationship seem to come back together again.

In fact, Megan's investigations of the Agency became more intense than Wades' efforts. When they last spoke before he left on his Tangier mission, Megan was into the next level of her investigation which had already included probing "Classified" files at the Pentagon on certain senior Agency officials involved in a drug investigation cover up.

Not to be outdone by her lover and junior officer Wade, Megan turned up the level of intensity on her own internal investigation. When it came to details and pure research Megan was more thorough than Wade. She used close friends working at the Pentagon to access documents which increasingly confirmed several of their mutual suspicions about certain officials.

Putting together smaller morsels of information led to an implication of higher-ranked military intelligence officers who were now retired. Her investigation exposed more ties between certain senior officials just before Wade departed on his undercover mission to Morocco. He never got to hear what Megan found in those last files before she disappeared.

Wade remembered frequently cautioning Megan about making sure her research sources and methods could not be discovered. She rebuffed his warnings indicating that she had that issue totally under control. She reminded Wade that this was her specialty and he need not worry.

While Megan pursued her investigation Wade pursued his own using different techniques and contacts. Even though the two always communicated on secure encrypted lines they rarely gave details or spoke about specifics of their investigative techniques. Wade wished now that he knew more about exactly how she was accessing files.

Working closely with homicide detective Morrison and his NSA friend, Harold Yankovich ("Yari"), Wade identified one suspect that appeared to be a likely member of the death squad team that had murdered Army vet Lockhart.

Additional homicide evidence revealed that after three tours of recon duty in the Mekong Delta Region of Vietnam this Special Forces vet was suffering from battle fatigue and was psychologically unstable. Discovery from his last Vietnam tour revealed that he also became aware of certain high-ranking military intelligence officers involved in private drug dealings in Vietnam. Field reports told that Special Forces

Lockhart snapped after becoming one of the only members of his platoon to survive the raid that got most of his team killed.

That raid was ordered by Daniel Spencer, an intelligence officer assigned to Lockhart's command. Spencer was to be a key witness in an internal drug investigation and one of several officers implicated in drug dealing. He never got to testify. His demise was met in a freakish hit and run automobile accident that was never solved after returning to North Carolina. Without Spencer's testimony, the drug investigation languished and was still pending when the Pentagon files were suddenly closed.

All of the parts of a clean Lockhart suicide fit except in the suspicious instincts of a keen-eyed Georgia homicide detective by the name of Gabe Morrison. Morrison saw small isolated pieces in the death scene that didn't support a suicide explanation. He followed his instincts and ordered his coroner to take a liver biopsy when none had been authorized by a pending court order.

After a court battle with Fort Benning over jurisdiction of the soldier's body, Morrison's instincts and subsequent lab tests turned out to be a turning point in the case. The tests confirmed evidence of the use of exotic paralyzing drugs. Despite the Army's adverse contention, this was a clear case of a sophisticated murder done by a professional death squad team.

Further investigation revealed that the murdered Special Forces vet may have been the only surviving member of his platoon with detailed knowledge of his superior officer, Daniel Spencer's drug dealings in Vietnam. Morrison speculated and Wade confirmed the drug involvement didn't stop with Spencer. It was too convenient that Lockhart's death followed the unsolved hit and run death of Spencer.

Wade became convinced that Spencer was a key player but not at the top of the food chain. With Spencer and Lockhart meeting untimely deaths it was uncertain who might be left to finger the chain of command behind the drug dealing ring in Vietnam and now death squad and off-the-books black operations.

With the help of Yari from the NSA, Wade was able to pinpoint one possible death squad member at the training location when the sniper incident occurred. That suspect was now conveniently out of reach of civil authorities on a classified undercover mission for the U.S. Military in the country of Belize.

Based largely on a hunch and without Megan's knowledge, Wade embarked on his own covert mission to find the suspect. Military and intelligence protocol all seemed to be standing in the way of Wade completing his mission to Belize. Not to be deterred and cleverly using intelligence resources, Wade found and interrogated the suspect. The details and purpose of his mission were never shared with Megan.

The mission not only extracted valuable information on how the Lockhart murder was conducted but confirmed the existence of a covert group still operating within U.S. Military Intelligence. It was that group which had issued the order to the death squad to remove Lockhart.

Wade learned from his suspect that this internal group of operatives he worked for would terminate anyone who knew too much or otherwise threatened the objectives or secrecy of the group. The tight network of "good old boys" included well-entrenched retired military and intelligence officers. Many of the senior leaders of this secret group, though now retired from the military, were the brains and resources behind private off-shore entities with lucrative contracts for mercenary services and off-the-book assignments for the U.S. Military and Intelligence Services. Unfortunately, his suspect just carried out orders. His superiors were clever enough to make sure Wade's suspect never knew the names of his superiors or the positions they held inside the military and government. Orders were always given through a chain of command that assured no uplinks to the higher command were revealed.

At this point Wade could only speculate which senior individuals were at the very top of the food chain that ordered the death missions. He was hoping more links and proof would come from Megan's file investigations which she was just starting when Wade left on his covert mission. Even suspecting that his own Agency might be involved, Wade didn't have an axe to grind with the government or anyone within his own department. He wasn't out to get anybody unless he found they were part of Megan's disappearance. If that became the case matters would quickly become very personal for Wade.

With Megan gone, Wade felt exposed and vulnerable to the same sources that were behind her disappearance. Committing himself to follow the trail wherever it led, Wade knew that he would not be able to apply accepted Agency protocol in his search. He wasn't big on Agency protocol anyway. He often had to circumvent rules and the law to get his missions accomplished.

Wade's investigative approach seemed unconventional when he applied skills he had learned from his early life in the Louisiana swamps. The only rules that mattered were the ones that worked. Spending long days solving mysteries of nature and understanding natural phenomena were just part of his early life in the primitive swamp.

11

His youthful curiosity and unconventional investigative techniques exposed him to some unpopular local notoriety. Around the time he was twelve his excursions led to tracking the illusive swamp creature known as the "Rougarou". After discovering long, reddish-blond hair snared on a cypress stump and a partial manlike footprint nearby, he tracked the creature deep into the swamp for several days, living off the land. Unsuccessful in his attempt to see or capture the beast, Wade turned to science for answers. He turned over the hairs and skin samples he had collected to local university scientists to have them genetically tested.

After eliminating bears, wild boars and other known mammals and vertebrates, scientists were unable to confirm which species the hairs belonged to. The scientists only indicated his samples were "primate-like". Not to be deterred, Wade continued his search for several more months ignoring local newspaper articles which referred to him as "an imaginative swamp-child subject to hoaxes".

He never faltered in his belief that what he had found was an unknown species that had survived in the depths of the swamp. His frequent response to the media calls and others who would listen was, "The mere lack of evidence doesn't disprove the lack of existence. Look at all the dinosaur species that existed long before their fossil evidence was discovered." Wade continued his tracking even though most of his friends and a few others ignored his systematic investigative approach. They laughed at him thinking he might be a little crazy.

Chapter 2

One of the things that concerned Wade about his Agency was that they knew far more about him and his relationship with Megan than he knew about them. He came to this belief when the Agency, perhaps without realizing it, exposed themselves just prior to officer graduation in Wade's final polygraph exam.

The required exam lasted several hours and by the questions asked Wade knew that the Agency was aware or suspected things about him that were beyond his imagination. The examiner questions probed into people's names outside the Agency's influence or knowledge, details about which the Agency could not have known even to the point of asking if he and Megan had sex. Questions from the examiner also told Wade that they already knew certain things about the Fort Benning incident and names of military personnel that went well beyond the incident or information he had provided. Their questions involved military personnel in the Vietnam drug trade, which told Wade that they were more deeply involved than Spencer.

Before copies of research files from Megan's investigation reached Wade, he had already departed on his undercover mission to North Africa. The couple hadn't spoken since he left and his return appearance at her office was to be a surprise. That plan quickly turned when Wade found it was he who was the one surprised. Not only was Megan missing but her entire department had been replaced. During his ride to the airport Wade felt alone. Contemplating his sole quest to find her and a future without her struck him hard. He would not rest until he got answers.

Emotions boiled in Wade's mind during the return flight to Alabama. He squirmed, strapped in his seat, not being able to stop his mind from systematically analyzing all the moving parts of Megan's disappearance. The process was too complex to understand. He couldn't separate fact from emotion. All he needed right now was quiet space and familiar surroundings to think things through. He couldn't wait for the plane to land on Alabama soil.

Thoughts of all the new and absent faces at Megan's old office contributed to Wade's uncertainty. From the new people he spoke to no-one even knew Megan's name. There was no trace of her name on the appointment calendar or the reception desk files he saw. It was as though she had never existed in that department. Her condo had been sold in an equally mysterious manner. The husband and wife who purchased the condo had no knowledge of Megan's name as the seller in the transaction.

Megan's department head, Tony Shaw, had been hurriedly transferred to a remote covert assignment in the Middle East and was unreachable. This was a wholesale administrative change of Megan's entire department. In addition to Megan, perhaps other identities were being erased. Wade's feelings bounced back and forth between feelings of personal loss and anger. He worried he might never see her again. That she was no longer alive. His anger boiled when he thought of her being held in the Agency's custody and what she might be subjected to if she were still alive. Like Shaw, they could have sent her on some covert mission deep undercover and erased traces of her prior existence.

As the plane's wheels touched down on the Alabama tarmac Wade felt that some pressure had been lifted, that some spiritual referee had just called a *time out* giving him a moment of mental relief. His mind finally went blank in tentative relaxation for the few minutes of touchdown and taxi as he listened to the engines whine down when the plane went from a slow roll to a stop.

On the drive to his apartment, the clean air and serene surroundings settled over Wade like a blanket of comfort. Pulling up to his apartment complex he finally felt at home. Exhausted from the non-stop tension of his foreign mission and Megan's loss he would try to sleep in a familiar bed knowing when he awoke he would face the same uncertain beast he had lived with since early that morning.

His night was restless but Wade woke early the next morning with hackles standing at attention on his neck. The waking memory of his dreams and instincts reminded him that a serious cover-up or death eliminating the person he cared most about was in progress. He knew first-hand that whoever was pulling the side strings at the Agency would stop at nothing, including murder, as a means of maintaining control.

Wade fought the emotion of striking back at anything or anybody that would cause Megan harm as he tried to stay focused on facts that were needed to get to the bottom of what had really happened. He had to think like a covert operative not a lonely lover because his new self-appointed mission of finding her meant he could be taking on an entire army of covert operatives. In fact, Wade had to think beyond the mind of a covert operative. He had to be smarter and become even more clandestine than the operatives he would be facing since they always seem to be one step ahead of him with far more resources at their disposal.

For the next few days he vacillated between deep longing for Megan's presence and recovery from his dangerous Morocco mission. Getting back to the simple drudgery of everyday life of doing laundry, cleaning house and running errands actually provided relief. All the while, his mind darted back and forth trying to put small pieces of unrelated parts into a complex moving mosaic.

After several sleepless nights, Wade recommitted himself to his old familiar strenuous workout routine. He set the alarm for 4:30 a.m. and headed to the college stadium track for a three mile run followed by an hour of heavy weight workout at the gym and two hours at the firing range.

After a few days, small pieces of the puzzle started coming together mainly in the form of questions. He knew from experience that it was almost impossible to completely erase someone's identity, even with the resources of the Agency. Somewhere along the way there would be a small clue, some overlooked piece of information that didn't get covered up. He would start there and follow every small lead that each piece gave him.

Throughout his investigation and search Wade realized he had to keep his eye on the big picture. If Megan got too close to the sources she was investigating about the death squad she may have been terminated. If that was the case he couldn't help her now but he wouldn't rest until he brought down whatever cell or system killed her to his own personal justice. In the process he had to avoid making the same mistake she had made. If Megan was still alive he needed to find her, hold her and tell her about his feelings for her that never seemed to come across over long-distance lines.

Wade's strategy for the next several days was straight forward. He approached his task of making detailed lists of every little piece of information he could remember with unprecedented discipline. He started with the details he could most easily remember – the conversations he had with Megan just before he deployed to Canada prior to his North Africa mission. He proceeded with details in reverse order working his memory like a muscle he was honing on his body.

Each day Wade's list grew. One detail led to another, then another. Most of the pieces seemed insignificant and isolated, not fitting with anything else he had written. Wade recorded thoughts as they came to mind without any time sequence or order. Each morsel of information stood like an island not linked to anything else. As he stood back and looked at his pages no magical scheme or seminal moment stood out.

The thoughts and facts on the page looked like small strands of spaghetti all going in random directions. He sometimes smiled as he remembered Megan making a silly comment. The silliest comments made the list even if Megan made them at the wrong time and place and had no particular meaning. At times Wade wondered if his exercise would produce anything but random sheets of memory.

He tried remembering small details of what she told him about her research while he was in Belize. Some of her comments made sense, others did not. He even wrote down references Megan had made about her father before he died when she was still a teenager. There were phone calls between them, names of friends she had dinner or lunch with, meetings she attended for the Agency in the evenings, events and committees she participated in for the Agency and other recruits in training she was handling.

By the end of the second day Wade's lists made up dozens of pages. He let the lists sit for a day, glancing only in their direction while he performed other chores. After a day passed he added a few more remembered pieces.

Soon he started drawing simple, light pencil lines between items on the lists even when the connection was faint or far apart in time. Space on the wall of his apartment was cleared to hang a large cork board he had acquired.

The board was quickly filled with the lists all pinned neatly in line but with no particular order of time or purpose. After looking at the lists periodically during the day he would change the order of a few pages and draw a few more lines. At one point during this process Wade was starting to detect a pattern and reordered the pages in what appeared to be a rough timeline.

By the end of the following day twenty plus pages of lists extended the full length and breadth of the board making up the seemingly endless array of free flowing thoughts, names and phrases. Some notations on the lists were merely abbreviations of Megan's comments or places which only Wade could interpret while other items were of feelings he had which just seemed to hang in open air, unconnected and without meaning.

He rearranged the order of pages several times before narrowing his focus on two major parts of the lists which kept grabbing his attention. He circled those areas. One area of the lists was comments made in conversations just before going silent for his North African mission. Highlighting those comments made Wade realized how strongly Megan had tried to dissuade Wade from going on his mission. Until that moment Wade didn't realize how strong Megan's intent was even though her comments were disguised as polite, what conventionally-correct protocol would allow.

Her concern for his safety must have been part of it but was there a hint of something else in her voice which he didn't recognize or suspect at the time. Only now did there seem to be a subtle warning. Was she trying to tell him something else but couldn't or wouldn't say it? There was something else that was bothering her. Both perplexed and frustrated at himself with his new discovery, Wade wondered what overriding suspicions Megan had at the time.

His mind flashed to another incident. He remembered a telephone call from Belize about what her investigation was turning up at the Pentagon. That's when Wade first sensed Megan's suspicions that someone higher up in the Agency was covering up a classified federal investigation of drug dealing in Vietnam. He remembered she followed up with a detective in North Carolina who had investigated Daniel Spencer's mysterious hit and run accident shortly after he returned to the U.S.

Wade circled those points on his board. He contemplated as he pointed the pencil at his circled areas. His memory jogged between those two points representing the point in time when he and Megan's concerns about the Agency's secret operations were most aligned.

Megan had confidence in her ability to access confidential files at the Pentagon – perhaps overconfidence, Wade thought. There was someone at the Pentagon she trusted to do the digging. It had to be an insider. He made the note and just scratched his head trying to remember if she ever mentioned her friend's name at the Pentagon.

From his board of thoughts and squiggly pencil lines Wade crafted a list of questions. He combined those questions with notes he made after listening to tapes of his interrogation of the murder suspect, Mashburn. Not realizing it at first, his list of questions became an outline of the facts he needed to start his investigation. He circled the most important items on the list and prioritized them before picking up the phone to call the secure line of his close friend and confidant Yari, at the NSA.

Chapter 3

The secure phone line rang several times before Wade heard a familiar voice.

"Yari here."

"It's me, Wade."

You could tell from Yari's voice that he was glad his friend was on the line.

"Wade, where the hell have you been?"

"I just got back from that covert mission in North Africa."

Yari craved more details, vicariously admiring his field agent friend who put it all on the line.

"I can't wait to hear about that."

Wade had to curtail Yari's enthusiasm.

"You know I can't talk about the mission. Let's just say it went well and I'm safely back in Alabama."

"Did you like overthrow a foreign government or something?"

"Something like that."

"Well, I'm glad you're back. A lot has been going on while you were away."

Wade hoped he was now going to be told about the personnel upheaval in the Agency.

"Fill me in starting from the beginning since we last spoke. I've been under deep cover and clueless about anything going on here."

Yari was quick to respond. "On the Lockhart matter, Detective Morrison has subpoenaed records and the deposition of several officers in military intelligence. The Army is fighting the production of any documentation every step of the way, but Morrison is not giving ground."

"That's good. Morrison is a tough cookie."

Yari was proud and anxious to tell his friend, "I've been given a small promotion here. I'm in charge of upgrading our encryption protocol."

Yari started giving details of his new promotion but Wade's focus was on Megan's disappearance and he needed to hear about the change that might provide clues. Out of politeness Wade remained silent as Yari went on with details about NSA politics that were of little interest. He held his silence for a few more moments until he reached a point where he couldn't hold back any longer. When Wade saw the conversation wasn't going to address the administrative changes he interjected.

"That's great about your promotion and I don't mean to interrupt your story but I have a few areas of concern that I want to talk to you about."

Yari realized he had been dominating the conversation and stopped, asking, "Sure. What's up?"

"When I returned from my mission I learned there had been a big personnel change in my training department. Do you know anything about that change?"

Yari quickly replied, "No I haven't heard anything. Aren't you technically out of that department now?"

"Yes, but I have friends that were in that department that seemed to have disappeared. Until I am assigned to a new posting I guess I still report to them."

"Haven't heard anything about it. Do you have any names you want me to check on?"

"Yes, I have two names for you. One is Tony Shaw and the other is Megan Winslow."

Yari didn't know Shaw's name but quickly recognized Megan's. "Isn't Megan the one you called from Belize?"

"Yes, she was helping do some research while I was on that mission." Continuing, Wade explained, "Tony Shaw is or was the head of our department. Both are gone."

After a brief pause, Yari responded, "That's strange."

"I agree. Does the agency or the NSA routinely record calls to and from the office?"

Yari thought for a moment before he responded. "Each department and Agency does it differently. I think most record incoming calls and some departments do a selection of outgoing calls. It's hard to say what they record and how long they keep those recordings."

Wade thought for a moment before asking, "What about encrypted calls."

"That gets more complicated. The recording procedure would be the same if they used an internal secure line. If it's an incoming call it depends on the encryption model they use and how secure the incoming line is."

Wade was thinking of his next question as Yari explained.

"What if the incoming calls are made from a secure line?"

"I will have to check. Each department has different policies. They want to remain secure even if the outside caller is using a secure phone. Of course if the phone is another agency's secure line I think I can decipher that call even if it is encrypted."

Yari continued with a question, "What time period do you have in mind?"

After pausing to think Wade responded, "If I can get incoming and outgoing calls for the last six-month period that would be great."

Yari hesitated before he replied, "Can you tell me what this is about? I don't want to be caught investigating our own people without some kind of authorization."

Wade thought about Yari's concern but needed to be emphatic. "I definitely don't want any attention called to this. My interest is these people were suddenly transferred or are on some covert mission and are no longer even listed as having even been part of their department."

"That's heavy."

"You're damn right it's heavy. It may tie to something I was doing on my mission to Belize. I just need to know where they are. I am especially interested in who Megan spoke with and any record of conversations she had with anyone in the last three months."

"I hear you man. We both could get in some serious trouble if I'm caught digging around in our Agency calls."

Wade thought for a moment before responding, "You need to have a good cover story for your assignment just in case anyone catches you."

Wade's comment puzzled Yari. "What kind of cover?"

"I'm not exactly sure how your department works but you need to have some kind of authorization in hand to cover yourself. Perhaps you could get a memo confirming that you are checking the encryption integrity of certain phones as part of your new promotion."

A light went off in Yari mind. "That's a great idea! One of my bosses here I know pretty well. He really helped in my promotion. Maybe I could ask him."

Wade considered Yari's last comment and felt he needed to be more careful in his guidance.

"As a suggestion I think you might have a memo authorizing you to do random checks of Agencies to see that the encryption protocol is consistent between Agencies and departments. Think like a covert agent in your mission."

Yari liked being considered as a covert agent on a mission. He was quick to respond to Wade's suggestion.

"I like that suggestion. It gives me an idea. As part of my promotion I am supposed to come up with a new job description. I can do this as a separate research project and get my encryption boss to sign off on it."

Wade was pleased with how quickly Yari picked up on his idea.

"That sounds good, just remember not to reveal either of those two names I gave you or reference them in any memo or report."

Yari was quick to acknowledge Wade's request. He was excited to be working with and unofficially under Wade again.

"This could be a fun project. I will have to see what they have in recorded files. Give me the last phone numbers and extension for Shaw and Winslow you have and I'll get back to you soon."

Wade provided Yari with the office and home numbers and the last dates he knew that they were in use before he replied, "Now you're thinking like a true covert agent."

Yari couldn't wait to get started. "I'll get back to you soon, partner. By the way, who do you report to now?"

"That's a good question. I am technically on leave from my last mission and hoping they'll forget about me for a while. I don't want to rattle any cages or draw attention to me. They'll assign someone for me to report to soon enough."

"I hear you."

They both exchanged farewell greetings before ending the call.

The next day Wade resumed his two-hour workout and equally long session at the firing range before he called his father and a few friends. On his way out of the apartment Wade stopped for a few minutes to examine the Megan list on his board. He would often add a few more items and connecting lines when he passed. Many additions were quick flashes of memory he had previously overlooked.

For the moment Wade concentrated on Shaw. He wondered why someone who had been in an administrative position so long and that high in his department would suddenly be sent back to the field. *Was he really in the Middle East or on another covert assignment?* It had been years since Shaw served as a field agent. He knew Shaw was too much of a career administrator and enjoying the suburban D.C. lifestyle to suddenly want to be in some undercover operation somewhere off the map in an unknown Middle Eastern town. Something wasn't right about his assignment or the reason for his sudden departure.

As far as Wade knew his training department was doing just fine. The move didn't fit him or the profile of his office. He couldn't rule out the possibility of a political hatchet job on Shaw. The thought seemed unlikely. Shaw shook too many hands with a smile and he was certainly considered to be in a "safe" if not cushy "training" department as far as drawing attention in Washington. Other than a few typical end-of-year budget contentions, his department drew little attention. It was considered a model of how good government intelligence departments ran. They made few political waves and were always parading their bright young officers before some congressional committee for awards.

From what Wade knew about Shaw he couldn't see his reassignment coming as a request from Shaw and he certainly didn't see it as a promotion. It was possible that it was a demotion but that didn't jive with all the accolades their department received about exceeding goals.

Perhaps, Wade thought, the Agency had reason to hide him outside of public or congressional investigating committee reach.

From all the internal memorandums and discussions he had with Megan, the department wasn't being reduced or shut down because of budget cuts or change in administration. The department now operated with the same complement of people, just different people in all the key administrative positions. There had to be an explanation, either officially or off the record, that only a few people knew about.

On further thought Wade reasoned that perhaps what happened to Shaw could provide clues to Megan's fate. His instinct told him that the two events were somehow connected. Wade thought long and hard about where he might go within the agency to find the "unofficial story" of the department reorganization without raising suspicions about his inquiry.

Chapter 4
Zurich, Switzerland

There was someone Wade knew that might have an answer or could get one. But reaching out with probing questions to any colleague at this point was not without risk. Wade concluded that the risk was worth it if Leo had or could find the answer. What he didn't know was how much he could trust Leo.

He had to approach the topic carefully with Leo. Even though they had bonded on his last assignment Wade knew Leo held everything close to the vest and wasn't sure who else in the company Leo confided in. Wade thought a direct approach with questions might get the best results from Leo. He knew Leo would pick up on the slightest uncertainty in Wade's voice or the slightest diversion in his purpose. Wade had to be straight with Leo. The last thing Wade could afford was Leo suspecting he was not being honest or had some ulterior motive.

Shaw was supposedly on an international assignment and when it came to covert international assignments Wade knew Leo had his hands on the pulse of most international operations, especially if they dealt with black ops. Leo was also no stranger to Middle East covert operations.

Wade wasn't sure Leo would share everything he knew but felt he trusted him enough that their conversations would be kept confidential. Before he made the call Wade made detailed notes about why he was calling and what he wanted. His approach with Leo would be critical. Wade knew Leo operated out of the Agency's Zurich Intelligence office but was never at that office. He was a ghost that operated everywhere and part of his survival plan was no one could pin him down. Wade had Leo's direct secure number but felt it was best to leave a nondescript message at the Zurich office knowing that it would be recorded.

The secretary picked up Leo's phone answering in German. Wade knew that she spoke perfect English.

"Good morning, Greta. This is Wade Hanna."

"How are you, Mr. Hanna? It is nice to hear your voice."

"I heard on the international channel that you were having good weather."

Greta answered without hesitation, "It's my favorite time of year."

"I don't expect that Mr. Leopold is in the office today?"

"No, you are correct, he is not here. You know he travels a lot."

"I know. I would just like to leave a message that I called to see how he is doing. Please ask him to call me when he gets a chance. It's not urgent."

"I should be speaking with him when he calls in a day or so and will give him your message. Does he have your phone number?"

Wade thought for a moment before he responded knowing Leo would never call unless he was on a secure, encrypted number. "It's the same number he has, no changes."

"Good speaking with you, Mr. Hanna."

As the call ended Wade thought he had said enough to get a call back but wasn't sure how long it would take. Leo was probably in the middle of a covert mission.

It had been four days since he spoke to Yari when the phone rang. The voice on the other end spoke with the excitement of a young kid winning a baseball game. After "hello" the excited voice of Yari was mixed with some concern and confusion.

"It's me, Yari. I think I have something but I'm not sure what."

Wade responded with an equal sense of uncertainly. "Well tell me what you have, maybe we can figure it out."

"It took me forever, but I finally got into Shaw and Megan's recorded departmental phone lines. It was strange that their department only recorded a small fraction of the calls. It was either that or a lot were erased after-the-fact."

Wade pondered Yari's statement before following with a question. "Were the calls you reviewed all encrypted?"

Yari responded, "Some were encrypted but that wasn't the problem. They used an older encryption program two generations behind what we use now. It wasn't difficult to decipher the encryption."

Wade responded, "Then what was the problem?"

Yari paused before responding. "I'm looking at this voice data we downloaded. It seems a lot of the conversations were broken off in mid-sentence or partially erased after the call was recorded. I don't know any department in the government that uses that technique or has that type of recording and security policy. I can tell you the recordings we looked at were all manipulated after they were taped."

Yari took a deep breath before continuing. "At first I thought there was a glitch in the recording system but I had my guys do a voiceover analysis and scan each voice sequence into small segments. Then I had them perform a technical analysis on each segment. In every case the erase or override distortion was applied after the initial recording was made."

Wade asked, "Then why the random pattern to all this? Why not just destroy the tape or erase everything?"

Yari was ready with a reply. "It looks to me that whoever did this went to the trouble of trying to make it look like there was some mechanical malfunction of the recording device. Like something was causing a scratching or erratic erasure process, like the recording device was skipping sections on the tape. It was not the work of a faulty recording device. We are breaking out segments of the conversations trying to separate the squeaky override noise and rebuild the underlying conversation but that is going to take some time."

Wade scratched his head before responding, puzzled by Yari's explanation and not totally understanding the technology Yari was describing. "I'm not sure that I understand you, but rather than giving me the technical description of how they erased the tapes can you summarize what you did find?"

"Well, I haven't finished capturing all the data and analyzing the technical side but it seems they took random segments of conversations. Each conversation is so chopped up I can't put my finger on exactly what was done, how or why."

Wade was quick to respond, "Let me worry about the 'why'. Let's just focus right now on what pieces of conversation you do have."

"Right, let me start with Shaw. We don't have much of any conversations involving him during the last two days leading up to his departure. A few sounds like code words were recovered in broken conversations the week before he left. That's all we have recovered right now."

"Can you tell from his conversation what Shaw's state of mind was?"

"What do you mean?"

"Did he sound concerned? Did he sound like there was anything urgent? Was he upset?"

Yari paused before he responded. "Perhaps a little urgent or surprised but not upset."

Wade was ready with the next question. "What were some of the code words you thought you heard in Shaw's conversations?"

Yari scanned the data in front of him before responding. "Let me see. I have a list here. One was Blue Sand. There was another term, Operation Spire and what sounded like Pawnee Blanket. None of these checked out on my list of covert operations in play. Also, the way the terms were used made no sense as part of the rest of the conversation we picked up. Do those names mean anything to you?"

Wade thought for a moment before he responded. "They don't to me but it gives me something to work on. Was there anything else you found on Shaw?"

"There seems to be a lot of conversation over scheduled meetings he had to attend. It looks like Shaw was going to be doing a lot of travelling."

"Were you able to get any dates or places of the meetings?"

"Nope, they were erased or the speech pattern was intentionally distorted."

Wade asked, "What do you mean by distorted?"

Yari tried to explain using as non-technical terms as he could.

"It was like a sound track of white noise of some kind was being inserted over the real conversation, like metal scraping or a loud machine running that drowned out the conversation when a code name was used."

Wade wanted to know why Yari used machinery to describe the sound and asked, "Did it sound like he was speaking from some machine shop or factory?"

Yari thought about where Wade was going with his question and answered, "No, I was able to separate the different sound waves into separate tracks. The machinery noise wasn't an actual factory background sound at the time. It was applied after the conversation."

The explanation didn't make sense to Wade. "Why would anyone go through the trouble to override the sounds in that manner when they could just erase it?"

Yari contemplated Wade's question before responding, "Good question and one that has been puzzling me as well. The only explanation I have deals with standard recording protocol employed by the Agency."

"What do you mean?" Wade asked.

"All the Agency tapes routinely go through a quality control check periodically like every two months. The tapes are run through a high speed sorter that doesn't listen to the conversation. It just looks for inconsistent fluctuations."

Wade quickly replied, "So when they do the QC check as long as there is sound in place they pass the distortion test?"

Yari was shaking his head up and down. "That's right. In other words, if there are no large spaces with no magnetic activity the tape is deemed to pass. Getting through QC means it could be months or never before anyone actually listens to the individual sound on the tape. Most tapes are just archived."

Wade was thinking. "So a tape that passes QC might sit on a shelf for years before a distortion is discovered?"

"You got it."

"Now that we have the distorted taped conversations how long do you think it will take to break them down and reconfigure them?"

"That's hard to say. I'm going to have to work on a sample before I can give you an estimate. I should have some answers in about a week."

Wade paused before commenting, "Why don't we just focus now on what little bits of information you were able to capture. You did a great job. Take your time and try to get as much of the conversations reconstructed as you can. Can we turn to Megan?"

Yari reshuffled his papers before responding. "We have a slightly different situation with the analysis of Megan's conversations. First, there are more gaps in her tapes."

"What do you mean?" Wade asked.

"There were days leading up to her departure where there were no telephone conversations using her phone lines at all but there were conversations from other lines on her tape. "

Wade was quick to react, "That's strange. She was on the phone constantly."

Yari responded, "I have been spending most of my time on the Shaw tapes but I did pick up a few of Megan's conversations. They were also partially erased or distorted."

Wade was listening to Yari's description intently. As he formulated his next question his eyes were glued to his memory board tacked on the wall in front of him.

Wade asked, "Do you know the dates for the conversations you have?"

Yari shuffled his papers. "During the four days prior to her departure we captured four partial conversations. Of those conversations, we were only able to identify two of the calls."

Wade had his pen poised upright between his fingers, anxious to hear Yari's next words.

"One call is to a Beverly at the Pentagon. Let me read what we have to you. It starts out with, 'Hi Bev, I was able to get reservations at the World indistinguishable Grille.' The rest of the conversation was distorted by a sound override."

At that instant Wade realized he had heard the name Beverly before. In fact Megan had mentioned her name several times before. They served with on several intelligence organizing committees.

Wade turned to his list on the wall. There were numerous times when Megan indicated she had a friend at the Pentagon that was doing research on the Vietnam connections. Wade's silence while he connected the dots seemed to unsettle Yari. He broke the uncomfortable silence by asking, "Did I say something that bothered you?"

Wade came out of his concentration but wasn't yet ready to share his thoughts with Yari.

"No, in fact you did really well. I was just thinking about something else. By the way, did you get a phone number for Beverly?"

"Well, of course partner, I wouldn't be doing my job if I hadn't."

"Great, let me have it."

Yari gave Wade the number. The prefix looked familiar and he confirmed it with Yari.

"Isn't that prefix from the Pentagon?" Wade asked.

"It sure is. I haven't checked the extension or from what trunk line that feeds it but that number is to a secure phone in the Pentagon. Do you want me to check it out further?"

Wade was quick to answer. "Yes, but don't call the number or leave a trace. It would be better if you can also come up with her home number."

"I'm on it partner."

After getting the time and date of that call, Wade shifted the conversation slightly.

"What about that other telephone call with Megan?"

Yari responded with more mystery in his voice. "That's a strange one. It's going from Megan's secure line to a secure Army line I traced to Maryland."

Wade couldn't imagine who she would be calling at an Army facility unless it was to arrange a training session for a recruit. He waited for Yari's answer.

"As best as I can tell now this call is going to an Army medical doctor at the Army's Medical Research Institute of Infectious Diseases."

Wade immediately responded, "What? Why would she be calling there and what is that place?"

Yari replied, "I did some research. It's the facility that replaced the Army's Biological Warfare Laboratories at Fort Detrick, Maryland. The current facility was erected after the treaty on biological weapons was signed. It's located in the same place as the previous facility in Fort Detrick and is called the United States Army Medical Research Institute for Infectious Diseases and goes by the acronym of "USAMRIID".

"Who the hell came up with that acronym?" Wade reacted.

Yari laughed as he replied, "Who else but our government geeks rearranging the alphabet to confuse the general public."

Wade's frustration came through the call. "I can't deal with that acronym. How about a more user-friendly code name like 'Bug House'?"

"That works for me," Yari replied.

Wade redirected the conversation trying to find out more information. "Were you able to tell who Megan was calling at the Bug House?"

"On different calls she spoke to different people. There was one researcher by the name of Cathy and the other calls were to a Dr. Palmer," Yari replied, but was obviously confused about what all this meant and where Wade might be going with his thinking.

Yari asked, "What do you think is going on here with Megan and the Bug House?"

Wade's mind was spinning through options and alternative scenarios involving Megan when Yari's question hit. "I have no idea but you can bet I'm going to find out. Do you have a name and phone numbers for these calls?"

"Sure. We traced the extension to a Dr. Isaac "Chip" Palmer but I haven't had time to do any background investigation on him yet. I assume you would like me to do that."

Wade didn't hesitate to respond. "Yes, but be extremely careful not to leave any traces of your investigation. This is serious stuff."

"I understand partner. I should have something for you in a few days."

Wade responded by thanking Yari for his good work.

That evening Wade had a lot of items to add to his witness list and names of several individuals he needed to approach. With new disconnected pieces of isolated fragments his circle of confusion grew wider. He didn't have a sense of what was going on and couldn't stop the many alternative scenarios that kept running through his mind.

Wade concluded that he had to not only plan within this confusion but he had to do so without raising suspicions. Given the number of people who were now involved he told himself his task was not going to be easy. Now he needed more information from Yari and wondered why Leo hadn't returned his call.

The next day he created a list of who he had to call to find out if Beverly was still employed at the Pentagon. Wade had already concluded she was Megan's friend and probably one of her secret researchers if for no other reason than she had access to Pentagon files. He had to find out for certain. If she turned out to be one of Megan's researchers the Agency might already know and Beverly's continued government employment might be the least of her worries. Beverly just might be on the Agency's kill list.

Chapter 5

Greenstone, Alabama

Between training workouts and the firing range, Wade spent most of his spare time in the library at the university finding out all he could about the Army Medical Research Institute facility in Maryland and Dr. Isaac Palmer. While he waited for Yari's call on the phone recordings there was a lot of background research he could be performing on the people and purpose of the Bug House.

Four days after his call with Yari, Wade was relaxing with a late night peanut butter and jelly sandwich and glass of milk when the phone rang. He could instantly tell from the line delay and static that the call was coming from an overseas secure line with encryption. A clearly recognizable voice came through after a stream of static.

"Hey Kiddo, I understand you wanted to speak to me."

"Leo, it's good to hear your voice."

Wade knew that Leo wasn't one to mince words and didn't like to chit chat. He got Wade quickly on point when he asked, "What do you need?"

Wade had his story prepared knowing he had to be brief. "I ran into an issue here when I returned from our mission. I don't know if you remember Tony Shaw but in the two months I was away he and most of the senior people in my training department were removed and replaced by new people. None of the new people knew anything about the administrative change or where they went. I am particularly interested in Tony Shaw and my handler, Megan Winslow. I was wondering if you have any information about that."

There was a pause while Leo thought through his contacts. He finally responded, "Sounds like a 'clean-out' to me. I know Shaw but why do you think I would know anything about where he is? The company doesn't exactly consult me on domestic issues."

Wade replied, "I just found out from the department that Shaw was transferred to the Middle East on a covert assignment and I knew you were familiar with Middle East operations."

There was a pause before Leo answered, "That doesn't sound right to me. Shaw's been flying a desk for too long to be useful to any covert operation."

"I thought the same thing. The explanation sounded suspicious to me," Wade replied.

"That might just be his cover story. I can make a few calls to my people in the Middle East."

"That would be great. I really appreciate it."

Wade continued, "Did you by chance know a Megan Winslow? She also disappeared around the same time as Shaw. There are other people gone from the department as well but those are the main ones I'm interested in."

Leo thought before he answered, "I don't know any Megan but I can snoop around with her name as well. Let me ask you why are these department personnel changes bothering you? Haven't you graduated? Why do you care?"

"For one thing it was my department and I found these sudden changes suspicious and disturbing. The second thing is I knew Shaw, and I was close to Megan. It was not like her to just pick up and leave. I also found out that her condo had been sold and the new buyers didn't even know her name."

Leo was caustic in his comment, "Maybe you had feelings for her but she didn't feel the same about you."

Wade replied, "I don't think she would leave without telling me."

Leo took the opportunity to give Wade some advice. "Remember, you're doing covert intelligence work. Did you tell her you were leaving when you were on my mission?"

Realizing Leo had backed him into an uncomfortable corner, Wade responded, "No, but at least she knew I was on some kind of mission. She just didn't know any details."

"How do you know she's not on a mission?"

"I guess I don't."

Leo changed the subject a bit.

"Speaking about women, you know Angèle always asks about you?"

"Really, I had no idea."

"You made a real impression on her during the mission. I think you should stay in contact with her. You never know."

"Yeah I will do that."

Leo changed the subject again, catching Wade off guard. "Hey kiddo, remember when we were in Zurich I asked you to set up a Swiss bank account."

"Yeah, I remember."

"Have you ever checked the balances in that account?"

Being caught off guard, Wade took Leo's comments as being accusatory. "No. I set that account up for you."

Laughingly Leo replied, "No, kiddo, that account was for *you*, not me. It was in your name and you are the only one who has the security number. I hope you still have the number."

"Yes, I kept the number in coded form, thinking you might need it."

"Good. I think you may want to check your balance. You may be surprised."

Stunned, Wade was still not sure where Leo was going with his comment. He replied, "My balance? I'm not sure I understand."

"Everyone on my missions participates in proceeds recovered if there are any. We recovered substantial amounts on that mission so I divided the pickings between team members and myself. That's just my policy."

"Shouldn't that be U.S. or U.K. government money?"

"No, none of that money came from either country. It was blood money, Sikes was going to be paid by Mabuto. It had nothing to do with any government advances. If anything our mission saved both governments millions, far beyond what was recovered. Neither government is entitled to it nor do they want any part of the money or operation. Remember the money wasn't recovered as part of any sanctioned mission. If you would have been captured or killed on the mission the U.S. would have denied your existence. You earned that money free and clear. If you have ethical qualms about accepting it just give it to charity."

"That's amazing. I had no idea. Thank you. I'll check the account."

Leo was preoccupied with another mission. "Look kiddo, I have to run now. I'm in the middle of another operation here. I'll check on your people and get back to you in a few days."

"Thanks, keep safe, please tell Angéle hello for me," Wade replied.

"I will."

As soon as the call ended Wade immediately started searching through papers from his last mission quickly locating the coded sheet that contained his Swiss bank account number and banker's contact information.

In other circumstances Wade would likely be giving any extra money he received to charity or a non-profit organization trying to preserve the Louisiana swamp but right now that money meant covering expenses he would incur finding Megan.

After checking time differences in Switzerland, Wade made a call to the bank in Zurich. To his surprise the banker remembered Wade and the two cordially exchanged greetings. Hoping that there might be a few hundred or even a thousand dollars he could use for expenses, he was ill-prepared when the banker told him his account contained $50,000. After thanking the banker Wade's hand remained frozen in space just above the receiver. For the next few moments he just stared in disbelief at the blank wall in front of him.

The cost of funding his search for Megan was no longer an issue. Wade turned to his list of two calls he had to make. Beverly would be his first call, but even with a secure phone patch from Yari he wasn't comfortable with a call directly to the Pentagon while she was still at work. He would wait until the evening and call her at home. Between the calls with Leo and the Zurich banker Wade felt drained and decided to go out for lunch, do some library research and spend another hour at the firing range just to keep his head straight and priorities in order.

Instead of calling from his apartment phone Wade decided to insert another security step and call from a payphone but not the one nearest his apartment. He spotted another payphone near the firing range under the shade of a large oak tree. He timed his call for Beverly's time zone, hoping that she would be home. Before calling Beverly, Wade dialed Yari to set up a double secure encrypted patch to insure additional protection like he had done many times before.

"Hi Yari, it's me. I'm calling from a payphone in Greenstone and wondered if you could set up a double patch for me to call Beverly?"

"Sure. Not a problem. I'll use my security clearance and take the payphone out of service. That way I can put both sides of the call through my encryption software."

"That sounds great."

"Just hang up and give me about ten minutes to set everything up. I'll call you back when her line is ringing."

"Make sure you call her home number."

"Right."

The phone rang several times. Wade began to wonder if she was home. Finally a soft voice answered.

"Hello."

Wade answered, "Hi Beverly, this is Wade Hanna."

A silence came over the line. Wade responded with a, "Hello?"

In a nervous, suspicious voice Beverly responded, "Yes, how can I help you?"

Although he had never met Beverly before, Wade was not expecting the distant response he received. Quickly realizing she was suspicious of him Wade replied in a gentle voice, "I'm calling you from Greenstone, Alabama from a secure line that is encrypted in both directions. I am calling you to find out what I can about Megan and her disappearance."

Another awkward pause threw Wade off guard, confirming for him that there was definite fear in her voice.

In an uncertain tone she uttered, "How do I know you are who you say you are?"

There was an enormous amount of pressure behind her voice. Wade felt that his next comments had to be reassuring and calming for the conversation to continue.

"That's a perfectly logical question on your part, Beverly. What can I tell you that will help confirm I am Wade Hanna, Megan's lover?"

The next pause was longer than the previous ones. The next question was unexpected, taxing Wade's memory.

"Have you ever written poetry to her?"

"Yes, I wrote a poem for Megan just before leaving on my last mission."

"Can you recite some of the verses of that poem?"

"Give me a second." Wade closed his eyes trying to remember the poem. It seemed such a long time had passed since he wrote it. He hummed quietly to himself trying to get into a poetic state of mind. Parts of some verses appeared as random segments. Wade began reciting what he could remember.

"Where nymphs among the fountains play
Under sea nets I search for prey.
I bide my time to love and pray."

He blanked out after the short verse and couldn't remember any more of the poem.

"I don't know if this is enough for you, but it is all I can remember right now."

Beverly replied, "That's fine. Megan was kind enough to share it with me. I know the poem very well. It was beautiful."

"Thank you," Wade replied and took a deep breath before Beverly followed with another question.

"I have another question for you."

"Sure."

"When you came to Washington what restaurant did the two of you dine?"

"Capittos," Wade answered.

Beverly's voice suddenly took on calmer tone. She was more relaxed.

Wade replied showing interest while respecting her need for security. He described his surprise at Megan's disappearance when he returned from his mission.

"When I returned from my mission I went to see her at her office and as you probably know most of the senior people had been replaced. I have been worried sick about her. Do you know what happened?"

Before Beverly answered she expressed another concern. "Before we go on are you sure this phone line is totally secure?"

"Yes, my best friend from the NSA has set up a secure patch with both sides of our conversation protected by encryption. I'm calling from a payphone that NSA has taken off line for security purposes. I don't know of any other way you can be more secure."

Satisfied that Wade's security measures were adequate she continued, "I consider Megan one of my best friends. We talked about a lot of things and I think we were as open as two girls can be with each other. In other words I don't think she would ever lie or mislead me. She was always a straight shooter."

"I understand," Wade commented before Beverly continued.

"It was on a Tuesday afternoon about 2:00 p.m. when she told me her boss Tony Shaw received a call from a senior Army Intelligence officer. She told me that Shaw called her into his office and described that someone at the Army's Institute of Infectious Diseases Laboratory in Maryland had uncovered a biological threat that needed investigating."

Wade was excited to hear the first witness report and was eager to jump in with more questions. He held back though, wishing to come right through the telephone line. Wade reasoned the information would be more accurate if he let Beverly tell the story in her own words and not jump ahead. He listened intently, making notes and being certain she didn't skip over any detail in her sequence of the story.

To help her continue in sequence Wade asked, "So Shaw got this phone call and asked Megan into his office. What happened after he told her he got the call from Army Intelligence?"

Beverly took a breath and continued. "Well according to Megan the call was disturbing to Shaw. The issue had to do with a new biological threat that the Army had picked up by analyzing the cells of some foreign nationals who had been recently hospitalized in the U.S."

She continued, "Shaw knew that Megan had three years of medical school and had taken courses in cell genetics and been involved in microbiology research."

Wade couldn't wait any longer to ask, "So why did Shaw need Megan's involvement?"

Beverly returned to what she remembered Megan told her. "Apparently Shaw didn't understand the technical or biological aspects of what he was being told and Megan simply said 'Shaw just told me to follow up on the call with the Army and get more details'."

"What happened next?"

"This is where it starts to get a little fuzzy for me."

"What do you mean?" Wade asked.

"Well, we spoke after she had a couple of calls with researchers at the Army's research facility and I could tell she was bothered by what they discussed."

"What do you mean she was bothered?"

"She only told me it was a big problem and a very serious biological threat. She said she needed time to think about it and do some library research."

Beverly continued, "I asked her if this was something that was going to involve her."

Wade was quick to jump in, "And what did she say?"

"She said, 'I hope not. It's very dangerous, but I can't tell right now'."

Wade asked, "Did she give you any other details?"

Beverly replied, "I asked her if she wanted to get together and talk about it. She replied, 'Not now'."

Wade was puzzled by Megan's sudden withdrawal. He asked, "Did you ever get together with her after that comment?"

"No. The couple of times we were going to get together for drinks she blew me off saying she was studying at George Washington University's medical library. The next thing I knew she was on her way to Maryland for three or four days to meet with these Army researchers."

"Did you see her before she left for Maryland?"

"No, but I spoke with her a couple of times after she got back."

"What did she say?"

"She said she spent four days looking into microscopes which she hadn't done since she was in medical school."

"Was that all she said?"

"Pretty much. She said she had a much better understanding of the problem and that they had been real nice to her at the laboratory. I had the feeling she actually liked being around all that research."

"Did she say who she met with at the laboratory?"

"She mentioned a department head. I think his name was a Dr. Palmenter."

"Could that name have been Dr. Isaac Palmer?"

"Yeah, I think that's the name."

"What happened next?" Wade asked, hoping that there were a few more pieces of information.

"That's about it. We had a couple of missed messages exchanged between us. The next thing I knew she was gone."

Wade was uncomfortable asking the next question but had to know the answer. He wasn't sure how Beverly would react.

"Aside from this biological thing were you and Megan working on anything else before the biological thing started?"

"Before this biological thing came up I was doing some research for Megan involving some old Pentagon files involving an older Vietnam drug investigation."

Wade's curiosity piqued, "What happened there?"

Beverly paused for a moment before she continued, "I turned over what I had to Megan about a week before the biological thing emerged. I also told her I heard a rumor at the Pentagon that someone was interested in knowing about the files I copied. When I told Megan about the rumor, she told me to stop all my research immediately."

Wade grimaced when he asked, "Did you find out anything more about the Pentagon rumor?"

Beverly's tone changed to a worried response, "Yes, I told Megan that I found out a Mark Shuman from CID was the one asking about my research. I was worried and still am that I might lose my job."

"Why do you feel you are going to lose your job?"

"The rumor mill here at the Pentagon can be pretty brutal. What I heard was that if anyone discovered that I was in those files there would be immediate disciplinary action against me. In other words we at the Pentagon consider that jargon to mean job retribution like being fired and black-balled from other government jobs. Megan said it could even be worse and not to even go back into that section of the file room," Beverly explained.

"What did you do?" Wade asked

"I followed Megan's instructions and stopped looking for files but I've been looking over my shoulder ever since. It wasn't long after I gave Megan copies of those files that she disappeared. I am worried that the two might be in some way connected."

"How do you think they might be connected?" Wade asked

"I don't know; I just know there are no coincidences in our part of the government," Beverly exclaimed.

Wade tried to keep calm although he felt the same way. He wanted to temper Beverly's apprehension.

"I think the more time passes, the more likely things will calm down for you. I assume Megan told you how to cover your research tracks?" Wade asked.

"Yes, and I did everything exactly as she told me," Beverly proudly responded.

"Do you know what Megan did with the files after you gave them to her?" Wade questioned.

"No. She said it was best I didn't know but that they were in a safe place," Beverly responded.

"Were you aware that Megan's condo had been sold?" Wade revealed.

"No! Oh my God!" Beverly started crying.

"It surprised me as well. I went by and spoke with the people who bought the condo before I left D.C.".

The broken sound of Beverly's crying voice was interrupted with sobs as she tried to maintain control asking, "What did they say?"

"They said they never heard of a Megan Winslow. Her signature was nowhere on the purchase documents," Wade replied.

"How can that be? She owned the condo."

"The only thing I can think of is the condo was transferred to a third party before the current owner purchased it," Wade replied.

Beverly seemed to muster some strength in her voice. "This is all too strange and I'm not comfortable with any of these explanations. Nothing I've heard is coincidental. She didn't disappear into thin air for God's sake and I'm worried about her,"

"I understand your feelings and I feel the same way. With your explanation I now have some confirmation of at least two pieces of information I didn't have before. They will be helpful in explaining her disappearance," Wade responded, trying to be as comforting as he could.

With her composure regained Beverly asked, "How did I help?"

Wade responded, "One piece of information deals with the investigation you and she were doing and the other is this biological issue she was working on. She may be in a deep cover related to that biological threat but I can't be certain of that yet," Wade explained.

There was a pause before Beverly began sobbing, "You have to find her. She loves you more than anything or anybody in her life," Beverly said with certainty.

"Thanks to you I have a lot more to go on. I want to stay in touch with you but I'm concerned you and I are potentially being watched right now. The only safe way to speak is through this double telephone security patch. I have to come up with a safe way for you to contact me if anything comes up on your end. I'll research how we can do that and get back to you. In the meantime don't do anything out of your normal day-to-day duties at work," Wade responded.

Continuing his warning Wade insisted, "No matter how tempting it is, don't make any inquiries about Megan or me or on any of the files you were investigating. At this point we don't want to raise any suspicions. I'll be back in touch with you as soon as I have something to report."

Wade could hear the steady flow of tears as Beverly's voice broke the silence pleading, "I understand. Please find her and thank you."

"I will do my best," Wade responded.

After hanging up Wade jotted down a few notes under the dim light of the payphone booth. He had to pass his school's university library on his way back to his apartment. It was time to find out everything he could about Dr. Isaac "Chip" Palmer before he made his next move.

Chapter 6
Frederick, Maryland

It was a clear day under a bright early morning sky in a suburb of Frederick, Maryland. Dr. Palmer helped his eleven year-old son, Randy, get his backpack into the car for their ritual morning ride to school. Chip Palmer took on more than just school taxi duties when it came to raising Randy and seemed to love every step of his son's journey.

The forty-six year-old distinguished microbiology university professor was present for most of Randy's important soccer games and basketball tournaments even though his son didn't often get the call to play unless his team had a substantial lead in the game. Randy struggled to make athletic teams but loved the sports he played and somehow managed to hold on to a second or third-string position despite his taller and more agile teammates. He and his father hoped that his teenage years would bring on a growth spurt that would change his odds, but until that time came Randy was fine using his strong work ethic and enthusiasm to stay on the team.

Randy's school, Pierpoint Elementary was just a few blocks out of Dr. Palmer's way to the expressway and a twenty-five minute ride from the suburbs to his research institute office at Fort Detrick, Maryland. The ride to school gave Palmer and his son a chance to talk about Randy's upcoming day. On this day the conversation centered on Randy's afternoon soccer practice and a class paper he had to prepare for science class. Randy asked for his father's help preparing that paper, which was gladly given with a smile and a great deal of fatherly pride.

Except for an occasional trip to the golf driving range and a rare nine-hole golf game, Dr. Palmer's life was very routine.

Work, household chores and scheduled youth sporting events seemed to take up most of Chip Palmer's spare time. Little would anyone suspect that his real job was as a researcher specializing in assessing biological threats to this country and countermeasures to international threats of biological terrorism which despite the international treaties for their prevention had become an increasingly frequent problem in America.

The white lab coat, horned-rim glasses and mild demeanor complimented the docile suburban existence Dr. Palmer shared with many of his fellow researchers working at the U.S. Army Medical Research Institute of Infectious Diseases. Before Dr. Palmer's time at the institute the facility operated during the 1950's as the Army's Biological Warfare Laboratories.

Palmer's true research passion had always been and remained gaining a better understanding of how the structure and behavior of cell membranes reacted to various foreign bodies. His research interests always outweighed any interest in trying to understand the workings of international terrorism.

Dr. Palmer had a stunning academic career holding both an M.D. and Ph.D. The internationally recognized, award-winning scientist held senior teaching professorships at three major universities prior to coming to the Institute. He now felt that the Institute rather than a university setting gave him the best opportunity to make further contributions to science in his specialized field of research.

A quick hug by his father and Randy bolted from the passenger seat to catch up with a group of young school friends. As he waved goodbye to his son and started to pull out from the curb, Chip Palmer didn't notice the dark green sedan three cars behind him. The car followed him from the semi-circle school driveway to the front security gate of the research

Institute. The two individuals following him had distinct Asian facial features and remained a comfortable three-car distance behind Palmer during his entire route to work.

By the time Dr. Palmer's car picked up speed approaching the expressway entrance, his mind quickly shifted to his upcoming meeting at the office. His first morning meeting was to give a presentation to his boss, Col. Riles Landry and several other researchers on the institute research staff. These monthly research meetings gave fellow researchers a chance to update each other on different research techniques and report their progress on their respective projects. As Dr. Palmer turned into the Fort Detrick security gate for clearance, the green sedan following him passed the main gate without slowing down.

Dr. Palmer drove past the security gate to the parking structure with enough time to make a few notes at his desk before his presentation began. Following the morning presentation, the rest of his day would be spent in more routine meetings with staff and overseeing ongoing research projects.

While Dr. Palmer parked the two men following parked their green sedan four blocks from the gate and noted his movements through binoculars. After Dr. Palmer passed through the glass front doors of the Institute the green sedan slowly pulled out and retraced its steps back to the expressway. Wade followed the green surveillance car back to Pierpoint School where they took up observation overseeing the playground where Randy's recess activities would take place.

After completing his presentation notes, Palmer's mind wandered to his schedule for the next few weeks, which included travel and seminar presentations at various university biological forums. After gathering his notes and research papers he walked over to the elevator and the conference room two floors above where the morning meeting was to take place.

Along the way several staff members bid him a good morning and he returned the same gesture with a smile. Researchers and other senior members of the committee gathered for coffee on a table in front of the open conference room door. Most had a cup of coffee in one hand and research folders under their other arm.

Dr. Palmer exchanged greetings as the group entered the conference room taking a seat near the end of a large oblong conference table as he walked past the coffee table into the conference room. The well-used white-board surrounding the room was shiny from being wiped down by the cleaning crew the evening before. Participants exchanged pleasantries about everything from weather to personal weekend activities, creating a low rumble of indistinguishable sound. Dr. Palmer took a seat and opened his files, taking a last quick look at the notes he would soon be presenting.

As was his custom, the Institute's chairman arrived three minutes after the scheduled start of the meeting, taking his seat at the head of the conference table. His contrived smile reminded the fifteen in attendance that he was everyone's boss. When Landry looked up, the tone in the room immediately quieted to a few isolated whispers as all heads turned toward him.

Col. Landry was a physician who came up through Army medical ranks as an orthopedic surgeon before achieving the rank of a full bird colonel. Unlike most senior researchers on staff Landry had Army stiffness to his administrative style that often made others feel uncomfortable.

When being addressed by Col. Landry you had that distinct feeling that you were a soldier exposed on a foreign battlefield rather than in the safety of one of the most secure and best equipped research laboratories in this country. After adjusting his papers, Landry looked up. His normal stern expression gave notice that he was about to address troops rather than the more acclaimed scientists sitting in front of him. Before he spoke the room went dead silent.

Col. Landry began, "Good morning. I trust all of you had a restful weekend. I would like to get our meeting started right away. We have a lot to cover and I am backed up with meetings today. We have visiting dignitaries from Congress touring our facilities today. I have the dubious distinction of playing tour guide and politician for this tour. They always claim these tours are to gather more information to better understand what we do, when in reality they want to take a closer look to see where they can cut our budget." Landry's facial expression showed the unwelcome role of tour guide he was going to be playing that day. He continued, "For our presentation this morning I would like everyone to keep their comments and questions brief. We can follow up on any details or question you have later."

The room remained silent as Col. Landry scanned the schedule of presenters. One of Landry's security protocols was that all projects only be referred to by their project code number and never about the nature of work being studied. He considered the practice critical to keeping closed lips and away from idle conversation protecting a project's secrecy even within the halls of the Army's laboratory.

"We're going to start today's presentation with Brenda. She is going to give us an update on the 507-D project. Is that right?"

"Yes sir," replied Dr. Brenda Levinson as she gathered her papers three chairs away from the room's center podium. Brenda was a sharp medical researcher holding both an M.D. and Ph.D. in microbiology from Princeton. She had served four years in the Army before transferring to the Institute. She had only been an Institute Fellow for a year but had already become a favorite of Dr. Landry who frequently reminded everyone that her four years in the Army is what really gave her all the training she needed to be a successful researcher at the Institute. In Landry's mind those "Army skills" far outweighed her substantial academic accomplishments. Her project dealt with the effects of radiation on cell structure. Today she would be talking about a project that measured the impact on different cells by various forms of radiation.

As Brenda took her position at the center of the conference table, Landry leaned over to Chip Palmer sitting to his left and whispered, "I have you going on next." Palmer acknowledged by shaking his head. After Dr. Levinson's presentation and a few follow-up questions, participants could see that Dr. Landry was ready to move to the next presentation.

"Thank you, Brenda. I'm sure there will be additional follow-up questions after this meeting. Next we have Chip who is going to update us on Project 461-C."

Dr. Chip Palmer already had his papers ready and proceeded toward the podium before Brenda took her seat. Sensing Landry's main concern to maintain a short schedule for the meeting, Palmer decided to skip the introduction he had planned in hopes that it would shave off a few minutes.

At least a third of those present already knew some of the background on Project 461-C or may have already been working on some segment of that project. Palmer reasoned that because of the highly sensitive nature of his project the rest of the participants didn't really need additional background.

"In view of the restrictive time I'm going to skip my normal background on 461 and just confirm to the group that we received our first stem cell tissue samples from the undercover operative on this project. Initial tests on the samples look promising. We were able to replicate sample cells in collagen substrates under a blue filtered UV light. A third of the samples seem to replicate the shadow cell prototypes we had hoped for. Remaining tests include establishing a prototype colony. It remains to be seen if the cells will have a problem interacting with normal cells in the colony."

Dr. Phil Hanson, sitting opposite Palmer, raised his hand with a question.

"Why is it necessary to comingle the new growth of shadow cells with normal cells this early in the testing?"

Palmer didn't hesitate to answer. "Good question, Phil. There are two reasons. First, we don't know how secure our source of new material is going to be or how long we can expect to get sample material. I already have concerns on that issue. Secondly, some of the shadow cells seemed unstable under the electron microscope tests we did. It was as though they were 'hungry' to attach to other cells and we aren't sure if this was a cell chemistry issue or an unanticipated interaction from the other cells. It's still too early to tell."

As Dr. Palmer finished his explanation an unexpected ring of the conference room telephone broke the quiet of attentive scientists. On the second ring, heads turned toward Dr. Landry. "Who the hell is that calling? They know I have strict orders about interruptions during my conferences. Rene, please see who is calling on this line."

The room remained silent while the staff researcher tentatively picked up the receiver answering, "Conference Room." There was silence as she listened to the voice on the other end. Putting her hand over the speaker Rene said, "Col. Landry it is your secretary, Marge. She says that the congressional committee has already started assembling in your office and thought you would want to know that."

Landry's face grimaced in frustration. "Damn it. They are not supposed to be here for another forty- five minutes." With a puzzled look on Rene's face she replied, "What would you like me to tell Marge, Sir?"

After thinking about the consequence of waiting politicians Col. Landry replied, "Tell her I will be up there in a few minutes. Ladies and gentlemen this is just one of the many reasons why politics have no place in our research facility. We are going to have to reconvene this meeting at another time. I will have Marge contact everyone for available dates and times."

As committee members stood gathering their papers, Col. Landry motioned to Dr. Palmer to come over. "Chip, I have a question or two about your presentation. Would you mind accompanying me to my office? Perhaps we can chat a bit on the way."

Palmer replied, "Surely."

Col. Landry's office was three floors up and a corridor away from the conference room. Palmer wasn't sure what he had said or didn't say that caught Dr. Landry's attention. He hoped his comments hadn't upset Landry.

In Palmer's view Landry was all right as a boss, reporting mainly to cronies in the military, but he didn't consider him a peer when it came to research. The room cleared as Landry and Palmer headed toward the elevator. It was while they waited for the elevator that Landry gave his first hint of what was on his mind.

"Chip, you made a comment in the presentation that I wanted to ask you about. In response to Phil's question you mentioned you weren't sure how long you could depend on getting stem cell samples. I assume you were referring to the undercover covert agent who's sourcing the specimen material?'

They waited in silence as the elevator door opened and four people exited nodding as they passed Landry and Palmer. The two entered the empty elevator for the ride to the third floor.

"That's right," Chip Palmer replied.

"What makes you think there might be a problem?"

"I just know how concerned the agent was when she left."

Landry responded, "Were you concerned about her research skills or her covert assignment? After all you did approve her."

"She was excellent in the skills department. She was concerned about getting sample materials back to us. I worry about her safety if she is discovered. I think her situation is very dangerous," Palmer replied.

There was a pause before Landry responded. "That's not your department. She is being handled by a joint task force of CID and CIA for this mission."

Chip Palmer contemplated before he responded. "I know, but I can't help wondering if she is okay. After all she is doing this assignment for my department."

Landry heard some sentimentality in Palmer's tone and responded in his typical Army manner. "Agents come and go. We are just a laboratory and don't run agents. The worst case scenario we have to worry about here is if we can't get any more sample material."

"I don't think we have enough material to complete my original testing protocol. We may get lucky but I think we are going to need several more shipments. I just can't sleep at night knowing someone is risking their life for these sample materials, which may or may not produce the results we need."

Landry stiffened his posture, "We risk lives every day in the Army. We wouldn't get anywhere if we didn't take those risks. That's what the public and these congressional bastards don't understand."

The elevator doors opened to a group of three individuals waiting to enter the elevator. The two men walked past the waiting line in silence. Their silence continued as they walked down the long corridor toward Landry's office. As they approached the large reception area outside of Landry's office five individuals made up of two congressional committee members and staff mingled around the sofa, chairs and coffee table in Landry's large reception area.

Col. Landry stopped twenty yards from his gathered guests and turned to Palmer. "I'm going to make a few calls to see if I can get a status report on the undercover agent. I need you to stay focused. We will need to discuss this further. When are you expecting your next samples?"

"That's one of the problems. We don't have any set schedule on when additional samples will be arriving. It's only whenever it's safe to get them out. My understanding is it takes several intermediary exchanges to get them out of the host country," Palmer explained.

Landry was quick to respond. "Let me do a little backtracking on this to see what I can find out and I'll get back to you." He extended his hand to Palmer. A big political smile emerged across his face as he turned toward his waiting political contingent.

Palmer shook Landry's hand as they separated. Palmer immediately turned back to the elevator not wishing to come any closer to the waiting politicians and any potential questions they might ask. All the way back to his office Dr. Palmer felt tension and anxiety about what the agent he trained must be going through to get his samples. He just hoped his research results would be worthy of the risk.

Chapter 7

Greenstone, Alabama

Wade paced his apartment floor rechecking his lists, frustrated that he had not heard anything from his many outstanding phone calls. Sometimes Wade's instincts got ahead of his planning. For two days he had his belongings packed for a destination he was yet to identify. He just knew he was going into action. His rigorous daily routine of workouts and firing range sessions helped relieve the tension, but he was frustrated that he had made such little progress on his next step.

It wasn't long after returning from dinner that evening when the phone rang. Wade was expecting to hear from Yari, but this call had that unmistakable delay that told him it was a foreign secure line.

"Hello," Wade answered.

"Hi. It's Leo. I wanted to get back to you on a couple of items. Your man Shaw as best as I can tell is not in the Middle East or on any active covert assignment."

Wade thought for a moment before responding. "I guess that is not too surprising. They were probably using that cover story to divert inquiries at the main office. That's what the department staff I interviewed was told to say."

"I guess," replied Leo.

"Do you know where he is?"

"Nope, but I don't think he's in the field active on any assignment as best I can tell."

Wade didn't understand Leo's answer, "What does that mean?"

Leo paused before answering. "They may have him parked somewhere."

"Why would they do that?"

"There are lots of reasons to park someone. It's mainly to get them out of the way. Most often it's to lead others down a dead end. How was Shaw connected to your other friend, Megan?"

Wade's expression showed he was puzzled, "I don't think the two were connected. Wait a minute, I did speak with a friend of Megan's who said it was Shaw that got a call having something to do with an Army biological intelligence project."

Leo was quick to pick up on that last comment. "There you go."

"What do you mean?" Wade responded, still showing that he was puzzled.

Leo smiled as he answered. "If Shaw was a link to Megan for this assignment they couldn't leave Shaw around. He's too vulnerable if they wanted to cut all links to Megan – both had to go."

"You mean 'go' as in disappear?"

"That's right, kiddo. In other words they both may be on the same assignment or Shaw could be on the other side of the world having nothing to do with Megan's work."

Wade couldn't let the obvious go without asking.

"Did any of your sources have any clues about Megan's whereabouts?"

"Negative. I checked around to see if anyone knew an assignment she might be on. I thought she might be in deep cover. Nobody had anything on her or her assignment. That doesn't mean she's not on assignment, it just means they did a good job with her cover. You said her friend told you it was Army intelligence. That's where I would go to look. Those guys aren't like us and they can be strange. We generally don't play well together – CID and CIA just have different ways of doing things."

"What do you think I should do now?"

"Start with what you know. Go back to investigating details taking baby steps until a lead breaks. There's nobody you can call to get a quick answer. I've already tapped out my sources and I know them well enough that if they knew something they would let me know. This mission is buried deep or she has been eliminated."

"Something else has been bothering me," Wade confided.

"What's that, kiddo?"

"I've been back from our Tangier mission about six weeks. I am wondering if the agency is going to reach out and give me a handler and assignment before I find out what happen to Megan or Shaw."

"I'll give Phil Damien a call for you. I think he can keep you out of the system for a while. He owes me a few favors."

"That would be great."

"I have to run now. Take care and move only one small step at a time."

"Thanks for all your help."

"Be safe."

The receiver barely rested in its cradle when the phone rang again. This time is was Yari. Wade answered, "Hello."

There was a pause before the friendly voice announced. "I tried to call a little while ago, but your line was busy."

"Yeah, I was talking with someone from my last mission. What's up?"

"No traces or communication from Shaw or Megan Winslow from the last time I updated you. I did get the contact information on Dr. Palmer."

"I'm not surprised. I think they have Shaw buried somewhere out of the way. The Palmer information will be helpful."

During the next five minutes Yari gave Wade the details of Dr. Palmer's contact information including phone numbers, address, credit card activity and bank accounts. None of the information seemed suspicious to Wade. This was the last lead he had of Megan speaking to someone outside the intelligence agency. She traveled to Maryland presumably to see Dr. Palmer just before she disappeared. It wasn't much but the only lead he had. He asked Yari for some additional information on Palmer before making a decision about how he was going to proceed.

"Can you find out what Palmer's specialty is or anything else about him? Right now he's all I've got to go on."

"I should be able to get that. No problem. What's your next step?"

"I don't know yet. I have to be very careful how I proceed at this point. I was hoping to get something on Megan or Shaw's location, that is, if they're still around."

"I hear you partner. If they are part of any U.S. Intelligence operation they're not using our communication system or I would know about it."

"I may just take a chance and see what this Dr. Palmer is all about. I'll check in with you later."

"I should have something in a day or two," Yari replied.

"That's great, talk to you soon."

There was a worried look in Wade's eyes as he hung up the phone. He kept vacillating back and forth between Megan being under deep cover on assignment or dead. Either way he didn't have sources that could provide the information to solve that mystery. He glanced at his board of notes for a few minutes before deciding that he needed to follow the only lead he had. He decided quickly on his next trip. One way or the other, he would be meeting Dr. Chip Palmer.

His backpack and fatigue handbag lay on the sofa partially packed. Details of how he would proceed to Maryland raced through his mind motivated primarily by instinct. His instincts told him that Maryland might not be his only stop. He made sure his passport and other fake ID's were in order and began packing his disguises, not knowing what exactly he would need or how he would approach Dr. Palmer. He just knew that somehow he was going to find out what Palmer knew before Megan disappeared. If he found Dr. Palmer had anything to do with her demise, his life as a researcher would soon come to an end.

After studying several maps and calling his buddy at his local airbase, the decision to fly military and not commercial was confirmed. It would take two connecting flights for his trip to Maryland but this would keep him out of watching eyes of airport cameras and the chance to run into close inspection of his gear.

With the help of his friend at in-flight operations at the local base the first leg of his flight could be done easily without his name appearing on the manifest. For his two connecting flights he would rely on disguise and his fake military ID. His final flight leg would bring him into Maryland but not to the Fort Detrick military base that Wade wanted to avoid. He would make the last part of his journey to the institute and Dr. Palmer's residence by rental car using his military fake ID and discount pass and cash.

After packing his camera, Wade decided on a few light weapons which included his silenced, semi-automatic Sig Sauer, combat knives, military choke cord and metal knuckles. He kept telling himself this was only an information gathering operation but his instincts kept telling him otherwise. After packing he made the call to his buddy at the airbase confirming his plane was leaving on time at 10:20 p.m. that evening.

By 4:00 a.m. the next morning Wade was parked in his rental car two blocks away from Dr. Palmer's home with binoculars trained on the front door. The upscale Frederick neighborhood was covered in darkness except for dimly lit street lamps and the shape of a glowing quarter moon above. Within the hour, lights came on in a sequence, reminiscent of most households rising to the beats of a suburban work day. Wade caught only glimpses of the outline of bodies passing across the light source and the loosely hanging curtain drapes.

For a brief moment Wade caught himself feeling envious of the life style he was observing. He visualized himself with Megan starting their early morning journey. Without Megan in his life those images were nothing but indiscriminate shadows. He quickly brought himself back from dreamy visions of her knowing they were not real but a wishful hope he held onto knowing that in reality it was more likely she was not alive.

It was a few minutes before 7:00 a.m. when the automatic garage door opened and Wade got his first glimpse of the outline of Dr. Palmer and a child getting into the car. Wade scanned his surroundings as Dr. Palmer's four door blue sedan rolled down the driveway. He waited a full three car lengths before pulling out to follow. Dr. Palmer wasn't checking his rear or side view mirror being preoccupied in conversation with his son. With little attention being given to his surroundings, following Dr. Palmer from his home to his son's school would not be difficult. He also took the most obvious and shortest route to the school feeling comfortable in his routine.

After several turns to avoid traffic lights, Dr. Palmer approached the half-circle driveway of Pierpoint School.

Palmer positioned his car in line with other cars waiting patiently for his turn while he and his son continued their pleasant conversation. When Dr. Palmer turned into the queue Wade found a parking spot a half block away where he could observe the driveway and allowed an excellent angle for photographs. As Palmer's car inched forward to the safety departure curb Wade grabbed his camera on the front seat and started taking pictures with his telephoto lens. The shots included the car's license plate and photos of Randy. Wade had to wait until Dr. Palmer turned back to get a fairly good shot of him looking back to make sure he was clear to pull out of the line. Remaining shots in this sequence included several shots of the school entrance and surrounding buildings.

As Wade continued his telephoto shots of the school area something immediately caught his attention just a half block away. Parked a hundred feet to the left of his position was a green sedan with two men inside. Wade quickly adjusted the focus ring to get a better look at the occupants, instinctively snapping shots as he scanned.

Two men with Asian features seemed trained on Dr. Palmer and his son each using a pair of binoculars. Wade turned back to get a few more pictures of Dr. Palmer's son and a better angle of the observing sedan. He was now sure the occupants of the green sedan were watching the same targets he was.

Wade's immediate thoughts were mixed. These men could be U.S. security agents or alternatively, observers with more sinister intent. As Dr. Palmer pulled away from the curb of the circular drive the green car followed. There was no mistaking that these men were observing Dr. Palmer and his son.

Keeping his camera trained on Palmer's car approaching the green sedan, he saw the two men suddenly turn to face each other pretending to be having a conversation. Wade waited until Dr. Palmer's car pulled past with the green sedan following. Wade got in line making up a caravan of three cars behind each other. At a stoplight before the entrance to the expressway Wade got close enough to take a shot of the license plate of the green sedan and got a good look at the occupants.

Having previously studied maps of the area Wade estimated Dr. Palmer's route to work. He was now less concerned about losing Dr. Palmer and suddenly wanted more information on who was following him and why. Dr. Palmer still seemed oblivious to his followers as Wade wondered how long his surveillance had been ongoing.

Chip Palmer took the route to work that Wade had projected. As Palmer turned into the guarded gate of the Institute he observed the green sedan remain on the main road passing the entrance gate and taking up an observation post two blocks past the entrance. Wade also drove past the gate and the green sedan position, taking his time to find a road that brought him up and behind the green car. The spot he found was ideal, recessed among some trees giving him ample vision of the front guard gate down the road and Dr. Palmer's followers.

With Dr. Palmer safely inside the Institute, Wade followed the green sedan back to the Pierpoint School where the green car took up position opposite the side playground yard where recess was held. Wade waited two hours taking pictures and making notes until the recess bell rang. Out came a hoard of kids joyful in their freedom from sitting in desks, doing math problem and watching chalkboards. Among the moving kids Wade found it difficult to distinguish one from another and instead focused on what the two men in the green sedan were observing. Their binoculars were trained to one section of the playground. Wade estimated the same angle and sure enough was able to pick out Randy, Dr. Palmer's son. Wade switched between binoculars and camera as Randy moved from one playground fixture to the other until he was satisfied both he and his Asian observers were watching the same person.

After school recess Wade followed the two men to the budget-priced Tudor Hotel in downtown Frederick. He parked a few blocks away from the hotel entrance and removed one of his disguises and his Sig Sauer semi-automatic with a silencer from his gym bag.

By the time Wade reached the entrance his targets had already gone to their room. Wade slowly entered the lobby taking careful note of the layout. He used the lobby restroom to change into his disguise which included a wig, mustache, dark sunglasses and hat.

Wade knew he might have a long wait in front of him and asked the bell captain for some local directions. He also asked where the entrance to the guest parking garage was and immediately headed for that door as soon as the bell captain pointed. After going up and down three flights of the parking stairwell, Wade spotted the green sedan, copied down the parking space number and took a close-up shot of the license plate.

Wade came back to the lobby and asked the woman at the main desk if she could help him locate his cousin who was staying in the hotel. He didn't know his cousin's room number, but had a message from his cousin that his assigned parking space was #385. The woman seemed anxious to please.

Shuffling across two reference directories she came back with
a room number of 557.

After sitting in the lobby to observe the cadence of
incoming and outgoing guests he planned his next task, which
was to walk the hotel halls looking for room service carts and
checking ingress and egress doors to the fifth floor stairwell
near room 557.

Wade took the stairs to the second floor and it wasn't long
before he found a cleaning cart parked outside the open door
of a guest room. Checking both sides of the cart he didn't find
what he was looking for.

He waited until the stout cleaning women who seemed of
European descent came back around the cart. Wade turned at
the last minute and clumsily backed into the large woman.
Showing surprise and apologies he repeated several times that
he was very sorry. She seemed to accept his apologies as a
guest tourist not watching where he was going.

Wade immediately noticed the large metal chain with
keys handing from the belt on her hip. The shape of the keys
told Wade they were master keys. Glancing up at the room
number she was cleaning Wade had to make a quick
calculation.

"Excuse me ma'am. I need some extra towels for my
room."

The woman returned Wade's request with a stern stare.
She reluctantly handed Wade two towels off the cart and
turned to go back into the room she was cleaning.

"Thank you. Oh ma'am, excuse me again but I have
another favor. I locked myself out of my room number 227.
It's just around the corner."

The woman's smile turned sour as she said in her broken
English, "I am very busy."

"If I can borrow your master key I will come back right away. I promise."

As he asked Wade reached in this pocket and pulled out a roll of $20 bills and started to unroll two.

Hands on her hips and clearly frustrated by Wade's imposition she shook her head and reached for her large key ring. Wade knew he would only have a few seconds to return before she would be right on his tail looking for her keys. The maid exchanged her keys for Wade's two $20 bills and pointed to the master key for the second floor. Wade quickly saw that each key was stamped with the number of the floor.

Thanking the woman profusely Wade bowed. She responded by immediately turning back to the room she had been cleaning. Wade reached into the cart and grabbed two bars of soap out of the accessories box and walked briskly down the hall with his towels. He turned the corner out of the woman's sight and quickly found the fifth floor key and impressed it into the clean bar of soap making sure it made an accurate impression.

To be certain Wade turned the soap bar over and made a second impression and wiped the key with the towel. He returned to the cart after having placed the towels in the stairwell and handed the maid her master keys, thanking her in the process. A partial smile returned to the maid's face as she turned to wipe the dresser.

Purchasing a newspaper, Wade returned to the lobby, taking up a chair with a clear view to the elevator doors. His wait was almost two hours before he caught sight of the two men coming out of the elevator and turning right toward the entrance door to the parking garage.

Wade immediately exited the front door breaking into a jog to his car two blocks away. He wanted to be in place by the time his targets exited the hotel garage. Turning the keys to unlock his door he saw the green sedan leave the hotel parking structure turning right on Marietta Street. Traffic was moderate and Wade quickly navigated a three car distance safely behind his targets.

After making several turns his targets parked behind the Ming Lo Chinese restaurant. The two men settled at a table on the outdoor patio as Wade found a parking space a half block away. As the men ordered, Wade crouched down below the window surface with his camera gear and telephoto lens. At this point Wade wanted some decent photos of these men.

One of the men was considerably taller than the other. The taller man did most of the talking and seemed to be in charge. Both men wore suit coats with open shirt collars and from the lay of their clothes neither seemed to be carrying any obvious weapons. Wade debated if he should go in the restaurant to get a closer view. He decided against that option and instead waited a half block away patiently looking through the viewfinder for each man to turn his head in conversation so he could get a clear head shot.

The other option Wade considered, but dismissed, was to get into their hotel rooms. He ultimately decided against that idea as well until he could find out from the photographs the identity of these men. The two men continued in leisurely conversation, ordering a second main course and obviously in no rush. Wade was able to get good photos from several angles on each man He reloaded his film canister realizing he had to find someone in Frederick or a nearby town to develop and print the film so he could get the photos to Yari.

Out of the corner of his eye Wade saw an empty phone booth at the corner. It was unlikely his targets would even notice him making calls while he kept an eye on them. Leaving his camera under the front seat Wade eased out of the passenger side of the car and proceeded to the corner phone booth. The phone book gave Wade several possibilities for developing and printing his film and the name and address of a wholesale key supplier. He made the call to the locksmith shop. Wade's locksmith training impressed the wholesaler and he confirmed his supply of blank keys and offered Wade the use of his key cutting machine. As Wade hung up, his two targets finished their meal.

Wade followed them back to Pierpoint School where they waited parked across from the school entrance for either Dr. Palmer or his son Randy. Wade estimated it would be at least two hours before school was dismissed and Dr. Palmer returned to pick up his son. He used that time to drop off his film and make his master hotel key. When he returned the men were still in the same position waiting for either Dr. Palmer or his son to appear.

Chapter 8
Frederick, Maryland

The uneventful tail of the two operatives ended with Dr. Palmer returning home safely with Randy. By that evening the developed pictures of the two men were wired to Yari who immediately checked them against the U.S. database and circulated them to Interpol for identification. Yari told Wade it would probably take a few days for Interpol to respond.

Early the next morning the same surveillance pattern repeated itself like clockwork. Wade concluded the two men following Dr. Palmer and his son were not waiting for an opportunity to act but were under orders to just observe. Perhaps, Wade thought, Palmer didn't have the information they needed. He didn't know why that was the case. His instincts told him that Dr. Palmer's situation could change at any moment once orders were issued to these two men. The pause after completing the morning routine of Dr. Palmer pulling into the gates of the Institute facility gave Wade time to place a call to Yari at a local payphone.

"Hello."

"It's me, Yari. Any news on the targets I sent you?" Wade asked

"Yeah! We got an Interpol hit. It seems like your men are contract operatives out of Burma."

"Contract agents for whom?" Wade asked.

"Good question. We don't know yet. They have worked for the Chinese and Russians in the past but it's not clear who they are working for on this operation."

"What kind of skills do these guys have?"

"They are contract assassins trained by several mercenary groups from North Korea and China. They have also been involved in kidnapping. I would say these guys are nobody to fool around with."

There was a pause while Wade considered alternative options. "Are you sure they are not U.S. or friendly government folks?"

"These guys really have a track record of working either for the Russians or Chinese as far as I can tell. They are wanted by Interpol for the murder of two agents several years ago but haven't been seen in Europe since then."

"How did they get into this country?"

"They came in through Canada about three weeks ago. Each has well prepared bogus passport documentation. We are working on trying to identify the forger. That may give us a clue on who was behind the bogus documents. I'm still working on that," Yari replied.

"What language do these boys speak?"

"According to Interpol their native language is Burmese but they speak a little English, French and Russian as well, and probably some Mandarin."

"My instincts tell me their mission has something to do with Dr. Palmer's project which may tie to Megan's disappearance."

"The timing is certainly coincidental with those events," Yari responded.

"No such thing as coincidence in our line of work."

"What's your next step?" Yari asked.

Wade responded, "I'm not sure exactly. I have to isolate Dr. Palmer and take these guys out of the picture. I first had to be sure they weren't U.S. backed operatives."

Yari replied, "I think you're clear on that last point but it sounds like you may need some help."

"I'm thinking about that as well. I still haven't decided on how I'm going to get Dr. Palmer to talk to me. I think he's going to be a hostile witness. Would you please check to see if Dr. Palmer has booked any travel reservations for the near future?" Wade asked.

"Sure, I'll check his credit cards and see if he booked any airline flights."

"Thanks, I'll get back to you soon," Wade replied ending the call.

Wade continued to tail Dr. Palmer and his targets as he thought about his next move. He didn't like the idea that there were two operatives trailing both Dr. Palmer and his son. All sorts of sinister prospects raced through Wade's mind as he followed the green sedan and Palmer's car back to Pierpoint Elementary.

Instincts told Wade that they were after information rather than this being just a contract hit on Dr. Palmer. Visions of torturing Dr. Palmer or his son rang loud in Wade's mind as a way to get that information. He wondered what missing piece of information they needed before they acted. There was little time to waste if Wade was going to intervene.

Wade realized that if the Russians or Chinese were behind this operation, taking out the operatives might mean they would just send replacements if the information they were seeking was important enough. Wade's jaw muscles tensed as he thought through the complexity of separating all the players and getting information out of both Dr. Palmer and these trained operatives.

The longer Wade waited the less likely he would find Megan alive. As long as the situation between Dr. Palmer and his followers remained status quo the more likely Dr. Palmer's routine would remain the same. Once the operatives got their orders, things would change for the worse very quickly. The only thing stable in the current condition was Dr. Palmer's and his son's repetitive routine. Wade had to find a weakness in his opponent's operation and also in Palmer's repetitive schedule before an order was issued to the operatives.

Except for changing where they ate meals, Wade concluded the Burmese operatives' routine was very predictable. From an intervention standpoint, it offered both opportunities and problems. The same was true of Dr. Palmer. For an intervention to work with the operatives, Wade would have to find a way to break their routine. By the same token he had to find some slight variation in Dr. Palmer's routine. The more Wade thought about options the more he realized he couldn't pull off both sides of this without some assistance.

If his instincts were right, the operatives were after something about Dr. Palmer's research and that research probably had something to do with Megan's mission and disappearance. Wade had to find a way to interrogate both Dr. Palmer and the operatives. Concluding that the Burmese operatives were well trained professionals, they would be difficult and dangerous to capture and not easy to interrogate. Perhaps they would have to be eliminated.

After making certain the afternoon surveillance routine had no variation, Wade broke off to get a bite to eat and call Yari. During his call, Yari confirmed that Burma had just received a shipment of arms from Russia. Wade and Yari's immediate thoughts were that Dr. Palmer's operation might somehow be part of a payback favor for the Russia arms shipment.

As evening approached Wade confirmed that Dr. Palmer was safely at home with his son. He jotted down a few notes on the motel stationery. With a sketchy plan in mind Wade made the few calls he needed to test the waters of his plan. He called through secure telephone patches already set up by Yari. The first of these calls was to Georgia detective Gabe Morrison who Wade had come to know and trust from his work on the Lockhart murder. Since he was a senior detective who had worked on thousands of cases over his career, Wade thought he might know someone in law enforcement in the Maryland area. Wade scribbled on the pad as he gathered thoughts while the phone rang in Morrison's home.

"Hello."

"Mr. Morrison, this is Wade Hanna. Sorry to bother you at home this evening. I just wanted to keep this call away from office ears."

"It's never a problem taking your call. What's on your mind, son?"

"I'm involved in the middle of an intelligence matter here in Maryland and thought you might be able to assist. It's a long story and I don't want to get ahead of myself with too many details."

Morrison responded, "That's not a problem. I'm going to take the phone over and sit in my easy chair so I can take a few notes while you're talking. Just start wherever you would like."

"I am in Frederick, Maryland on assignment overseeing an internal investigation into the disappearance of an intelligence agent. The agent was last seen working with one of the scientists by the name of Dr. Chip Palmer at the Army's Medical Research Institute on Infectious Diseases."

"I don't know that name," Morrison was quick to reply.

"I wouldn't expect that you would and I don't know much about Dr. Palmer except that our missing agent and he were working together just before her disappearance."

"I see," said Morrison.

"While I'm here doing my investigation I learned that Dr. Palmer is being followed by two Asian men that my people tell me are not friendly. I took photos of the men following Palmer and just received word from Interpol that these men are trained intelligence operatives out of Burma probably contracted out as operatives by either Russia or China. They are not only following Dr. Palmer but are also observing his young son Randy who goes to Pierpoint School."

"What the hell are Burma operatives doing in our country?" Morrison questioned.

"We still don't know for sure, but my guess is Russia is looking for some information Dr. Palmer has."

"What the hell? We probably have a basis for bringing these Burma characters in right now for questioning."

"Hold on. That might not be the best idea until I get information on my missing agent from Dr. Palmer. My question to you is if I am able to detain these Burmese characters do you know anyone in Maryland that can handle their formal arrest. I will turn over all the Intel on their backgrounds. As an intelligence officer I just can't be involved in their arrest, I hope you understand."

There was a silence while Morrison thought. "Let me think. I worked with a great guy in Maryland on a case some years back by the name of Darren Wherter. I think he might be retired now. When I last spoke with him he was living in Bethesda. He was former FBI then went to work as a senior detective for the Bethesda Police Department. He was a great guy to work with. I still have his number. With your permission I'll give him a call."

Wade thought for a moment. "Sure, that would be great. Remember I'm not asking for him to do any legwork here. If everything goes as planned I hope to hand these guys over on a platter. I just can't be identified or as part of the arrest loop to protect my cover."

"Darren will understand that. Give me a few days to track Darren down and call me back. I should have something for you."

"You're the best, Gabe."

"I'm just old enough to have worked with a lot of people in this business."

"I'll talk to you soon."

Wade didn't want to provide more information at this time and ended the call with a polite,

"Thank you very much."

The next call Wade made was to another friend he had not spoken with or seen since his mission in Belize. As the phone rang just outside of Houston, Wade wondered if Max Yeoman had completed his physical rehab from the wound he suffered as an army Special Forces sergeant in Vietnam.

"Hello," the quiet voice of Max answered.

"It's me, soldier Wade Hanna, calling you from Maryland."

"Wade, how the hell are you? The last time we spoke was the Belize mission. I've spoken a few times with Yari who was quick to fill me in on your escapades," Max replied.

"Yari has been a great friend to both of us but I'm sure he exaggerated about any imaginary escapades I was on." Wade downplayed Max's comment.

"I'm not so sure. Rumors spread through our group at Fort Benning. We all kind of follow your missions. Like the one in Morocco."

"Don't believe everything you hear, buddy." Wade was quick to reply.

"What country are you in now?" Max asked.

"How does the state of Maryland sound?"

"Last time I checked they were still part of the union. What are you doing there?" Max was anxious to get to the purpose of the call.

Wade diverted the question at first until he could assess Max's physical condition. "Before we get into that I want to ask about your wound. The last time we were together you were limping pretty badly."

"Yeah, I kind of messed it up a little during my Belize extract. I took a few steps back in rehab but I'm good to go now," Max was clearly playing down his injury.

"Are you sure? Now don't play games with me, soldier. What exactly is your status?" Wade firmed up his tone when he asked the question.

"Well, I'm technically on long term disability. After Belize I rehabbed hard and put in for another tour in Nam but was denied again. To tell you the truth I don't think they are going to let me back into combat," Max reluctantly admitted.

Wade could feel the disappointment in Max's voice. "That must be a hard one for you, partner."

"Yeah, I took the rejection to heart. I live for the fight, man, but it's not all about me. I have my family to think about. I work out hard every day thinking I'm going to get my body back the way it was. It gets me down sometimes when there's little progress," Max admitted.

"I know there is no one better in the field and it must be hard but I want to see you healthy so you can take care of that family of yours."

"Thanks boss. Coming from you that means a lot to me," Max replied.

"Don't thank me yet, man. I'm going to test your fitness before we start anything."

"I'm ready for anything you throw at me. The newly minted special forces graduates can't keep up with me during training." Max was confident he would keep up with any mission assignment Wade threw at him."

"Let me get back to why I called. By the way I am speaking to you over a secure patch Yari set up for us so it's okay to talk," Wade assured Max.

"That's cool," Max replied having total confidence in Yari's ability to set a secure patch.

"I'm on a mission here near Fort Detrick in Frederick, Maryland and could use some help."

Max jumped in, "I'm ready, just say the word."

"Hold on, let me give you some background."

Max listened intently as Wade conveyed the story about Dr. Palmer and the missing agent, Megan Winslow. He gave enough detail so Max knew what he was getting into without certain background just in case Max were to become captured or arrested as part of the assignment. The fewer details he knew about Megan the better since this part of the operation didn't directly involve her.

After describing the two Asian operatives and what evidence Wade had gathered on them Max needed a few questions answered to help him understand his role in the assignment. Wade welcomed Max's questions as he was always upfront with him and wanted him to totally understand his role and the risks involved.

When Wade finished his lengthy explanation Max asked, "Say boss, I still don't understand why we just don't take the two operatives out right away."

"There are several reasons. The first is they may have information U.S. authorities can get out of them involving their backers, especially if they are being sent by the Russians or Chinese. I would like to give the U.S. authorities that chance to interrogate them. However we have to be careful because I don't want those operatives giving the U.S. authorities any information on us."

"Secondly, if we just eliminate them they are likely to send new operatives whereas if the U.S. has them in custody those countries might at least think twice before they send another team in after Dr. Palmer," Wade explained.

"I get it but you know as well as I do that capturing experienced operatives can be more dangerous than just eliminating them."

"I know that. I also know that during the heat of engagement circumstances I may have to change my current thinking to protect us. If these operatives somehow manage to compromise our position or threaten us or Dr. Palmer I will not hesitate to eliminate them. I'm not going to put you or me in any unacceptable danger level because of information the two Burmese operatives may have. You should know me well enough to know that's not going to happen."

"I hear you, boss," Max replied.

The next topic of discussion was equipment, weapons, timing and Max's travel arrangements. As Wade spoke Max was already making equipment lists knowing he had the best opportunity as a part-time Special Forces instructor to "borrow" base equipment.

They ended the call by setting dates when Max could be available. Wade agreed to make the final flight arrangements through his buddy in flight operations at the airbase in Houston. He wanted to make sure his flight records didn't show his real name in case those records were ever examined. After checking the equipment list one more time Wade bid his friend Max a safe trip and confirmed he would be waiting at the Maryland terminal when he arrived in two days.

Chapter 9

There was a light rain falling as Wade pulled up to the terminal at the Naval Air Station at Patuxent River, Maryland, also known as "Pax River", to pick up Max. After parking Wade entered the terminal and saw Max standing behind two duffle bags full of equipment at his feet. As he approached the two men smiled at each other.

"You couldn't get the equipment in one bag soldier?" Wade asked laughing.

Max replied, "You wanted 'stuff' man and I brought it."

Both were glad to see each other and exchanged military hugs. As Wade picked up one of the bags he commented, "What the hell do you have in here? I didn't ask for a tank."

"I just thought of a few extra things we might need," Max replied.

As they walked to the car Wade paid particular attention to Max's stride which looked a lot better than his limp when they were on the Belize mission.

"I see you're walking better on that leg," Wade commented.

"I told you I'm fine. They just won't let me back on combat missions right now. I think they feel if it flares up I might let my team down."

"Like we talked the other day, maybe that decision is the best one for you. I want you to tell me if that leg of yours starts acting up on this assignment. Not like you failed to do in Belize. Okay?"

"I will. No problem," Max replied.

"Let's go put this stuff in our rooms and I'll show you the lay of the land and who we're up against."

"Has everything remained quiet since we last spoke?" Max asked.

"Yeah, everything's as I described it on the phone. The two operatives just trail my scientist and his son. I think they're waiting for a call from whoever is running their operation before they make their move. We want to take full advantage of the lull in their routine. Once they get the call it's going to be run and gun."

On the drive back to Frederick the two men strategized options, taking time to analyze alternatives and discuss back-up if things went wrong. Wade explained routes from Dr. Palmer's residence to Pierpoint School and the Institute. Driving through town, Wade showed Max the hotel the operatives were staying at and pointed out some of their favorite restaurant haunts.

Wade had almost forgotten how quickly Max's mind picked out details and how much they thought alike. When the two strategized it was like two minds meshing into a single well-oiled machine; each seeming to know the other's thoughts before they spoke.

After getting a lay of the land Max commented, "I want some time estimates on each of these routes."

Wade replied, "I've already done some of that on the major routes both in heavy and light traffic. I have those notes back at the motel. I also have a copy of the ID photos of the operatives and their rap sheets as well as photos of Dr. Palmer and his son." Max asked, "I assume the operatives have a rental car?"

"Yes, I checked that out as well," Wade responded.

"How long did they rent the car for?"

"They rented the car for a month and have another week to go."

Max quickly picked up on the length of the rental, "Sounds like they expected to be here a while from the beginning. We should check their hotel to see how long they booked the room as well."

Wade replied, "I agree but I don't want us waiting around for their call to action to come. I was thinking about getting into their room this evening to see if there is any evidence or documents around."

Max responded, "That's fine by me. I guess we can do that when they go out for dinner."

"I was thinking the same thing."

"I'll cover the operatives. Do you think you can get into their room without a problem? Hotel locks are not that difficult to pick."

"Why take that chance when I have a master key?" Wade replied.

"You're unbelievable man," Max commented before he continued with a reminder.

"My guess is they are too smart to leave anything around the hotel but be careful that nothing is left out of place that would alert them. We don't want to mess up our big surprise."

"I hear you," Wade replied.

Wade asked, "I assume you brought the two-way radios that work?"

"Do you really think I would forget those?" Max signed off.

They returned to their motel and sorted through Max's supply of armaments for the operation. After a quick bite the two gave a brief check of radio transmitters and earpieces and Max dropped Wade off at the Tudor Hotel and proceeded to follow the two operatives to one of their regular restaurants.

Wade came up the parking entrance to the hotel and entered the hotel lobby.

He was already in disguise as a hotel waiter in a bellman's uniform he had taken from the hotel laundry room the previous day. To complete his disguise, he carried a service tray cheek high to partially block any outstanding facial features. He proceeded to the fifth floor where the operatives were staying and carefully looked up and down both hallways leading away from the elevator.

Knowing no one would reply, Wade knocked on the operatives' door announcing "Room Service." After an appropriate pause he used his master key and entered the room. Slipping on his rubber gloves Wade first checked the room for bugs and cameras. After finding none he systematically proceeded with his search for evidence.

Carefully opening the top drawer of the first dresser, Wade looked for anything unusual in the drawer. He ran his gloved fingers across the sides, back and bottom of the drawers searching for anything that might be taped to the surfaces. Finding nothing he moved to the next lower drawer and completed his inspection of the dresser before moving to the writing desk nearby.

Everything on the writing desk looked in place except for the slight indentations he caught on the blank surface on the hotel notepad. He held the pad up to the light at an angle to confirm they were slight indentations from pen marks used to write on the page above. The top page containing the writing had been removed.

The handwriting was difficult to see and clearly not in English but the impressions on the paper were definitely there. Slowly he removed the top five pages of the pad being careful to keep the pages flat without causing any bend that would make reading the impressions complicated. He kept the pages flat, placing them in a small bag he carried strapped to his back.

Wade continued his search of the two-bedroom suite taking time to do a sketch diagram of the furniture layout in each room. He also photographed each room making notes on his sketch pad. The positioning of these objects could become important if they had to take the men down by force into a dark room with two exit doors.

As Wade turned to search the small refrigerator in the built-in bar under the counter a voice broke the absolute silence in his earpiece.

"Sparrow to Base, do you read?" Max's voice rang out loudly.

Wade turned down the volume on his earpiece and replied.

"Base here, I copy you, what is your status?"

"Still at the chop house. Party starting on third main course for the evening," Max stated.

"I need another twenty minutes, over," Wade replied.

"That's not a problem the ways these guys are eating, over."

"Good. I'll confirm when ready to extract, over."

"I'll pick you up at designated rendezvous point, over," Max confirmed.

"Out," Wade replied signing off.

Wade continued searching the rooms, opening dresser drawers, looking under the beds and opening both of the operative's suitcases. He found copies of passport and flight documentation, which confirmed what Yari had already obtained on the operatives. To be certain, Wade laid the documents out on the floor and photographed each one along with papers written in Chinese.

After completing his search of the rooms and finding very little Wade turned to the small refrigerator. Amidst some stale cheese and crackers he found two dark brown vials with eyedropper caps that looked out of place. He opened and smelled the contents of the bottles which gave off a strong medicinal odor. The unmarked bottles didn't appear to have any medically prescribed use. The strong pungent smell reminded him of sedative pills he had to take once when in the hospital. Puzzled by the lack of obvious use Wade returned the bottles back where he found them when his earpiece rang out again.

"Sparrow to Base, Do you read? Over."

"I read, over," Wade replied.

"Our boys look like they're getting ready to leave. Over," Max warned.

"I'm almost done. Will extract in ten minutes," Wade replied.

As his last task Wade wanted to photograph the position of the furniture in each room in case they had to do a forced entry in the dark to take down the operatives. Just as he closed the door behind him the green sedan pulled into its assigned parking space in the hotel garage.

During the meeting at the extraction point Wade and Max decided that they would both need a car for the rest of the mission and proceeded to a rental car company downtown a half mile from the hotel. The two separated with Max following Dr. Palmer while Wade went to get his photographs developed.

Max's persistent tail of Dr. Palmer caused him to see an unusual break in his regular pattern. Wade listened intently to Max as he radioed in his report.

"It seems Dr. Palmer has a new sport we didn't know about. This evening he didn't go directly home from work. Instead he stopped at the city golf course driving range to hit golf balls."

"That's interesting," replied Wade. "Does he have the swing of a beginner golfer or pro?"

"Somewhere in between," Max replied. "It's not the first time he's swung a club but he looks a little rusty to me although I'm no expert at the game."

"Are our friends there watching too?"

"Negative. They broke off the tail when they thought he was headed home."

"Good. They may not know about his new golf hobby yet."

"I think we should try to keep it that way," Max replied.

"How late does the driving range stay open?" Wade asked.

"I think till 10:00 p.m. I'm going over to check out the range and find out what's going on there," Max replied

"Good. I'll check on our Asian friends. Stay with the good doctor until he gets home."

"Will do, out," Max signed off.

Max watched Dr. Palmer for an hour hitting golf balls into the misty clouds that formed over the floodlights. He picked up copies of the driving range schedule and noted that they were connected to the city golf course just down the road.

While Max watched Dr. Palmer try to improve his golf swing, Wade followed the green sedan from the hotel parking structure to a new restaurant which was a scale up in lavish dining from their usual haunts. The newer Golden Gate Restaurant sported a large Oriental-designed bar with a band playing an odd mixture of American, Latin and country swing music. Chinese lanterns hung above Asian-dressed waitresses and waiters to complete the strange international scene.

The operatives were enjoying themselves and the music. The taller of the two operatives, who Wade had named "Tallman", stood at the bar trying to charm one of the waitresses as his cohort sat drinking at the table alone, tapping his foot to the music.

Wade entered the bar in disguise and immediately found a small table the end of the crowded bar where he had a good view of his targets. He noticed Tallman write something on a piece of paper and hand it to the waitress as they spoke. He soon returned to the table to join his cohort.

Wade moved to the rear wall of the bar. Turning his head away from the crowd so he could hear over the loud band noise Wade radioed Max. He was anxious to hear what Max had found out about Palmer's routine at the driving range. After they discussed the details, Wade asked Max to get even more details about where Dr. Palmer preferred to park and more information about parking lot lighting at the driving range. Since Wade had both operatives under his watchful eye at the restaurant, he saw no need for Max to continue his surveillance of Dr. Palmer that evening.

Tallman and Shortstop were having the best of times as the two settled in for a long night of drinking and eating. Wade concluded he could better observe them undetected without the large crowd and high noise level from across the parking lot. Through the large glass window abutting the operative's table Wade spotted a location that would give him a clear view from across the parking lot without the crowd and noise. After

94

paying his tab Wade headed for the more peaceful observation point.

As Wade watched half-drunk couples trying to dance the salsa, Max wandered to the driving range offices. He made notes on the number of staff who worked there, hours of operation and of course the number and type of security locks on the various doors.

At one end of the driving range patio Max noticed a white-board hanging outside one of the closed office doors. He walked over and scanned the names posted on the schedule. The list of people taking golf lessons included Dr. Palmer's name. He was third on the list with dates of Wednesday and Friday lessons scheduled with someone by the name of Louis. It was a Thursday night and Max concluded Dr. Palmer was at the range practicing between his scheduled lessons.

Back at the restaurant Wade watched the operatives consume five rounds of hard liquor and eat four main courses of Chinese food with all the side dishes. His targets were carefree and totally smashed. They pushed each other back and forth and laughed like two drunken friends each trying to drink the other under the table. After paying the bill, Tallman spent more time with the waitress and tried to hug her before leaving through the front door. They stumbled out of the restaurant back to their car. Wade followed well behind them as they wove their way back to hotel parking.

Max and Wade reconvened at their motel exchanging more details of the evening's activities, trying to contemplate how they might use Dr. Palmer's newly rediscovered golf hobby in their plans. At one point in their discussion a light bulb went off in Wade's mind when he blurted out in the middle of one of Max's sentences, "Wait, I think this golf interest of Dr. Palmer provides just the right opportunity for the intervention we've been looking for. After all, look at how golf changed his uncle Arnold Palmer's life."

Max asked, "Are you serious? Are they related?"

"No. Just kidding but I do think the golf thing might work in our favor," Wade replied.

"Sometimes I never know when to take you seriously," Max responded.

Their discussion suddenly got more serious when they shifted back to the operation plan as each began to build on the other's suggestion of how Dr. Palmer's golf routine might fit into the plan. The conversation continued through a late dinner that evening and started fresh again early the next morning at breakfast.

At times the operational scenarios Wade and Max came up with ended in a dead stop. There were too many unknown variables to contend with, too many pieces that could go wrong. Nothing seemed to completely address all of the divergent moving parts and their consequences.

The next day they discussed scenario after scenario until the late afternoon when things finally started to come together. After a day of rejected alternatives, each suggestion by Wade and Max built in a positive way until an "Ah-Ha moment" came early that evening when each turned to the other at the same time saying, "I think we have it."

They talked through more details and settled on a single plan. This exhaustive exploration of details seemed to always be the way it worked when Wade and Max were on an operation together. Sleep was the only remedy for their exhaustion when both agreed it would be best to take up Plan B alternatives in the morning.

Wade and Max shared breakfast the next morning, both committed to finalizing alternative tactics of a Plan B the next day. One Plan B alternative they agreed on was that in the event of problems with the operatives they would terminate them. They were expendable to the overall mission of obtaining information on Megan's whereabouts and as intermediary subcontract assassins they could probably provide little intelligence information that would be valuable to the U.S. government. The two men further reasoned late that night that by eliminating the operatives at least Dr. Palmer and his son would be out of immediate danger. Tomorrow Wade and Max would finalize details of the main plan and various alternatives and begin execution of their plan.

Chapter 10

At 5:30 the next morning after only two hours of sleep both men struggled to remember details of last evening's discussion. After a cup of coffee and a refill, details started coming back and neither of them had any major corrections to their operational plan. Each emphasized to the other that dates and timing would be critical to the plan's success.

As with most good covert plans, even with the complexity of moving parts, the plan itself had to remain simple in its structure. Both felt confident that their plan met all the criteria that their collective Intelligence and Special Forces training had taught them - Diversion, Separation, Take-Down, Interrogation, and Extraction. Both men agreed the next day that the plan had passed the overnight "sleep test" in flying colors. They started laying out the activities for the day's operation as each consumed two more cups of strong coffee.

Wade had his list already prepared, which included contacting several individuals including Detective Darren Wherter of the Bethesda Police to confirm whether he was on board with the pick-up plan for the operatives. Wade gave Max the duty of checking that Dr. Palmer's routine had not changed. Max's other assignment was to scout out sites they needed for the take-down phase of the operation .

After completing several calls, Wade returned to the Golden Gate Restaurant where the two operatives had partied two nights before. Wade arrived in disguise two hours before the restaurant opened and approached the handsome bartender who was also part owner and manager. He told the bartender that he was local FBI and showed an authentic FBI badge.

Explaining to the manager that they were investigating a crime in the area, he believed that a person of interest had recently visited his restaurant and was served by a particular waitress. Wade gave a detailed description of one the restaurant waitresses and emphasized that he wanted to speak with her. The bartender knew exactly who Wade was referring to and left for the kitchen area. He quickly returned escorting the waitress with him. The bartender suggested that they occupy a booth in the far corner of the restaurant where they could speak in private.

Wade introduced himself to the waitress speaking in a calm tone, describing what information he needed. "My name is Agent Nelson of the FBI. We are working on a case and you may be able to assist us."

"Am I in any kind of trouble?" The waitress nervously asked.

"No, you are not involved in the case or under any investigation. You just may have some information about two people we are investigating in connection with your work here."

The stress on the face of the waitress suddenly turned to curiosity, "How can I help?"

Wade smiled, "The two persons we have under surveillance you served here two nights ago. I have a few questions to ask you about those guests."

The waitress looked puzzled trying to recall all the guests she served. Wade began his description, "The gentlemen I am referring to had Asian facial features. One man was quite a bit taller than the other and did most of the talking."

Pointing to a table a few feet away Wade continued, "The two men sat at that table and were here for a long time. In addition to ordering several main courses they did a lot of drinking. Do you remember them?"

The waitress's eyes moved back and forth rapidly before answering, "Yes, I remember them."

"Have you ever seen these men before?"

"Yes, I think the two men came in another time or two."

"Do they always come in on the same evening around the same time?"

"No, I think the other time I remember they came in was a Tuesday evening."

"Did they leave you a nice tip?"

"Yes, they were very kind. I think he gave me fifty dollars."

"I would call that a nice tip. Do you remember if he gave you anything else when they were here last?"

"What do you mean?"

"Did he write anything on a piece of paper and give it to you?"

"Yes, his phone number. He said he wanted to have a date with me and take me out to dinner."

"I assume he meant somewhere else besides here?"

The waitress broke into a smile. "No, we wouldn't come here."

"Did you understand his offer to go on a date was with him alone or also with the other man?"

"No, just with him, not with the other man."

"And when would you have gone on this date?"

"I told him on my night off, which is on Monday."

"Have you called him back at the number he gave you?"

"No. He was drunk. I'm not going to go out with that man."

"Do you still have his number?"

"I don't know. I would have to look for it."

"Where would you go to look for it?"

"I think it might be in my changing locker here in the staff ladies room."

"I would like you to go see if you can find that piece of paper. It may be important."

"You want me to go now?"

"Yes, I'll wait for you at the bar."

Wade and the waitress walked over to the bar together before she separated to go back through the kitchen door. Wade turned to the bartender.

"She's going to look in the ladies room for a piece of paper I need."

"Is she in any kind of trouble?"

"No, I don't think she's involved. She just innocently came into possession of a phone number we need."

"Good. She's one of my best waitresses. I wouldn't want to lose her."

"She's been very cooperative. From what I see so far I don't see our investigation involving her in any way."

A smile of relief by the bartender was soon followed by the waitress emerging from the kitchen and handing Wade the piece of paper with the phone number. Wade pointed and the two returned to the booth they previously occupied.

"I just have a few more questions for you."

"I'm going to copy down this number and return the paper to you."

An insulted expression came over the waitress who quickly responded, "You can keep it. I don't need that number any more. I wasn't going to call that man, especially if he's in some kind of police trouble."

Wade smiled as he responded. "Actually, I want you to keep this number. I may need you to call him and arrange to meet for that date."

Her facial expression suddenly turned sour, thinking she had to go on a date with the man. Anticipating her response Wade quickly explained, "Don't worry, you won't actually be going on the date with him. Our officers will handle everything. I just need you to make the call."

Wade's explanation seemed to calm her as he continued. "I will need your contact information so I can reach you when we need you to make the call."

Making notes as she provided information, Wade also confirmed the work schedules of the other waitresses before he reminded her to maintain her normal schedule.

"One last thing, it is possible that one or both of these men will come into the restaurant again. I want you to serve them just like you did before, not giving any sign that you are worried. I don't want you to speak to anyone here at the restaurant or at home about our conversation. You don't need to engage in long conversations but if the tall man comes in be sure to smile showing him that you are still interested. You will be under close surveillance by my men all the time. Do you understand?

"Yes. When will all of this happen?"

"It's hard to say for certain but I think soon, perhaps within the week."

"That's good," replied the waitress, relieved that the incident would soon be over.

Wade wanted to leave on a positive note. "By the way, I told your boss you were very cooperative to our investigation, so there won't be any problems over this matter with your job here. In fact, your boss complimented you by saying he feels you are one of his best."

"He told you that?"

"Yes, he did."

"He never tells me anything like that."

"Neither does my boss. I think all bosses are alike in that regard."

The waitress smiled at Wade's comment as they both got up from the booth.

On the other side of town, Max drove down the dusty back roads of Frederick looking for the right isolated locations for the remainder of his day's assignment. Max radioed to exchange updates.

"Rover 1 to Base, over", Max called through the receiver.

"Base copy, over."

"How did your interview go at the restaurant? Over."

Wade answered, "Fine, I think we have at least one new intervention we can deploy. How is your search going?"

Max responded, "Good. I have one location set and am working on the second. We'll need to get a couple of good locks but it looks safe. I'm on a country backroad looking for spot two. I have a couple of ideas to discuss when we get together."

Wade responded with a reminder. "Remember, the closer to the golf course for the second location the better. I don't want to be driving around with the package for very long."

"I hear you, boss. We'll talk later this evening."

"Copy and out," Wade replied as he signed off.

That evening they caught each other up on details while they checked radio batteries, weapons and maps. They rehearsed each operational step, timing them with a stopwatch. Both men knew no matter how detailed their plan was, there would always be unknowns with uncertain events occurring that neither could control. They ended the evening session by walking through as many responses to unforeseen events as they could imagine.

As the weekend approached, each man took turns following Dr. Palmer and the operatives through their unchanged daily surveillance routines. On Saturday, Wade met with the waitress and rehearsed the call, setting up the date for Monday evening until he thought she was ready to make the call to Tallman.

Mid-afternoon the waitress made the call in Wade's presence. Her voice was gentle, but a little nervous providing the ideal demeanor of a shy innocent girl showing a reserved interest for a first-time encounter with a man she had just met. Using a payphone near the restaurant Wade shared the receiver with the waitress so he could hear Tallman's voice. The Burmese operative was anxious to meet the younger waitress away from the crowded bustle of her workplace. While Tallman didn't speak the King's English he confirmed to Wade that he clearly understood and could communicate in English.

The waitress was convincing in her explanation of why she didn't want a new man coming to her door, which would be upsetting to her elderly mother who lived with her. With the lot being just a short distance away it would make life easier for her to meet there. Tallman's acceptance of the location Wade had previously selected went smoothly.

Shaking hands after the call, Wade thanked the waitress for her cooperation and reminded her again not to discuss anything about her role in the investigation or their conversations. Wade assured her that nothing identifying her would be kept in the official investigative records. The waitress thanked Wade in return and turned toward her restaurant only a half-block away. Everything was now set for the meeting on Monday evening.

While Wade was with the waitress, Max checked the golf course schedule board confirming Dr. Palmer's golf lesson on Tuesday was still in play. Everything was in place for the take-down phase of the operation. From here the hardest part of the operation would be waiting for Monday evening to arrive. Each man kept busy checking out locations, weapons, equipment, and timing routes making sure that there were no loose ends and they hadn't missed any details.

Saturday evening Wade spent sleepless hours preoccupied with how he was going to convince Dr. Palmer to provide information on Megan's whereabouts and her project. While Wade contemplated Palmer's interrogation, Max lay awake contemplating everything that could go wrong with apprehending or eliminating the two operatives.

If they were going to successfully pull off the operation sequence, timing would be critical. For the third time on Sunday Wade and Max checked radio reception, weapons and reviewed maps as they had rehearsed numerous times before. Both men knew that no matter how long and detailed their plan was there would always be unknowns and uncertainties that neither could control. They ended the evening session by walking through as many responses to unforeseen events as they could imagine.

Monday morning both men rose early, each a little apprehensive of the day's events. For Max it was like the day before a Recon mission in the jungles of Vietnam. For Wade it was about putting his anger into check to focus on action steps to find Megan. The two men shared breakfast with their game faces on, each exchanging personal comments unrelated to the mission and showing a care-free professional front in the face of their pending mission.

Even though the men knew each other well, feelings of nervousness or apprehension, which they both shared, were now buried in confident references to mission details and expressions of commitment to the same operational goals. Each was in a military-assured calm mode, projecting nothing but mission focus and success.

After breakfast the men went over each other's steps, timing, and routes one last time prompting each other with surprise questions of what they would do if some unexpected event occurred. Both had their routines so well memorized they could recite them down to the last detail and in reverse order in their sleep.

Monday morning started out with Wade taking first watch on Dr. Palmer and the operatives' surveillance positions while Max checked site locations making sure the equipment they needed was all hidden in the right places. Around 1:00 p.m., after performing morning tasks, the men returned to the motel to start mission countdown procedures.

As the mission time grew near for their individual departures, they tested transmitters, receivers and radio frequency settings one last time. They both checked each other's disguises. Max was using one of Wade's disguises which he had modified to better reflect Max's facial features. They wished each other well as Wade was the first to depart to his assigned location.

Chapter 11

Wade had scouted the designated parking lot location for the meeting before the scheduled date. He drove past the actual lot without slowing down just to ensure that it was empty and lighting would not be a problem. He made several turns down side streets until he found a vacant residential lot that gave him good vision of his target location and surroundings through binoculars. A large tree grew on the other side of the vacant lot and he parked under its several overhanging branches.

He scanned all sides of the horizon including the area behind his current location. Wade wanted to be certain Tallman was not also surveying the same location and that there were no operative reinforcements waiting in the surrounding area.

Thirty minutes after Wade's departure Max headed to a street parking position near the Tudor Hotel. Approaching the hotel, he first checked the parking structure to see if the operatives' green sedan was still parked in its assigned space. Max radioed Wade that the targets' car was still parked at the hotel before he proceeded to the lobby.

Picking up a newspaper from the stack at the registration counter, Max settled in a chair where he had good vision of the hotel lobby. A line was forming in front of the desk to register new guests that had just arrived by bus. The lobby was a bustle of activity of incoming people with suitcases and bellmen giving directions.

It wasn't long before Max spotted Tallman coming off the elevator. He paused to look over the line of new guests before leaving through the door to the parking structure. Moving from his chair to a corner where he could be less obvious he spoke into the small microphone on his lapel.

"Rover to Base, do you read?" Max called to Wade.

"Base, I copy you."

Max added, "Your target is leaving the garage now."

Wade replied, "Right on time. I'm in place, over."

Wade asked, "Do you have eyes on Shortstop, yet?"

"Negative, over," Max replied.

"Give him some time. He starts to get hungry about now."

"I copy, over."

Max returned to his chair and resumed reading the paper. The line of incoming guests had grown to more than double its previous size and was blocking a portion of his view of the elevators. After moving to another chair which gave him a better vantage point over the lobby Max carefully scanned the registration line. He was looking for anything suspicious that might represent reinforcement troops for the operatives. Of all the faces he observed none posed a threat.

After an hour of waiting Max saw his target enter the lobby out of the elevator door to his right. Shortstop paused at the crowded lobby looking around at the proliferation of new guests and confusion around the front desk. Max watched carefully to see if his target spotted anyone of interest. Ignoring the lobby crowd Shortstop turned and exited through the front hotel doors.

Max followed closely in his footsteps, mixing in with the growing crowd of commuter pedestrians going in both directions on the sidewalk. Shortstop took a sharp left turn and picked up his pace. Max traversed in and around commuters to keep the same distance from his target. The crowd had now splintered into only five pedestrians between him and his target. The sidewalk was a bustle of activity. Everyone was in a hurry to get home from work.

Having turned left at the last corner Max knew that his target had eliminated one of three possible favorite restaurant choices. Wade had memorized the routes to all those restaurant options from the hotel. Max brought his lapel speaker closer to his mouth.

"Rover to Base, over."

"Base copy, over."

Max reported, "I have Shortstop en route to one of two possible locations. Do you have sign of Tallman? Over."

Wade replied, "No sign of Tallman yet, over."

Max responded, "I would give him more time but be careful he's not observing your location, over."

Wade answered, "I am well away from the meet site, checking traffic and bystanders in all directions, over."

The green car came into Wade's view as it passed the meeting site without slowing down. Only one occupant, the driver, appeared in the car through Wade's binoculars. The car drove two blocks past the meeting site and turned right. Anxiously waiting to see if the empty lot was too suspicious for Tallman, Wade patiently watched. The green sedan made a second appearance this time passing the lot from the opposite direction. After driving past the lot for a block and a half Tallman parked the car and shut off the engine. Wade had already started running through take-down alternatives thinking a waiting game had ensued. He radioed Max.

"Base to Rover do you read? Over."

"I read four by four, over," Max replied.

"I have target in sight on a side street from lot. He is parked observing meeting spot from two blocks away. I may have to change approach, over."

Max replied, "I would be patient. The waiting game works against him after he feels she may not show if he is not there."

"Good point. Waiting works both ways when it comes to a date. What is your status? Over."

"I am a block away from the Golden Palace Restaurant. I guess Shortstop decided if he was going to eat alone he would go for the more expensive dining, over."

"Does that restaurant change any of your take-out plans?" Wade asked.

"Negative. Either one works for me. In fact this one is actually a little better, over," Max replied.

"Good. We both should check in when anything changes," Wade instructed.

"Copy, Boss."

According to Wade's wristwatch it was fifteen minutes before the scheduled meeting time. He wondered how long Tallman would push his luck of not being there when she was supposed to arrive. The next few minutes seemed like an eternity. Wade didn't want to go to Plan B if he didn't have to because his odds for a positive outcome would change dramatically.

His best Plan B alternative at the moment was if Tallman didn't approach the lot, Wade would have to pin him into his parking place for an open street take down. In the mostly residential neighborhood where Tallman had parked that might mean a messy gun battle on the quiet streets of Frederick.

Wade watched Tallman surrounded in darkness remain still in his car. His watch ticked one minute before the meeting time. The waiting game of who was going to break first was now intense. Perhaps Tallman was waiting until he saw the waitress arrive before he pulled into the lot. By the same token the waitress not wanting to be alone in a vacant parking lot might not be willing to show herself until she saw him and his car. Wade hoped but had no way to verify that concerns of not showing without him in the parking lot were weighing heavily on Tallman's mind.

By Wade's watch it was fifteen seconds after the scheduled meeting time before the light and engine of the green sedan came on. Tallman's car rolled slowly across and down the street into the lot to park at the far end. Wade felt his timing was now critical. He wanted his target to get comfortable, but not too comfortable before he came bolting in.

When the green sedan rolled to a stop at one of the concrete wheel stops at the far end of the lot Wade counted seconds as he reached for his ignition key. Suddenly to Wade's surprise Tallman's door swung open. Caught off guard at the movement Wade's hand froze in mid-air inches away from the ignition.

Tallman got out of his car and pulled out a cigarette. After lighting it, he began smoking as Wade took a deep breath as his heart raced, wondering if his suspect saw something that made him suspicious. Tallman wandered around to the rear of his car casually looking around the lot and at the half-moon sky above. He seemed to be unconcerned about having to wait for his date or he was sizing up distances across the lot carefully plotting his next move.

Wade considered new options. To be most effective Wade reasoned his approach had to be direct and quick not allowing Tallman time, space or opportunity to take evasive action. He had to wait until Tallman finished his smoke and see what unfolded. The sun was below the horizon and the street lights on the main avenue hadn't come on yet. The lot became a little darker every minute.

Shortly after his stroll Tallman tossed the remainder of his cigarette and returned to his seat, closed his door and put down his window. Wade instinctively knew this was his cue. He slowly turned down a side street which led directly to the empty lot and made a sharp turn picking up speed as he turned into the lot. Wheels squealed as Wade's car came to an abrupt halt crossway behind the rear bumper of the green sedan. The exit for Tallman out of the lot was now blocked.

With his gun drawn Wade quickly approached the driver's window and pointed his automatic weapon directly at Tallman's head. Wade was in disguise, which included a police uniform and bullet proof vest. He said in a loud firm voice,

"Police, put your hands in the air where I can see them!" His gun was pointed less than a foot from Tallman's head. His next instructions were given in an equally forceful manner.

"Using your right hand open the door using the outside handle, slowly."

When Tallman complied, Wade continued.

"Now slowly back out of the car keeping your hands on the roof of the car at all times and spread your legs."

Tallman complied not showing any particular surprise. Wade's voice as well as his intent conveyed if his suspect showed any unauthorized movement he would not hesitate to shoot him. Wade proceeded to pat the suspect down. After telling Tallman to leave one hand on the roof he took one hand behind the suspect's back Wade cuffed the one hand then the other before completing his pat down.

His search revealed a model .044 leather ankle holster and a low caliber short barrel Beretta semi-automatic and a fighting knife in a scabbard along his beltline. The knife rested in downward position in the center of his back.

Wade asked, "What is your name, sir?" The suspect didn't respond.

Trying to get the suspect to speak Wade asked again, "What is your name?" Still the suspect remained silent.

Wade had his captive but was not about to take any chances and certainly wasn't worried about the suspect's rights. After removing all of his identification, money and car keys, Wade attached ankle cuffs leaving ten inches of chain between each foot and marched Tallman in small steps over to the rear of his car.

Tallman now seemed both surprised and annoyed at the unconventional police procedures. He had already started thinking that this was no normal traffic violation stop. Concluding he had been set up Tallman's thoughts turned to more serious consequences.

The change in Tallman's expression continued as Wade gagged him and put a black hood over his head. Tallman heard the snap of the trunk latch open and felt Wade's firm hand helping him into the confined trunk space. Wade told the suspect to lay face down flat on the trunk floor as he applied the last precautionary gesture of bending his knees and attaching a chain between his ankle shackles and his handcuffs. Wade called the foolproof procedure - *"hog tying"*- and checked to make sure the bindings were tight before slamming the trunk lid.

Slowly pulling out of the parking lot, Wade radioed Max to update his status speaking in a low voice so his passenger, no matter how well detained in the trunk he was, couldn't overhear the conversation.

"Base to Rover. Do you copy? Over."

"I copy. Over."

"Package in tow without problem. En route to Holiday Shores. What is your status? Over."

Max reported, "I am at the bar of the Golden Palace watching Shortstop eat and trying to pick up his own waitress."

"Do you need assistance? Over."

"Negative. I have two possible interception points identified. Just have to wait until dinner and romance is over here. Over."

"Copy. Will report after next phase. Over," Wade confirmed.

"Roger, out," Max replied ending the transmission.

Holiday Shores was a forty-five minute drive down a back road just outside of Frederick. That code name was used for the holding spot for the two operatives until law enforcement could arrive for formal arrests. The out of town holding pen accommodations were older storage units that were only manned three days a week in the morning by an elderly gentleman that called his place -*"The Ranch"*-. The large rental figure the men were offering the old man ensured that whatever went on in their units would stay on the ranch.

Max and Wade made a few modifications to the basic units to make certain they were secure and ventilated enough so their captives could survive for several days. They also rigged water bottles with tubes leading to where the captives could draw water when needed. The design of the water system was compliments of Max, who saw first-hand how the troops were kept alive as captives in Vietnam.

As Wade turned off the highway down a gravel road toward Holiday Shores he thought about taking time to interrogate Tallman since his part of the operation had gone so smoothly. He had an extra hour before he had to entertain Dr. Palmer that same evening. Wade thought it might also be a good time for Tallman to consider talking as he had further time to contemplate his predicament as a U.S. held captive.

Chapter 12

Knowing Wade had everything in hand with Tallman, Max focused more closely on his task at hand. His situation was different than Wade's, which had in some ways more risk. Max and Wade realized that Shortstop would be on foot and depending on which restaurant he chose different take down points had to be identified for each location. At the last minute Max decided against a police uniform believing it would cause more street attention. He settled on a facial hair disguise and street clothes.

After his suspect entered the restaurant and took his seat, Max entered the bar and picked a corner table where he could observe the back of his suspect in the larger well-lit main dining room. Without his cohort for company Shortstop took more time than usual to study the menu, even asking the waitress to explain certain dishes.

The stocky frame of the shorter operative aptly described his code name "Shortstop". Max noticed that what the code name didn't reflect was the muscular build under the street clothes and the heavily callused hands and forearms Max or Wade had previously failed to notice. Max had seen those fighting marks before in the many martial arts competitions he attended and participated in during his Special Forces training. The unusually wide stance and thick thighs on Shortstop also went unnoticed. Knowing the body type, Max immediately concluded his target was a kicker and probably in martial arts training since childhood.

Like some sixth sense, just after ordering the suspect suddenly showed nervousness, turning his head back and forth. At one time he turned around as through looking for someone in the bar. Max didn't feel he had been seen but felt it was time for him leave and prepare for his street take down. He radioed his status to Wade who had just secured his witness to the heavy eye rings they had installed in the storage unit.

"Rover to Base. Do you read?"

"I read. Give me time to step out of the unit so I can talk. Over," Wade requested.

"Take your time," Max replied.

"I'm clear, Rover. What's your status?" Wade asked.

"Just left Shortstop at the restaurant. He may be in there for a while. On the way to move the van closer to the contact point. Over," Max reported.

"Any surprises with Shortstop?" Wade inquired.

"No, except our boy may be a fighter. He has all the marks."

"Do you need assistance? I can be there in less than an hour. Over."

"Negative. Nothing I can't handle. Over."

"Are you sure? No time to take chances."

"Life's a chance," Max replied.

"Life's also what you make it, man," Wade countered.

"I'm fine on my end. What's your status?" Max asked.

"I just gave Tallman a talking to about how he is in no position to stay quiet because the people he's going to be turned over to are not going to be as nice and accommodating as I am."

"What did he say?"

"Nothing. That's pretty much the way it's been with him since the take down. I don't think we're going to get much out of him. Perhaps spending some discomfort at Holiday Shores will soften him up when we speak to them together."

"What's your plan from there?" Max asked.

"I leave here in a half hour to meet golfer unless I'm coming to meet you."

"I'm fine with this guy. Just proceed to your next stop. I'll call if something comes up."

"Okay partner. Be safe," Wade responded.

"You too, partner," Max replied as he signed off.

Max retraced his route deciding on one particular interdiction point that he liked. The space was an empty flat lot surrounded by what remained of an old brick wall from a building that had been torn down many years ago. He carefully studied the lot and determined the best direction to approach Shortstop.

Walking around the perimeter of the lot he looked for viewpoints where they might be observed by others. The lot was a block from the main avenue and backed up to the rear doors of shops, which had all closed for the evening. Max was satisfied that the view into the lot by pedestrians on the main avenue was limited. After parking his van closer to the lot Max retraced the route back to the restaurant to see other options Shortstop might take. He had to be ready to quickly change his preferred interdiction point if Shortstop decided on another route.

Max took up position outside the restaurant where he had a clear vision of dining guests. The wait seemed forever, but eventually Shortstop brought his check to the front cashier and left the building. Keeping a half block distance behind, Max watched his target cross the restaurant parking lot taking the route he had expected. His target seemed unaware of his surroundings and consumed in thought, perhaps thinking of his cohort having a better time that evening with his new girlfriend.

118

At the third block past the restaurant Shortstop made the expected right turn to take the shorter route back to the hotel, avoiding a busy intersection crossing on the main street. He was now headed directly for the vacant lot. As Shortstop approached the vacant lot, Max moved to his right and circled around to the position where he wanted to intercept his target. Max was wearing a baseball cap with a police emblem and a bullet proof vest with "Police" printed across the chest. He had his gun out as he approached his target from the side.

"Police, stop where you are and put your hands over your head," Max rang out in strong voice.

The suspect stopped and started to raise his hands halfway above his head slightly turning in the process. With gun drawn and pointing at the suspect Max said, "You are under arrest. Keep your hands in the air."

The suspect smiled while Max noticed a slight shifting of his weight from front to rear leg. His next step closer to the suspect was met with a lightning-fast quarter round kick that caught Max slightly off guard. Max's well-trained quick reflexes rebounded causing the operative's blow to be only glancing. The kick shocked Max's forearm holding his weapon but didn't dislodge the gun from his hand.

Max used the momentum of the suspect's kick to spin and follow with his own kick which landed hard on the suspect's neck and jaw. Before Shortstop could recover, Max landed a second hard frontal kick to the solar plexus. The second kick put the suspect on the ground dazed. Max thought the confrontation had ended with the last blow and began approaching the suspect for cuffing.

To his surprise Shortstop jumped to his feet throwing a barrage of fists and kicks at Max which he either blocked or avoided. Both men stood opposing each other in a martial arts stance. Shortstop ignored the fact that Max was still holding his silenced Sig-Sauer 9 mm semiautomatic weapon on him. There was a brief momentary pause when each man looked ready, daring the other to make the next move. Max hesitated from using his weapon, feeling confident he could take this guy in any hand-to-hand confrontation.

His opponent initiated the next move with a quick flurry of kicking and punching moves. Max was even quicker, moving from side to side and backward to block or avoid his blows. His opponent slowly circled Max looking right into the barrel of his gun somehow believing Max would not use it.

Shortstop made another volley of several more quick kicks and spins which missed their mark. His shorter opponent surprised Max when he seemed to pull back from his position and turned his head like he might consider fleeing the scene. That was not to be his next move, however. His real purpose was to draw Max closer. Max suddenly saw the blade of a fighting knife in his opponent's hand that he had pulled out from under his shirt. The five inch blade was black in the center with highly sharpened edges glowing on both sides.

Shortstop initiated more kicking thrusts combined with slashing movements of his hand with the knife. Max avoided the kicks by moving back and blocked one of the thrusting blows of the knife a foot before it reached his vest. Max didn't understand his next act or his own emotions which prompted it. Instead of using his weapon, Max returned his gun to his holster so he had both hands to contend with his opponent's knife. Something had triggered a momentary response in Max that the fight was no longer part of the operation but had become personal.

As the suspect lunged forward with his knife, Max grabbed his wrist and followed with a hard punch of his other

120

hand on the suspect's jaw. The suspect went down again. As Max went in for another blow the knife grazed across Max's forearm making a four inch gash. Max could feel the blood already starting to run down his arm. His opponent was dazed from the last blow unable to come to his feet when Max landed another blow to his face. This knife flew from his hand landing a safe distance away.

Max stood over the suspect who slowly rolled to his side while Max reached for his handcuffs thinking the battle was over. His suspect wasn't ready to give up quite yet. With his hand under his body the suspect reached into the lining of his jacket and pulled out a sixteen-inch tube. Before Max realized it there was another weapon involved in his suspect's arsenal. With a quick movement the suspect inserted a small dart and fired the blowgun at Max. The small dart, probably coated with a drug, landed in Max's bullet proof vest but didn't penetrate the vest or Max's skin.

Without thinking Max reacted to the dart, which he could see from the corner of his eye sticking out of his vest like a miniature carnation. Max responded with another strong blow of his gloved fist into the suspect's face. The metal blowgun added to Max's strong blow breaking the suspect's jaw and removing several teeth in the process. The suspect's face was now a bloody mess.

Tired of secret weapons and the relentless stamina of his opponent Max pulled back from the suspect on the ground and drew his weapon. Max instructed the suspect to turn face down. Again disobeying the order, the suspect went to one knee then jumped up to a standing position attempting another roundhouse kick and a flurry of fist blows this time yelling through his bloody face. Even though he was now dodging more feeble blows Max was done with the challenges and his opponent's attitude.

He took a step back, aimed his weapon and shot the suspect in the leg just above the knee cap.

Shortstop rolled to the ground grabbing his leg in pain. Max wasted no time pulling the suspect's hands behind his body and cuffing them. Max knew the pain he was going through because this was the same location Max had suffered his wound in Vietnam. Perhaps his shot was part anger, part redemption. He left the suspect curled on the ground not worried that he was going anywhere while he walked the half block to get the van.

On his way to the van Max took out his small flashlight and examined his own forearm wound. It was an ugly gash but no arteries were severed. Max pulled the van on the lot between the street and the suspect. He approached the suspect carefully and ankle cuffed both legs. Max pushed and dragged the heavier suspect to the side door of the van and managed to get him inside. He checked the leg wound, tore off a piece of the suspect's shirt and bandaged it. He tore another piece of the suspect's shirt and bandaged himself. Finally he bent the suspect's leg and attached a chain from the ankle cuffs to the hand cuffs so he could report to his boss that his captive was hogtied.

Climbing in the driver's seat Max looked around and didn't notice anyone standing around the vacant lot and considered himself lucky that a crowd hadn't appeared. He drove the van out of the lot and adjusted his radio for a call to Wade.

"Rover to Base, do you read?"

"Base. I read you loud and clear."

"I am with package en route to Holiday Shores, over."

"Did you have a problem securing the package?" Wade asked.

"You might say so. The package is a bit damaged but suitable for presentation. Over."

Wade could hear a little adrenaline shake in Max's voice and knew his propensity for dry humor.

"Are you all right?" Wade asked.

"A few bumps and bruises but I'm fine," Max answered.

Wade knew better than to accept Max's casual explanation knowing something more had happened. Wade commented, "I'm not buying the story. I'll meet you at Holiday Shores."

"Unnecessary, boss. I'm fine. You should follow your own mission instructions and proceed to the next phase."

"I have time and I know you too well. I'll meet you at the Shores," Wade firmly responded.

Wade checked his watch. He was about ten minutes out from the storage units on his way to apprehend Dr. Palmer. Worried that his partner wasn't giving him the whole story he pulled to the side of the highway and when traffic cleared turned around and headed back to the storage units. Fifteen minutes later Max's white van pulled up. He took one look at Max and knew he was not okay. Max got out of the driver's door and Wade motioned him over to better lighting where they were also out of earshot of his captive.

"Now tell me the whole damn story from the beginning and don't leave anything out," Wade demanded.

Max gave Wade a truthful blow-by-blow description of what happened. Wade was shocked that there had not been more damage to both Max and the suspect. Wade saw the hastily-wrapped bandage on Max's arm.

Pointing to Max's forearm Wade said, "Let me get the medic bag out of the car and take a look at that under the light." Wade walked toward the car as Max leaned in exhaustion against the side of the van. When he returned Wade could see in Max's pale face the comedown after the adrenalin rush.

"I'm fine. You need to be getting Dr. Palmer."

"Let me worry about Dr. Palmer. I'm fine on time."

Wade opened the medic bag on the car hood and removed the shirt bandage.

"Who taught you how to field bandage?" Wade asked.

"I was asleep in that class," Max replied.

"You sure were. You need a few stiches, my friend."

Wade cleaned out the wound, stitched it and taped a compression bandage over his forearm.

"You've got blood all over your shirt and vest," Wade commented.

"You should see the other guy," replied Max pulling open his shirt to show Wade the red tail end of the dart sticking out his vest.

"You better be thankful that didn't go through. I suspect you'd be sleeping now or worse," Wade responded.

"I'll bet our other guy Tallman has the same blowgun and darts in his coat lining," Max commented.

"We'll check him in a minute. Let's check your guy first," Wade replied.

"Whatever you do, don't let his feet loose. He's got a kick like a mule," Max warned.

"I'm not letting anything on him loose. I just want to check his bullet wound to make sure he doesn't bleed out on us," Wade replied.

Wade and Max turned Shortstop over to expose the shot in his leg. Leaving all his constraints in place, Max held his flashlight on the area while Wade examined the entrance and exit wound.

"It's a flesh wound that passed through the thigh. Either you're a damn good shot or he's real lucky you didn't hit an artery or his bone," Wade reported as he looked over the captive's broken jaw and teeth.

"I'll accept either accuracy or luck. The guy was a beast," Max replied.

"He'll need some medical attention but he's okay. He's going to need a good dentist or his smile will never be the same. I guess he must have gotten you real pissed off."

"Something like that," Max replied.

Wade cleaned out the bullet wound with alcohol and applied a compression bandage. They both wrestled the suspect out of the van and dragged him into the storage unit where they secured him to the wall bracing.

The two men went three units over to Tallman and found the blowgun and a set of small darts hidden in the lining of his jacket just as Max had suspected. After removing the dart weapon they locked the doors to the storage units and walked back to Wade's car.

Wade looked into Max's eyes.

"I want you to stay here for at least another half hour before returning to the motel. You know as well as I do that you're coming down from the adrenalin rush from your battle with this guy. It takes your body at least two hours to come down from that even when you're in great shape."

"I hear you. I've been there before,'" Max responded.

"Your cut is bad but going to heal just fine but you'll be sore as hell for the next few days."

"I've been banged up more in training exercises," Max replied.

"I want you to check in with me every half hour."

There was a pause and look on Max's face of some disapproval.

"Do you read me, soldier?" Wade waited for his answer

"I read you, boss," Max replied.

"If I'm with Palmer I may not reply but I still want to hear your update and where you are. When you're back at the motel clean up and get something to eat, but no caffeine."

"Yes, mother hen," Max replied.

"You did a great job tonight. You're okay and you brought your man in alive. That was the mission." Wade complimented Max for his effort.

Unsatisfied with his performance Max replied, "I hesitated, boss."

"What do you mean you hesitated?" Wade asked.

"I should have shot the bastard right away. I hesitated to see if I could still handle myself in combat with my bad leg."

"You know damn well you can handle yourself in combat whether Special Forces thinks so or not," Wade responded.

"I won't let you down next time, boss," Max replied.

Wade quickly responded. "You didn't let me down, man. Stop thinking that way."

"Thanks," Max replied.

"I've got to go or I'll miss Dr. Palmer's golf swing," Wade stated.

"Good luck."

"Don't forget to report in," Wade commented before leaving the storage units. He waited for Max's nod that he heard the order.

Chapter 13

Greatly exceeding the speed limit, Wade was anxious to get back to the driving range before Dr. Palmer left. As Wade wove in and out of traffic, his earpiece rang with Max's first report since he left the storage units.

"Rover to Base. Do you read? Over."

"I read loud and clear. What's your status?" Wade asked.

"I am heading back to point zero. I verified that our packages are safely resting at Holiday Shores, over."

"How are you feeling?" Wade inquired.

"Good. I'm fine now. What's your status, over?" Max asked in a worried voice thinking his delay may have caused Wade to miss his window of opportunity.

"I wasn't sure you were fine before, partner, but you sound better now. I'm five minutes away from target and okay with the time. Over," Wade replied.

"I'll clean up and get back to watch the packages. Over."

"Negative on returning to Holiday Shores. Packages are fine for now. I may need you here. Try to get some shut-eye but keep your radio on," Wade instructed.

"I copy and will wait for your call. Over." Max replied, ending the call.

Less than an hour after leaving Holiday Shores Wade turned into the driving range parking lot. He could see the balls of mist swirling around the flood lights of the driving range. There were at least ten people in open stances hitting balls into a black sky, hoping to see a white dot drop somewhere near the distance markers where they were intended. As he drove closer for observation Wade hoped one of those men swinging at the balls was Dr. Palmer.

127

He pulled up closer to the fence for a better view. Dr. Palmer was four positions from the end. Watching him swing at a few balls confirmed Max's assessment. It was not the first time Dr. Palmer swung a club but he wasn't going to give any of the pros a run for their money anytime soon.

Wade returned to the area of the parking lot where he saw Dr. Palmer's car. It was parked off to one side well in the shadow of one of the overhead lights. Wade approached Palmer's car trying to decide on the best angle to intercept his target. He decided that surprising Dr. Palmer would not be to his advantage so he decided to park in a spot parallel to his car so Dr. Palmer could easily see his parked car about ten feet away.

Disguised and in police uniform Wade didn't want to draw any unnecessary attention to his presence. He settled low in his seat keeping track of Palmer's activity through intermittent scans of his binoculars. The long row of hitters started thinning out as one after the other emptied their basket of balls. Four golfers remained, each swinging from assigned stations separated by chalk lines. It was a half hour before closing time.

Dr. Palmer's metal basket was about two-thirds empty. With nothing better to do, Wade calculated that at the rate Palmer hit balls it would take him another fifteen to twenty minutes to empty his basket. Wade used those minutes to relax and control his breathing while he rehearsed exactly what he was going to say when he approached his target.

After hitting the last ball, Dr. Palmer stared out at the lighted field as though he recognized his particular balls among the thousands before him. Bidding farewell to the field, Palmer put the last club in his golf bag and turned toward the office exit and parking lot. He stopped for a short moment to speak to one of his fellow golfers two stations away.

With his bag over his shoulder, Palmer came down the steps and through the range's iron entrance gate walking towards his car. Although the parking lot was mostly empty, Wade's approach had to be spot-on not to attract unwanted attention. Dr. Palmer was paying little attention to the fact that Wade's dark sedan was parked parallel to his car ten feet away. With keys in hand Palmer moved to the rear of his car to open the trunk for his golf bag. Wade approached slowly with a smile on his face. He held a badge in one hand while the other hand rested casually on the butt of his weapon.

"Dr. Palmer, my name is Detective Nelson of the FBI. Can I have a word with you, sir?"

Thinking something must have gone terribly wrong at home or at work Dr. Palmer politely said, "Certainly. Is there a problem?"

"I'm not certain at this point. Please put your clubs in the trunk and step over here."

Palmer complied. His face showed the strain of pending horror. Wade followed Palmer to a spot between the two cars. Wade maintained his hand on his holstered automatic weapon keeping a calm but serious smile.

"What's happened?"

"Sir, my department is working with one of our intelligence agencies on an investigation that might somehow involve you and I have some questions for you in connection with that investigation."

Palmer thought the worst, wanting to know the exact meaning of the detective's statement. He responded with a question. "Is anyone in my family or at work in danger?"

Wade responded, "We are not certain. That is part of the information I am seeking."

Wade continued before Dr. Palmer could get out another question.

"There could be sufficient danger in this situation that we have an operational safe house set up near here for me to ask you a series of questions and share some intelligence on this matter. I am asking you to accompany me there for approximately one hour. I will return you to this location immediately after that so you can proceed home."

Palmer was becoming suspicious of the set-up. "What's the subject of this investigation and why aren't we having this discussion in your office or mine?"

"Sir, the discussion involves a highly sensitive intelligence matter and requires we maintain a high level of security. I'm going to have to insist that you come with me," Wade affirmatively stated.

"This seems totally out of protocol and I don't like it. What if I don't agree to come with you?" Palmer indignantly replied.

"Sir, my orders are to take you into custody whether you cooperate or not," Wade responded.

"Am I under arrest? What am I being charged with?" Dr. Palmer protested.

"Sir, those are legal issues that I am not authorized to discuss with you at this time. For now you are under protective custody for the purpose of answering questions critical to a U.S. Intelligence investigation and that is all. The matter is very serious requiring the highest level of security and could involve the lives of American citizens at risk. You may unknowingly have information which is important to this investigation. I can assure you that I would not be here if your immediate cooperation and testimony was not essential at this moment. If you have done nothing wrong in connection with these matters you have nothing to worry about. If you are somehow involved you will have due process and the opportunity to involve your own legal counsel. At this point is we are only interested in you answering a few questions."

"How long did you say this will take?" Palmer asked.

"It will take less than an hour," Wade replied.

"And you will bring me back to my car when this is over?" Palmer asked looking for confirmation.

"I will personally bring you back here unharmed in any way."

"I guess I don't have a choice with that weapon strapped to your side," Palmer commented

"I was hoping it would never become necessary for me to use it, sir," Wade replied.

"Okay, let's get this over with but I have no idea why you want to talk to me," Dr. Palmer said in frustration.

"Thank you, sir. The answer to your questions of why will become clear very quickly," Wade responded.

The two men turned to Wade's car. Dr. Palmer reached for the front door handle.

"Dr. Palmer, I'm going to have to ask you to indulge one more inconvenience. Because of the high security nature of this matter I am required to cuff and blindfold you until we get to the safe house," Wade politely instructed.

"Do you think I'm going to flee the scene and outrun you guys?" Palmer sarcastically replied.

"No sir. There will be other intelligence officers in the room whose identity we cannot disclose to you at this time," Wade responded.

"Crap. This is ridiculous. I've never heard of this before," Palmer responded in disgust.

"I agree the security measures are extreme, but I can assure you they are necessary to protect the lives of innocent citizens who may be involved," Wade replied.

Palmer turned around as Wade cuffed him then placed a black sleeping mask over his eyes and gently helped him clear the roof of his car as he came to rest awkwardly in the front seat.

Wade drove a circuitous route with plenty of turns while he engaged Dr. Palmer in conversation about his golf game. His intention was to take Dr. Palmer's mind off memorizing the route to the safe house destination. Pulling into the back lot of the restaurant off a side street Wade parked saying to Palmer, "We're here."

Max found the empty restaurant and thought it would make a great safe house. The empty building was close to the driving range. According to the real estate agent, the facility had been vacant for more than a year with no showings due to the fact that it was tied up in litigation among partners and their lenders.

After gaining access to the main dining room Max positioned a table and chairs, installed a ceiling light and dusted off the scene to look like the perfect stark room you might find in any office building.

Gently bending Dr. Palmer's head to clear the roof of his car Wade led the good doctor up the short path and staircase to the front door. There was reason why Wade wanted to give the impression that others were inside the secure building. He approached the front door and knocked in a deliberate pattern of short and long knocks.

He leaned over to Dr. Palmer's ear and whispered, "I have to give them my code."

Dr. Palmer nodded as he heard three reply knocks of short duration, which Wade supplied hitting the side of the building.

Wade responded with, "Code 7003 reporting." There was a quiet pause as Wade unlocked the chain. He kept his hand on Dr. Palmer's arm just above the elbow leading him through the door.

Replying to an imaginary officer, Wade said, "Are we over here?"

He turned back to Dr. Palmer and said, "We'll be turning to our right." While applying light pressure to his arm, Wade guided Dr. Palmer in a right turn and positioned him in front of an upright chair with substantial arm rests.

"Here's the chair. It's okay to sit right after I remove your cuffs."

After removing one cuff Wade helped Palmer get comfortable in the chair. Moving to the other side of the chair he cuffed his other hand to the armrest leaving his right hand free.

"Are you comfortable, sir?"

"I'm fine," Palmer replied.

Wade moved to the other side of the table. He reached for his tape recorder and file folder, which he put in the middle of the table before taking a chair opposite his witness.

"Our session will be taped and I am ready to begin as soon as I record a short introduction on the tape," Wade commented.

"Let's get this over with," Palmer responded with frustration.

In the few moments it took to take his seat Wade saw Dr. Palmer's expression turn from apprehension for his life to concerned interest to curiosity. Wade made his introduction into the tape recorder sounding official.

"This is Agent Nelson Code 7003 marking the beginning of a taped interview with Dr. Isaac Palmer as part of covert operation, 'Black Veil." Wade followed with the date and time of the interview.

During the introduction, the real tape in front of him was never turned on but Wade felt the formality of the introduction added credibility with Dr. Palmer and the setting. He needed Dr. Palmer to buy into the whole procedure and provide the information he needed.

The introduction seemed to be working. Palmer stiffened, sitting straighter in his chair. The official introduction caused Palmer to straighten his back sitting in a more erect position waiting for his first question.

Questions had been carefully prepared by Wade. The order was as important as the questions. He wanted to start with something that would immediately get Dr. Palmer's attention and involve him in a way that gave him reason to be concerned. Wade offered his witness bottled water which Dr. Palmer politely refused.

"I'll come right to the point Dr. Palmer. Are you aware that you and your son Randy have been followed for the past three weeks by a pair of national felons out of Burma? These men are wanted for kidnapping, torture and murder."

"No. I'm not aware of that at all. What makes you think any of that is true?" Dr. Palmer responded in a sarcastic manner.

"Dr. Palmer, I'll ask the questions. We will go over some of that evidence in a moment but I take it your answer to that question is no?"

"That is my answer, no."

"Can you think of any reason why you and your son are being followed?"

"Hell no. What does my son have to do with this?"

"Again, Dr. Palmer, let me ask the questions. Please try to concentrate on the question."

"I said no."

"Is there anything you are working on at work that might cause you to think these men or whoever they work for are interested in you or your son?"

"No. I work in a secure medical research facility for the U.S. Government and why do you keep bringing up my son? He's eleven years old for God's sake."

"I am aware that you are employed at the Army Medical Research Institute. I am referring to any particular project you may be working on that might interest a foreign government that is unfriendly to America."

Palmer paused before he answered. Wade could see his expression change as he thought about his research projects.

"There might be one or two projects that an unfriendly government might like to get their hands on," Dr. Palmer replied trying to be somewhat circumspect.

"As for your son, Dr. Palmer, our concern is that Randy is being targeted as a means of getting information out of you."

"That sounds like some crazy hypothetical Intelligence theory. I wouldn't accept that proposition without seeing some evidence," Dr. Palmer replied as though it was some research project, still rejecting the hypothesis.

"Dr. Palmer I really don't think you understand the seriousness of this matter. We are talking about your son. The foreign nationals I am talking about are well-trained assassins with a track record of kidnapping and torture. You don't seem to get the point. We are not talking about some theoretical plot.

These men have been following you and your son to Pierpoint Elementary every day for the last three weeks. They have documented every one of Randy's recess breaks and soccer practices. You have to visualize the consequences here. If these men kidnapped you and your son I can assure you from their track record they would not hesitate to strip Randy and horribly torture him in front of you until you give them the information they want. They would probably kill you both after they were finished with you."

Dr. Palmer cringed at the disgusting vision he was having from Wade's description. He had difficulty responding. Wade felt it was time to show him the evidence.

Chapter 14

Wade let Dr. Palmer stew in his own thoughts about visions of his son being tortured in front of him. He turned off the recorder making sure his witness heard the noise of his moving chair before getting up from his seat.

"Dr. Palmer, I'm placing before you on the table a security file which I would like you to review. I'm going to stand behind your chair to remove your blindfold and uncuff your right hand, so you can turn the pages of the file. Under no circumstance are you to turn around and look at me. There is a man across the room who has a gun pointed at the middle of your chest should you make any sudden moves. Do you understand?"

"Yes," replied Palmer.

Dr. Palmer could hear Wade approach the rear of his chair. Wade first uncuffed his right hand then removed the mask before stepping back into the shadows behind his chair. Palmer was momentarily stunned by the strong illumination of the light above the table. The file on the table soon came into focus. After his eyes adjusted the doctor pulled the file closer and with his free hand opened the cover of the folder.

Silently and slowly, Dr. Palmer studied each of the numerous photographs of himself, Randy and the two assassins. As he turned the pages he saw photos of the foreign operatives observing his house, work, Randy's school playground and soccer practice field. He saw picture after picture of the assassins intruding his personal space and his stomach sickened. He put his hand to his face in awestruck disbelief.

He stopped turning the photos and asked, "Why haven't these people been arrested?"

"There are two reasons. First, as for you and Randy, they haven't actually committed a crime yet. Secondly and more importantly, they are just paid operatives and not the people behind all this. These operatives are expendable to those behind this plot. The two men would be quickly replaced with others unless we get to the top of the organization behind all this," Wade replied.

"These people look Chinese. Doesn't that tell you something?" Dr. Palmer said in frustration.

"Not really, one country often uses operatives of another country to disguise their true identify. We have reason to believe that is the case here," Wade replied.

With his hand covering the lower part of his face Dr. Palmer now showed the personal concern Wade had been trying to instill, causing him to freeze. He remained motionless with the file open to the same page. Dr. Palmer showed little interest in turning more pages. Wade directed him back to the task of reviewing the file.

"Dr. Palmer, there is more I would like you to see in the file. I think it is important. Please continue."

The next four pages were photographs of his son Randy at recess. Shaking his head, Dr. Palmer turned the next two pages. Each of the following pages included Interpol mug shots and long rap sheets on each operative. It listed the crimes they were wanted for and gave a gruesome description of crimes already committed and time served at various international prisons and all the crimes each operative was wanted for.

The rap sheets showed each operative was wanted for kidnapping, torture and murder of family members of four European intelligence officers and which European countries considered these men as fugitives.

Dr. Palmer broke his silence. "There's no question these guys are bad news."

Wade was pleased to see reality set in and that Dr. Palmer grasped the seriousness of his situation.

"Dr. Palmer, I'm going to put your mask back on and cuff your hand back to the chair so we can continue our discussion. I told you we would not be more than an hour and I would like to keep that promise."

"Certainly," Palmer replied.

After returning to his chair Wade continued with a question. "Dr. Palmer, I would like to now focus my questions on why these men are here. I think you will surely agree after seeing the evidence they are not here to observe Randy's next soccer game."

"Yes, I agree. While I was reviewing the file I already started thinking about some of the projects I'm working on," Palmer replied.

"In those projects you were thinking about did any stand out?" Wade asked.

"Yes, I think there might be two projects that I think unfriendly foreign nationals might want to get their hands on."

"Please hold those thoughts. I am anxious to hear about the projects but before we get into those I want to ask you a few other questions about your work in general."

"Sure," Palmer replied, now eager to participate.

"Do you know a person by the name of Megan Winslow?"

"Yes. I spent some time training her," Palmer answered quickly, without hesitation.

"And what were you training her to do?" Wade followed.

"I was teaching certain procedures in cell microbiology for one of my projects," Palmer answered.

"Did you know that she was an intelligence agent?" Wade asked.

"Yes," Palmer replied.

"And how did you come to find out she was an intelligence agent?" Wade followed.

"She was provided to me by an intelligence source for one of the projects."

"Who assigned her to you?" Wade asked.

"My boss, Col. Landry, head of my department and director of the Institute," Palmer replied.

"How did Col. Landry come to know Ms. Winslow?"

"I think he got her name from Army Intelligence but I think she was CIA or from some another covert agency," Palmer replied.

"Do you know why she was selected for this assignment?"

"Yes, her name was given to us because she already had quite a bit of medical research training," Palmer answered.

"Why was that particular medical training important for this job?" Wade inquired.

"Well, because she was both an intelligence agent and a medically-trained researcher. You don't get that combination very often," Palmer responded.

"Was this project of yours that involved Ms. Winslow one of the projects you previously said you thought foreign operatives would like to get their hands on?" Wade asked.

"Yes. In fact, it was the primary project I was thinking about," Palmer quickly stated.

"Without getting too technical I'm going to have to know the nature of this project Ms. Winslow was working on," Wade said affirmatively.

"That project is classified," Palmer replied.

"I understand your concern but let me assure you that everyone in this room has a top level security clearance, including myself. Also, my questions won't explore the chemical or medical details of your research. We are only interested in the nature of work being performed by Ms. Winslow. Quite frankly none of us here would understand your detailed medical explanations anyway. We are only interested in knowing the nature of work Ms. Winslow was engaged in," Wade explained.

There was a pause while Dr. Palmer pondered Wade's explanation. Surprisingly he responded by asking permission to ask a question. "Can I ask you a question first?"

"Sure, go ahead," Wade replied.

"Is Megan okay? I mean is she in serious danger now?" Palmer asked with a worried face.

Wade paused while he considered his reply.

"We believe she is in serious danger at this time. That is one of the main reasons we are here. Why in particular did you ask that question?" Wade asked.

The worried expression on Palmer's face grew. Seeing the expression on Dr. Palmer's face worsen, Wade saw that Dr. Palmer had special feelings for Megan's safety or he was feeling guilt for having placed her in harm's way. Wade gave Palmer time to compose himself.

"I've been worried sick about her to the point I can't sleep at night. I've discussed my concern with Col. Landry," Palmer responded with genuine worry. Wade saw the complexity of Palmer's worry shift from danger to himself and his son to Megan and whoever was behind the assassins sent to capture him. Wade could see Palmer's mind wandering over these concerns and tried to keep his answers on point.

"And what did Col. Landry say?" Wade asked.

141

"He said he would check with his intelligence contacts and that I should not concern myself with it. He said she is a trained intelligence agent under another command. We are not responsible for them. We just utilize intelligence agents when we need them. It's not our job to worry about them."

"Do you feel that way?" Wade asked.

"No, of course not. She is a fine person and working on my project. How can I not be worried about her? It was my project that put her in harm's way. I don't give a damn what Landry says." Palmer's outburst showed his frustration for the system and Landry. Wade wanted Palmer to calm down and get back on point.

"Let's not get ahead of ourselves here. I still need you to tell me in non-technical terms how Ms. Winslow was involved in your project."

Palmer paused having come down from his former outburst. Dr. Palmer was now showing signs that he felt more like he was part of Wade's intelligence team than the Institute. At least here he felt Wade's team was trying save his family and Megan. During the pause Palmer contemplated how he was going to explain Megan's work without losing his audience in medical and research jargon they wouldn't understand. He prefaced his next statement by taking a deep breath.

"It's difficult not to get a little technical here but I will try to give you the background," Palmer commented.

"If you start to lose me, I'll let you know," Wade replied.

"The research which led to my project started two years ago before I got involved. A researcher at the Center for Disease Control and Infection in Atlanta was performing statistical research on children that became infected with debilitating diseases. Even though the diseases these children had contracted were all different this researcher found that there were strange similarities among them."

During Dr. Palmer's pause as he thought through the next sequence of events he was going to describe Wade interjected, "I follow you so far. Please continue."

"While studying the medical records and statistics of these children patients, this researcher found that all of the infected patients were children between the ages of nine and twelve. All had contracted a different debilitating disease within six weeks of each other. Each child came down with their disease in a different city in the United States and there were no contacts between the children or their parents," Palmer explained.

"So far I hear different unrelated children contracting different diseases in different parts of the country. Do I understand you correctly, Dr. Palmer?" Wade interjected.

"Yes, that's correct and most researchers would have stopped there. But this researcher had a hunch something wasn't right and he kept on digging. Following nothing more than his instincts he found other connections. I don't suppose you would like to hazard a guess what he found?" Dr. Palmer asked.

"No sir, I have no clue," Wade replied.

"After checking birth records in the various states he found all these children had been adopted by American parents."

"Please go on," Wade prompted with interest.

"Not only had these children been adopted but all came from the same country. And the similarities didn't stop there," Dr. Palmer emphasized before continuing his story.

"Not only did these children come from the same country, they came from the same orphanage," Dr. Palmer revealed.

"Even I know the odds of that occurring naturally are astronomical," Wade interjected and was now totally hooked on Dr. Palmer's unfolding mystery.

"There's more, a lot more, and the researcher realized this as he dug deeper. Soon your astronomical statistical odds will become a lot greater to the point of being unbelievable," Palmer commented.

Dr. Palmer turned his head toward Wade. He took a deep breath under his mask then surprisingly asked a question that Wade thought might be changing the subject.

"Do you know what a 'shadow cell' is in the human body?" Palmer asked like he was addressing a freshman class in medical school.

"I can't say that I do," Wade replied.

"The best way I can describe them is that shadow cells make up a very small part of everyone's body. Some shadow cells have a nucleus but many are often devoid of them. They are usually pale pink in color and typically will not accept a stain. We see them in concentrations as part of some tumors where we sometimes use them to provide vague tissue landmarks. Shadow cells are also referred to in the medical literature as "ghost cells," Dr. Palmer lectured.

Wade was already lost in the explanation and knew things were probably going to get more technical. After considering interrupting, Wade decided to keep quiet and let Dr. Palmer continue. In the short duration of Dr. Palmer's explanation, Wade had already concluded that the two operatives didn't have sufficient background to interrogate Dr. Palmer even at this level. They might be here for his take down but someone else with the higher level of medical training would be conducting Dr. Palmer's interrogation.

Dr. Palmer continued, "It turns out in our story of the researcher that all of the infected children had abnormally high counts of shadow cells in their bodies."

"Could this have come about from the disease?" Wade asked, trying to make sense of the anomaly.

"No. Several of the children unfortunately died from their disease but the ones that survived continued to produce high levels of shadow cells," Dr. Palmer explained.

"What happened next?" Wade asked.

"You know that Houston scientist I spoke about? He's the one who continued studying those children who survived." Dr. Palmer paused before he continued.

"That's when I became involved. The Houston physician contacted me after studying those children for eight months after their ordeal. We met and he sent me blood and tissue samples and copies of his prior research study. For the last year my research team discovered these were not ordinary shadow cells but special variations probably mutated from normal shadow cells. They had unique properties that when injected with certain proteins would behave like 'carrier cells'."

Wade was lost. He didn't understand how protein caused a cell to change but he wasn't here to learn medicine. He just needed to know how this applied to Megan and didn't want to see Dr. Palmer get off point.

"Dr. Palmer, this is all fascinating but can you focus your explanation on what the cells do when they become carrier cells and how Megan was involved? I seem to be missing something."

"Sure, I was coming to that anyway," Dr. Palmer continued.

"Please continue," Wade responded.

"In simple terms, when a cell becomes a carrier cell it works like a transmitter. The unique properties of a purely transmitting cell are that it is immune to the disease or toxin it is carrying but can carry and deliver that disease or toxin to the rest of the body. In other words, a carrier cell is nothing more than a shadow cell with a mission," Palmer explained.

"How does a shadow cell know it needs to become a carrier cell and what it needs to deliver?" Wade asked showing his ignorance, but completely immersed in Dr. Palmer's description.

"Very good question. It shows you were listening. Much of that answer is still unknown. What my research discovered is a protein tells the body to produce shadow cells. We still don't know how certain shadow cells know when to become a carrier cell or where to concentrate in the body," Palmer responded and paused before he continued.

"Is that where Megan comes in?" Wade asked.

"Yes. That's the point I wanted to make. Megan is involved in getting essential stem cell materials which I believe are the source of shadow cell production. It is necessary for me to have stem cell material to continue my research," Palmer explained.

"How is Megan involved in that task?" Wade inquired.

"I'm coming to that. Before we could find how the carrier cells did their mission we had to find out how the body was producing shadow cells. To do that I needed stem cells because those along with certain proteins are what I believe are being injected into the children. That's what I trained Megan to do, how to source and preserve the stem cell material and she learned very quickly. In fact she is a damn good medical researcher. I don't know anything about her skills as an intelligence agent," Palmer confessed.

146

"Now that you explained the medical part of this tell us what you know about the intelligence threat part of your project," Wade ordered.

"Once we put the medical side together we realized that the children from this orphanage were being injected starting at a young age then put up for adoption in the U.S. Intelligence people got involved investigating how they were getting these children illegally into the country and past U.S. Customs and adoption protocol."

"Dr. Palmer, let me interrupt you for a moment. While all of this is intriguing and terribly abusive to children, not to mention violating lots of other laws, I seem to be missing the intelligence threat here. Why was someone going to all the trouble of using these children for this purpose? Was this just some kind of money-making scheme in human trafficking?" Wade asked in wonderment.

"No, you're missing the much bigger picture here. You don't seem to be getting the connection that because of their shadow cells, each one of these children, once implanted with a contagious disease, becomes a walking biological weapon. A contagious biological bomb that can be released into any major city in the U.S. Once released, they would kill millions of Americans." Dr. Palmer paused to allow his last statement to sink in. He continued his explanation with the same vigor.

"My Intelligence sources have told me that once there are a suitable number of these children in place and their cells are turned into disease or toxin carrier cells the larger part of the American population is at risk depending on one or a combination of diseases or toxins they use. We would have unheard of levels of catastrophic infectious diseases spreading that rivaled the great plagues of Europe." Palmer said this emphatically hoping he emphasized the serious impact of his project.

This time Wade paused while he digested Dr. Palmer's statement. The magnitude sunk in. He was almost overwhelmed in disbelief.

"Do your intelligence sources have reason to believe this plot is sponsored by some other country or group?" Wade asked.

"They have their theories but they haven't shared those with me. Because of the sheer magnitude of organization required here my guess is this would take the resources of a country to pull it off. However, the initial research and testing phase could be done by a well-financed smaller group. Whenever I ask that question to my intelligence contacts I'm told the information is above my pay grade," Palmer confided.

"How does Megan get these tissue samples shipped back to you?" Wade asked.

"That process is complicated and involves the intelligence side of the operation. I have a few of the details as it relates to protecting the material but don't know any of the parties or other details involved. I know the tissue samples have to go through several intermediary hands before they get into our hands and ultimately to me," Palmer replied.

"Has Megan delivered any of this tissue material to you as part of her operation?" Wade asked.

"Yes she has delivered two good samples of material that allowed me to do the protein experiments but the last one was almost two months ago," Palmer responded.

"Do you know why no additional materials have been sent since her last shipment?" Wade asked.

"No. That's why I'm so worried about her," Palmer answered with evident stress.

"How many more shipments is she supposed to deliver?" Wade inquired.

"Ideally I would like to receive samples every other week but I realize that might be impossible because of all she has to do to preserve the samples and get them out. I am told she is under armed guards all the time," Palmer responded.

"How do you know she is under guard?" Wade inquired.

"The Intelligence side tells me she is in a very dangerous deep cover situation. Please understand I was never involved on the intelligence side. I was just teaching her about the research for the project," Palmer pleaded.

"But you said the intelligence side would tell you things. What kinds of things did they tell you?"

"One of the Intelligence guys told me if she were ever discovered she would be immediately tortured and killed," Palmer replied.

"Do you know where Megan is right now?" Wade asked firmly, wanting a direct answer.

"Megan is undercover at the research facility responsible for preparing the formulation and injecting the children from the orphanage. That biological facility is in a small village by the name of Realta in Argentina just a few miles from the orphanage," Palmer replied, his voice cracking, showing his feeling of guilt for Megan's precarious situation.

"What is the name of the orphanage and where is it located?" Wade followed

"The name of the orphanage is Heritage Children's Home and it is located in Realta just a few miles from the biological facility," Palmer responded.

"Do you know the name or names of the U.S. intelligence officers involved in this case?" Wade asked

"I just know the names they told me to call them by, Barry and Conrad. I don't think those are their real names just like I don't think your name is really Nelson," Palmer replied.

"Most likely those are not their real names, but it gives me something to go on," Wade responded.

"I have a few more questions about Megan before we end the session. At the time Megan started working with you did she seem like she was under pressure to take this assignment?" Wade inquired.

"No, at first she was trying to just help with the technical side. I got the feeling she really didn't want to become involved further than on a technical or advisory level," Palmer explained, pausing before he continued.

"For what it's worth I think most of Megan's pressure came from herself. What I mean by that is at first she didn't want to take this assignment. When she saw these kids being used as carriers her emotions changed. We would talk about this in the evening after work. She was very incensed by the thought that any human being could do that to another. At some point Megan's emotions for these children took over. The next thing I knew she told me she had decided to take this on as the primary undercover agent and work things out on the intelligence side," Palmer explained.

"What was her cover story? In other words how did she think she would be accepted by another country and not be seen as a U.S. spy?" Wade curiously asked.

"All I know from the Intelligence guys was that her cover story had to be documented extensively going back to her high school. I wasn't involved in all that but remember it being a big issue and taking months to set up. I just remember it was all very involved and included them wiping out her identity back to her childhood. I can tell you one thing," Dr. Palmer prompted.

"What's that?" Wade responded.

"She was good enough as a microbiologist to pass any questions about her medical expertise. She could work in my department any time," Palmer proudly stated.

"That's an important part to her cover. I hope it's enough," Wade responded.

"What happens now?" Dr. Palmer asks.

"I am almost done with our interview. As I told you before I'll bring you back to your car and you will be free to go," Wade responded.

"No. I mean what happens to me and my son and for that matter Megan after I leave here?" Palmer aggressively retorted.

"Well as it now stands, in 24 hours I think the operatives following you will be in custody. After that what happens depends largely on you," Wade responded.

"What do you mean on me?" Palmer replied with a questioning expression on his face.

"What I mean is, technically the operatives following you haven't acted on capturing you or your son but I think that could happen any time. My guess is they know you haven't completed that last part of your research," Wade advised.

"How would they know that?" Palmer questioned.

"You probably have a mole in your research group," Wade postulated.

"What! All of my people are security screened from top to bottom before they come to work for the institute," Palmer replied.

"My best guess it's one of your lower level researchers. Someone who has access to the research results perhaps through the paperwork. I suggest you look there first," Wade recommended.

"I don't know how to investigate that and what about my family's safety?" Palmer showed his frustration.

"I can't tell you what to do from here but I can give you some recommendations. I think you start by finding someone in the FBI or Intelligence community that you can trust. You might want to call Detective Wherter of the Bethesda Police department. Tell him that 'Nelson' suggested you get in touch. He has a lot of contacts in the FBI and Intelligence community. Tell him your story about what you learned about the operatives and a little about your project. I wouldn't tell him about the Megan side. Let him handle the domestic side of security for your family. You can also tell him that I suggested you may have a mole in your group. Listen to what he says and follow his suggestions."

Wade paused before he continued, "There is another thing you can do. You are clueless about your surroundings. You need to be more aware about who is around you, what routes you take to work, school and home. At no time during my surveillance of you did you become aware of anyone following you. You didn't change your route or routine or even look in your rear view mirror." Wade was now instructing Dr. Palmer and he was taking the advice to heart.

Wade continued his recommendations. "There's another thing, according to my records you are married yet I didn't see a woman around the house. Are you raising Randy alone?" Wade asked.

"My wife has been in Minnesota for the last two months taking care of her ill mother," Palmer responded.

"Where is Randy now?" Wade asked.

"I have a nanny. She comes when I have my golf sessions and have to go out of town," Palmer replied.

"You just need to become more aware of your surroundings. Take different routes to school, home and the office. Purposely take note of anyone following you. Whether you like it or not your job makes you part of the intelligence community. That means you also have enemies."

Dr. Palmer thought for a moment, taking in the advice Wade had given. "Thank you for your help. I will take your recommendations seriously," Dr. Palmer commented.

"One last thing, I don't think you should have any further discussions about Megan with your Col. Landry. Don't show that you are concerned about her anymore. Whatever you do don't tell anyone about our conversation. That alone could endanger your life," Wade advised.

"Why is that?" Palmer asked.

"Because my group will be taking a close look at your Col. Landry and the people he reports to on the hill," Wade replied.

"Will you be around? I mean is there any way that I can contact you if I come under surveillance again?" Dr. Palmer asked hoping Wade might be there for help.

"I'm afraid that won't be possible. I was brought in to do this one mission and will be out of the area before you wake up tomorrow," Wade replied.

"Well, I know I'm still blindfolded and never got a look at your face but I want to thank you. I somehow feel all of this was worthwhile. I guess I can't help but wonder what would have happened if I hadn't decided to cooperate?" Palmer inquired.

"Three unfortunate events would have unfolded. First the operatives following you wouldn't be brought into custody and would remain on your tail until they were instructed to act. Secondly, Megan's chance of getting out of Argentina would have become more remote and she would be less likely to survive and thirdly, it has to do with your own physical well-being this evening and I will let your imagination run with that one."

"But, I always intended to cooperate." Dr. Palmer tried to assure Wade.

"I'm going to uncuff your hand from the chair but procedure requires that I bring you to your destination cuffed."

"I understand," Dr. Palmer replied.

Wade pulled up behind the right side of Dr. Palmer's parked car. Only one remaining overhead parking light was left on to defeat the encroaching shadows of the deserted lot. Wade came around and assisted Dr. Palmer out of the car and escorted him to his own vehicle. When he was comfortably in the driver's seat Wade handed him the car keys and told him to keep facing forward while he removed his mask. He instructed Dr. Palmer to count to twenty without looking in his rear view mirror before he drove off.

After twenty seconds Palmer looked in his rear view only seeing the dark shadows of a vacant parking lot. Wade was already gone.

Chapter 15

A few blocks from the driving range parking lot Wade doubled back to check that Dr. Palmer was heading home. He spotted Palmer's sedan two blocks ahead. Wade was pleased that Dr. Palmer was heading home but wasn't taking his normal route.

Wade wasted no time updating Max who was anxiously awaiting word at their motel. Using the pre-agreed code from his interrogation of Dr. Palmer, Wade radioed that he had been successful.

"Base to Rover. Do you read?"

"Rover here. I read you loud and clear," Max replied.

"The chef prepared an excellent meal of scrambled eggs and bacon," Wade advised.

"That's great. Are you now en route to Point Zero?" Max asked.

"Negative, I am en route to advise our mark on package pick-up. Will return to Point Zero in one to two hours. Over." Wade replied.

"I copy. What are my instructions?" Max asked.

"Prepare for Plan B – Evac. Over." Max knew exactly what he had to do which included breaking down all the weapons and packing them for shipment by military transport to his base in Houston.

"I should be ready when you return to Point Zero, over."

"Good, I will advise if further eyes are needed on packages. Over."

"See you at Zero, out." Max replied, signing off.

Wade already had previously identified the payphone he would use to call Yari to set up the encrypted call to Detective Wherter. The meeting with Dr. Palmer ran over its scheduled time. Wade hoped that everyone held their posts for his expected call that evening.

The welcoming voice of Yari answered after Wade dialed his secure number.

"Yari here."

"Glad you're still awake, my friend," Wade replied.

"Wade, where the hell have you been?"

"Did Max tell you I had a date tonight?"

"Yeah, but he told me you would be calling in an hour or two ago. I just got worried," Yari replied.

"Some dates go better than others and some you end up spending the night. Look partner, I don't have time for details right now. I need you to set up a double-encrypted patch right now for a call to Detective Wherter. I need to have my voice go through one of your distorter programs because it will probably be recorded."

"Okay, give me five minutes to set everything up and I'll call you back on this payphone," Yari responded.

"Before you leave I need to talk to you about some Intel research I need but I'll call you back after my call with Wherter. By the way don't forget to take this payphone offline so it can't be traced."

"I got you. I'll get back to you in five." Wade heard his line with Yari disconnect. He opened the bi-fold doors of the phone booth to get some air while he waited for Yari's connecting call.

"This is Detective Wherter."

"Detective Wherter, this is Nelson calling you back as we discussed to report that your suspects have been detained and are ready for pickup and arrest when you are."

"Nelson, it's good to hear from you. I was beginning to wonder with the late hour and all."

"There were a few complications that caused my delay. My apologies."

"Were you able to detain the two suspects we spoke about?" Wherter asked.

"Affirmative, both suspects are cuffed and blindfolded at a secure location on the outskirts of Frederick. I am ready to give you that location whenever you are ready," Wade reported.

"Hold on, I was looking at my map and have it just on the corner of my desk here. I'm ready."

"The suspects are located in two separate storage units located just off State Highway 26 about seven miles north of Frederick. Coming from the city you turn left off the highway just past the intersection of Highway 70. Four miles past the intersection on Highway 26 you take a gravel road until you see a farm with a sign marked *Townsdale*. Make a left until it ends at a farm gate. The storage units are actually on the farm."

"How the hell did you find that place?"

"It's a long story. I'll have to explain at another time but it turned out to be perfect for what we needed."

"Does the owner of the farm know anything about the contents in the units?"

"No. In fact we arranged for the rental of the units without ever meeting him. We just left him the money in an envelope."

"That's clever. I'll have to remember that one."

"When you get to the farm gate there is a large silver mail box. In that box there is an envelope marked with your name on it. The envelope has all the keys to the storage and locks for each of the suspects. The suspects are located in Unit 209 and

214. They have been separated since their detainment and I recommend you keep them separated."

"Just so you know, I have contacted the local Frederick police and my friend at the FBI who will be accompanying me and my man on the arrest. I want all the right political connections involved so the paperwork is done correctly. You understand I hope," Wherter replied.

"It also helps keep the political credit properly distributed as well. I really don't care who you bring into the arrest," Wade replied.

"Now my understanding from Morrison is you or your department doesn't want any credit or involvement in that capture. Is that correct?" Wherter asked.

"That is correct. This is your show to do with as you please. You were just given a tip from a concerned citizen and acted on it," Wade replied.

"That's fine by me. What else do you have for me with these guys?" Wherter asked.

"I think you'll find everything in the folders on these guys. The leader of the two is who we refer to as Tallman is stored in Unit 214. Inside that unit to the right of the door you will find a wooden foot locker. That locker contains an envelope of all surveillance photos, falsified passports and entry documentation, Interpol rap sheets, weapons and material we found in their hotel room."

"Where were these guys staying?"

"They were staying at the Tudor Hotel in Frederick, Room 557. You will want to get a warrant to search that room. They didn't have time to destroy any evidence before our take down. In the bar refrigerator you will find two brown bottles of solution that look like medicine. When you have those tested I think you'll find the solution to be a strong sedative for the darts in their blow guns."

"Blow guns?" Wherter replied.

"That surprised us as well. There are other weapons involved but you will see from their rap sheet they are very skilled at using these blow guns in their other kidnapping cases," Wade explained.

"What else do we have on them?" Wherter asked.

"As I explained before they are paid operatives interested in Dr. Palmer and his research project at the Institute which has significant international Intelligence projects in play. You have them both here illegally on falsified passports, illegally carrying weapons, and as wanted felons of Interpol on a long list of major crimes. I think you are in the driver's seat where you go from there. I would suggest you involve both the Intelligence community and the FBI. Both will have interest in these characters. You also have the option of extraditing them if you don't want to hold them here. All of that will become apparent when you see the rap sheets and other evidence," Wade described.

"Is there anything else I need to know about these guys?" Wherter asked.

"I didn't have enough time to interrogate them properly. I would really work on that end. It's worth it if they give up who they work for. You might want the Intelligence folks to handle the interrogation. I think they will know more about who all the international players are in these," Wade advised.

"Good suggestion. I will definitely involve them," Wherter replied.

"Two last things. The suspect in Unit 209 needs some medical attention. It seems he incurred a bullet wound, broken jaw and some cracked teeth resisting arrest. The bullet wound is a flesh wound that I cleaned up and dressed with a compression bandage. The rest is cosmetic. He wasn't beautiful to begin with," Wade commented.

"That's not a problem. I'll have the local law enforcement people provide medical support. You said there were two things,"

"Yes, in my opinion, Dr. Palmer and his family, who were the targets, are going to need some protection until things can be sorted out. I have advised him to call you directly. I would appreciate it if you can direct him to somebody you trust in either the FBI or Intelligence that can cover him and his family while he's exposed." Wade paused before continuing.

"He's doing important work at the Institute but doesn't have a clue as to how to protect himself. I think the importance of his work is so crucial to U.S. interests that whoever is behind these operatives would not hesitate to send more resources to get information out of Palmer," Wade explained.

"I know just the people who can help him. If he gets cold feet and doesn't call me, I'll call him," Wherter replied.

"Good. That's about it. When do you think you will be picking up the packages?" Wade inquired.

"Unless you feel otherwise my team and I are scheduled to pick up the suspects at first light," Wherter replied.

"That's fine by me. They have water and aren't going anywhere," Wade replied.

"Is there any chance of us meeting so I can thank you in person before you leave town?" Wherter inquired.

"Perhaps another time. I have another part of this mission that needs my immediate attention," Wade replied.

"I understand. Morrison told me you would be gone faster than you arrived. I just want to thank you for all you have done," Wherter responded.

"Not a problem, just doing a citizen's duty." Wade ended the call.

After hanging up, Wade dialed Yari back and gave him a list of research questions he needed answers on. Using notes from his meeting with Dr. Palmer, Yari copied down Wade's requests as fast as he could write.

When they finished the list Yari asked, "So what's next for you?"

"I'm headed north," Wade responded.

"North? From the research destinations you gave me shouldn't you be heading south?" Yari asked.

"Not until I complete my research and find the right cover story. I have a plan in mind," Wade answered.

"Far be it from me to ask about your plans. I guess I'll just wait for your next call," Yari replied.

"You'll be hearing from me within the next two days. See how much on that research list you can get completed. It's all very important."

"I'm already on it, partner. By the way, how is Max?"

"He's fine. He got a little nicked up on this trip but he will be back with his family by this time tomorrow," Wade replied.

"Good. I'll catch up with him separately. I still don't know what you guys were even there for."

"It's not important for you to know all the details. Remember, knowing details just makes you vulnerable. You must have learned that in one of the classes we took together," Wade replied.

"I know. I just miss not being in the field with you guys," Yari answered.

"It's no picnic out here my friend. Besides, you wouldn't have any computer friends to talk to. Look, I have to run now. We'll talk soon,"

"Talk soon," Yari responded ending the call.

Wade returned to Point Zero and his room at the motel. He met with Max and gave him just enough details of the Dr. Palmer interview so that he had a general overview. Both men agreed that the less Max knew the less he could reveal under the "need to know" protocol in case he was ever interrogated. The two went over Evacuation Plan B and did a final check on their gear.

Max's orders under the Evac Plan were to keep eyes on the formal arrest of the operatives from the safe location of a distant farm they had already scouted.

After making his own evacuation arrangements and two hours' sleep the bud in Wade's ear rang out as morning light shone through the side of his motel room.

"Rover to Base. Over."

"Base to Rover. Copy."

"The packages have been picked up and are safely inside an escort of four pony express vehicles. Holiday Shores is now closed for business. Over."

"Did the pony express find all of the party favors?" Wade responded.

"Affirmative. Everything secure, over," Max replied.

"Is your next stop soldier drop-off?" Wade replied barely awake.

"Affirmative. After that, Dulles International and home to chicken fried steak," Max replied.

"You earned the steak soldier. I can't thank you enough. Have a safe trip," Wade said in appreciation.

"You too, boss. I'll be cleaned up in two days and ready to party on the next trip," Max replied.

"I'll give you that call when something comes up," Wade replied.

"Always ready to help, boss. Over," Max ended the call.

Wade needed time to think and plan for the next phase of his mission. Most two-phase missions left tell-tale signs of an operative's presence that must be covered if he was going to avoid exposure. No matter how many times he was in disguise or how careful he was the fact that he spoke to a lot of people and was seen by many left uncomfortable trails that Wade had to remove.

It was necessary for him to disappear from the face of the Earth for a while. His training and more importantly his instincts, told him how to do that. His rules were clear and they started by not communicating with anyone from his Maryland mission. He had to immediately leave the area using non-traceable transportation and remove all traces of his ongoing presence like credit card transactions and unsecured phone calls. He needed a new disguise and a quiet location with resources for him to do research on the second phase of his mission. Ideally, it would also be a place where he had Intelligence contacts he already knew and could trust. The place he picked met all of his needs and he used secure, untraceable connections to ensure his safe arrival.

Chapter 16
Vancouver, Canada

Every bone in Wade's body urged him to find Megan. His instincts and training tempered those feelings knowing that if he acted hastily without proper cover and research and Intelligence connections, he would put Megan as well as himself in danger.

Covering all traceable steps of his current mission was the first order of business.

He had to disappear cleanly and without any trace of where he had been or who he was regardless of who might be inquiring. His first step in getting out of Maryland and the U.S. was through two inter-connecting flights to and from Montreal using two different identities and disguises. His last flight was a small commuter flight followed by a train ride. The two small airports and local train station gave Wade ample opportunity to check anyone that might be following.

Wade knew that he wanted to be somewhere out of the U.S. that was quiet where he could conduct his own research, develop his cover story and where he knew Intelligence sources he could trust would help document his cover.

The place was Richmond, Vancouver and the immediate area around Vancouver, which was his transition site for his mission to Tangier. From this location for his last mission, Wade saw his real life's history disappear and a new personal history created out of thin air. Wade met and worked with Leo's support intelligence staff on that mission and stayed in touch with them hoping they would be of assistance if he needed them. Until now he had never tested that relationship. His uncertainty was whether they would assist him without specific instructions from Leo. Wade would soon find out.

His arrival in Vancouver came with equal diligence on a small chartered plane from a private airport less than a hundred miles out of Vancouver. With his passport and identity papers already cleared in Montreal, Wade rented a car under an alias and drove to an extended-stay hotel he knew Leo had used in the past.

After a restful night Wade spent the day at the University of British Columbia Library north of Richmond a few miles off BC-99 on SW Marine Drive answering as many questions and learning as much about Argentina as he could.

His research included everything from Argentina history to newspaper articles on recent political conflicts. He learned the names of government officials and the positions they held.

Wade studied maps learning the location of major cities, roads, transportation systems and most importantly ingress and egress from the villages where the orphanage and research facility were where Megan remained undercover or by now in custody. After hitting the books all day and a quick meal Wade settled into one of the payphone booths outside the library for his call to Yari. His notepad and questions were in front of him as Yari's secure line rang.

"Yari here," the response came.

"It's me, Wade."

"I thought I might be getting a call from you today. You guys really hit it big in Maryland," Yari commented.

"What do you mean?" Wade asked.

"Headlines, man, *Two Suspects Arrested by FBI. Believed to be Foreign Spies.* That just has to be your guys," Yari commented.

"Don't believe everything you read," Wade replied.

"Turns out it's a big deal here," Yari answered.

"What did the article say?" Wade asked out of curiosity.

Yari read from a part of the article. "The FBI is following up on a lead from an undisclosed source and apprehended two suspects believed to be part of an intelligence spy ring operating in this country. Investigation continues into international sources behind the ring."

"Interesting, they decided to let the light shine on the Bureau. That may not be a bad way to handle that problem in the long run," Wade commented.

"You guys are awesome," Yari exclaimed.

"Thanks, but were you able to get any answers to my research questions?" Wade asked, hoping to get Yari back on track.

"Yeah, let me get my paperwork. I have lots of stuff," Yari responded. Wade could hear the papers shuffling.

Yari asked, "Do you want this in any particular order, boss?"

"If you could stick to the order in which I gave the questions to you that would be great," Wade responded.

"Okay. Let's see. I'll start with who the U.S. backed on the recent election upheaval. That would be the guy that didn't get in. It was all done behind the scenes but didn't work because Jorge Videla got in and all hell is breaking loose."

"What about ongoing Intelligence operations in the country?" Wade inquired.

"As best I can tell we have three covert operations in play. They go by the code name of Long Bow, Sandbox and Recluse." Yari read from his notes.

"Do you have the names of the Intelligence offices handling each operation?" Wade inquired.

Yari provided Wade with the names and contacts of the Intelligence offices. Wade didn't recognize any of the names and none seemed to be remotely involved in the orphanage operations.

"Do you know what operatives are heading up each of these missions?" Wade inquired.

As Yari went through the list nothing caught Wade's attention until he started describing the third, Operation Recluse.

"What do you know about Operation Recluse?" Wade asked.

"Not much. I started with the name which sometimes gives a clue," Yari replied.

"What did you find?" Wade asked.

"Let's see, a person in seclusion, a very deadly spider and a mountain range in Argentina. They spell the name without the -e-," Yari replied.

"What about the Operation itself?" Wade asked.

As Yari provided sketchy details, this mission became more intriguing to Wade.

"The only thing I was able to find out on Operation Recluse is that it was shut down right after those recent Argentina elections. It might have become an off-the-books Operation shortly after it was shut down. The authorization request memo I read indicated the Operation involved tracking down the sons and relatives of Nazi fugitives that came to Argentina to escape Germany. Apparently there is a loosely connected network of old Nazi officers that became part of Argentina society after the Second World War. That network is still being operated by the sons and relatives of those original members. These organizations have grown and apparently infiltrated legitimate businesses and politics and are influencing the country. That's why they are 'persons of interest' to the U.S."

Listening carefully, Wade saw elements to this Operation that triggered his instincts.

"Who is the operative handling Operation Recluse?" Wade asked.

"That's the problem. The Operation hasn't existed for two years. There's no one listed as heading it. The last memo I found was two years ago requesting authorization for funding by the CIA but it was turned down," Yari replied.

Wade hummed loud enough that Yari heard his reaction. "Do you know something I don't about this Operation?" Yari asked.

"I don't know for sure but I see fingerprints I recognize all over it," Wade responded.

Wade kept any suspicions he had about Operation Recluse to himself. The fingerprints he saw were those of Leo. He went on to the next topic thinking he would investigate that one himself. Yari was still curious about Wade's silence.

"Anybody's fingerprints I know?" Yari inquired.

"I don't think so." Wade changed the subject, "Were you able to find out anything about the orphanage?"

"Yes, the orphanage has been run by an order of nuns, the translation is The Sisters of the Adoration. The sisters came upon some rough financial times during the revolt. Some unnamed backer stepped in and now owns the property and other assets. The nuns still work for this unknown owner and take care of the children. There are some strange Intel docs I came across with this facility. I got access to some Intel photos showing there are armed guards around the place. The guards are dressed in military uniforms but are not part of the regular Argentina army. They look to be like someone's private army."

Wade wanted more details. "When did this group take over?"

"It looks like about three years ago. It may have been around the time of the Videla revolt."

"And you can tell who owns those assets now by the government records?" Wade asked.

"The ownership is by *Nominee*. The Nominee of record is some attorney in Buenos Aries. He represents the actual absentee owner and shareholders," Yari responded, looking at copies of the ownership records in his hand.

"The attorney is the front man. I'll need his contact information and a background check. Did you check on the ownership of the medical facility?" Wade inquired.

"Yes, also held by Nominee. Guess who?" Yari asked.

"The same attorney?" Wade quickly replied.

"Correct my friend, another one of those intelligence coincidences," Yari responded.

"Do you have any Intel on whether the medical facility is guarded?" Wade asked and waited while Yari shifted through lots of paperwork.

"It appears the facility is guarded by the same uniforms as the orphanage. How strange," Yari commented.

"Another coincidence," Wade replied.

Wade moved to another topic he had asked Yari to research. "Did you find out anything about the investigation being conducted in the U.S. on violations of these orphanage kids getting past the authorities in this country?"

"Yeah, actually that investigation resulted in several rather high-ranking individuals losing their jobs in adoption. One person is still under criminal investigation for their action in the scheme," Yari responded.

"I'll need the name and background on that individual and the FBI contact handling that case," Wade requested.

"Sure thing. I'll have that ready for you the next time we speak," Yari replied.

"What's the general climate for our intelligence operations in Argentina?" Wade asked.

Yari thought for a moment. "I would describe it as being very dangerous. It doesn't seem like we can trust anyone. Things are very unstable. I don't think we know who to back and who we can trust. That's my assessment from reading everything," Yari replied.

"From what I gathered in my research I think you are spot on in that assessment," Wade replied.

Wade continued with more questions. Putting together what he learned from Yari and his prior Intelligence research he started developing a plan.

"I need to know ingress and egress possibilities. What has been the U.S. policy and how much leeway do they have getting in and out of the country?" Wade asked.

"That looks pretty open right now. Military has airspace restrictions, but other than regular commercial passenger flights we seem to have a brisk commerce going with the country. We bring in a lot of machinery and equipment and they export a wide variety of food and other products to the U.S. I don't really see any restriction if you have the right permits and all. Those probably require that someone gets paid off, but I don't see any quarantine zones around most of the air space. Travel within the country seems open as well. You don't want to go out without your passport, but I think any restrictions on travel are very limited."

"Good. That helps," Wade replied.

"You're going down there undercover? Not in any official capacity I presume?" Yari asked.

"Have you ever known me to go anywhere on official business?" Wade replied.

"I should not have asked the question," Yari answered.

The two men spoke for another half hour covering details that were important to Wade. At this point Wade concluded that he had enough information to craft his cover story and began his back-up documentation. For that he would need help and arranged a dinner meeting with the former MI-6 Agent Reggie who worked on document profiles for Leo on his Tangier mission.

Wade and Reggie spent little time reminiscing about the Tangier mission in favor of concentrating on his cover story for this mission. Their document plan included everything from Canadian citizenship documents and passports to dog eared photographs of Wade with his wife of three years. The photos included aunts, uncles, and nieces which rounded out his cover story of a Canadian produce importer who along with his wife was looking to adopt a child.

It would take another three days to have everything prepared and officially stamped before Wade could depart. In the meantime, he had reservations to make and one important call to someone he respected and never wanted to cross accidently or otherwise. He knew it would take one or two days before he received a reply to his call, so he left the message that evening.

The next evening the phone rang in Wade's room.

"I see you're back in a familiar place, kiddo," Leo replied.

"I couldn't resist Leo. I hope you don't mind," Wade said.

"It's a good location to depart from," Leo answered.

"I had a few things I wanted to get your advice on," Wade prefaced.

"I guess you heard they caught some spies on our soil in Maryland?" Leo asked.

"Yes, I read something about that in the paper. Are you involved in that project?" Wade asked.

"No, not yet, kiddo, but I expect to get a call to check out who some of the real players are," Leo replied.

Wade started feeling uncomfortable about why Leo would bring up Maryland. He didn't want Leo's curiosity to go too much further not knowing how much he knew or didn't know. It was time to change the subject.

"I was calling about an operation I may be involved in soon and wanted to get your advice," Wade remarked.

"Go ahead. Shoot, kiddo," Leo replied.

"I am probably headed to Argentina and I understand there are a few intelligence operations going on. My mission doesn't have anything to do with U.S. existing operations there and I want to keep it that way. I thought you might have some advice on some agency people I can trust in that country and how I might be able to contact them."

There was an awkward pause before Leo answered, "Yeah, I know people there. It's a dangerous place right now."

"Yes, I've heard that. As part of my research, one project has come up and I just wanted to see if you might know anything about that operation. It's called Operation Recluse." Wade inquired.

Avoiding a direct answer to Wade's question, Leo followed with his own. "Does your mission have anything to do with your missing lady friend or Shaw?" Leo asked.

"Yes, my lady friend Megan Winslow. From my research, I don't think Shaw is involved in the mission any longer," Wade replied.

"What part of the country is your lady friend operating in?"

"She is in the Rio Negro region of Argentina. She's at a medical facility connected with an orphanage in a village by the name of Realta," Wade explained.

There was a brief pause. "I don't see any problems there," Leo replied.

Wade wasn't sure he understood Leo's response other than Leo wasn't going to confirm or deny any involvement with Operation Recluse. He decided not to probe further.

"Well, that's good to hear."

"When are you leaving?" Leo asked.

"In two days I think," Wade replied.

"It's a nice climate down there this time of year," Leo said.

"Do you have any suggestions for me?" Wade asked.

"Avoid making any of your connecting flights through Santiago or Bogota," Leo strangely advised.

"Okay. That's good advice."

"I have to run, kiddo - lots of projects going on. Good luck. Call me if you need help," Leo commented.

"Thanks, I'll be sure to do that," Wade replied, ending the call.

Although Wade was nervous about what Leo *really* knew, he felt he had accomplished his task of letting Leo know that he would be operating the same territory as Operation Recluse. The last thing Wade wanted to do was to surprise Leo, blindly getting in his way.

Chapter 17
Argentina

Wade's flight to South America was long and tiring in part because he avoided direct flights to large international airports. Instead his route took him to cities where passport stamps would confirm that he had visited produce export areas during his trip to bolster his cover story.

Letters of introduction were sent in advance to the heads of Argentina produce farm operators. He spent the next two days as a guest of the farm operators, touring their fields and packing houses. Showing interest by asking well-researched questions and checking the quality of fruit and nuts enhanced his creditability with the farmers all of whom supported his cover story. Wade was seen by the farmers as someone who would be buying and importing their products to Canada.

Going from one farm to another Wade also saw how effectively their "grapevine" communication operated. Long before he arrived at the next farm they already knew he was on his way and what he asked about at the last farm. If Intelligence communication worked anything like the farm communication network Wade knew he had to be on his toes at all times. His third tour that day was with one of the largest farm operations in the area run by an established well-known family headed by Don Juan Carlos Mendoza. Everyone called him Don Carlos.

After spending the afternoon of the second day and most of the third day with Don Carlos, Wade felt he got to know the man quite well. They hit it off and liked each other's company. The Mendoza family had been farming for five generations and Juan Carlos was a very wealthy man. He always played in the background but had a lot of political clout over area politics.

Feasting at Don Carlos' palatial estate over a wonderful steak dinner and several glasses of fine Argentinian red wine from his farm, Wade turned to Don Carlos and said, "Thank you for your wonderful tour today. I was very impressed."

"Mr. James, I am honored that you have selected my farm to review."

"Believe me, it was *my* honor," Wade responded.

"I was particularly impressed by the way you use the latest agriculture equipment, your research laboratory and how you apply excellent agricultural practices," Wade commented.

"Do they compare favorably to agricultural practices in Canada and the United States?" Don Carlos asked.

"In most cases they exceed our practices," Wade replied as the two men continued to talk about crop rotation, natural fertilizers and production levels for the next two hours. After several glasses of wine the conversation seemed to be slowing down. Wade changed his expression to a lower, more serious tone and leaned closer to Don Carlos' chair.

"Don Carlos, I have a personal matter I wish to confide in you. I was wondering if you might be able to help me," Wade said.

"In my family there is no difference between personal and business matters. All matters are of the heart. Please let me know how I can help," Don Carlos replied.

"The matter deals with my wife. We have been married three years and want children very badly. She has been unable to conceive and is very troubled by this," Wade reached for his wallet and pulled out a picture of Wade and his wife smiling and shared it with Don Carlos. Wade continued, "She is very happy in this picture, but has grown very sad now. The doctors in the U.S. say that she may not be able to conceive. I understand there are many beautiful children in Argentina that could be adopted if the proper arrangements are made. I found out about one such orphanage here run by the nuns. I have the name but don't know anything about them. I was wondering if you could inquire and see if this orphanage is a good one. Perhaps make an introduction for me. I told my wife I would check this one out."

"What is the name of the orphanage?" Don Carlos asked.

"I don't remember the name, but I have it written on a piece of paper." Wade fumbled through his wallet for the folded paper. "I can't pronounce the name properly. Perhaps you know this organization?"

Wade showed the paper to Don Carlos and read off the name out loud. Don Carlos paused trying to remember if he knew the name. He returned the paper to Wade.

"I'm afraid I don't know this one, but I would be pleased to inquire about it. When do you wish to visit them?" Don Carlos asked.

"I have another farm inspection tomorrow so the day after would be great. I'm not asking for a commitment at this point; I just want to meet the people running it and get a sense of the children," Wade explained.

"Contact me tomorrow afternoon after your tour. I will try to have something arranged for you," Don Carlos replied.

"I am most grateful, Don Carlos," Wade exclaimed.

"It is nothing. I am happy to help you. And if this one doesn't work out I will come up with more places for you and your wife to consider. Perhaps you can bring her down on your next visit and stay at my place," Don Carlos offered.

"You are most kind, Don Carlos," Wade toasted his glass showing his appreciation for the kind offering.

After broaching the adoption issue, Wade returned to the topic of produce, which he knew Don Carlos was always keen on discussing.

"Now let's get back to some business. Your cantaloupe and table grape season is just the opposite of what we have in North America. What months and quantities do you produce that would be available and how many tons would you be able to provide me in those peak months?" Wade asked.

"Let me get you last year's production schedule and what we predict for this year for those crops," Don Carlos replied and walked back from a table in the corner with many pages of production schedules. The men spoke for the next two hours about everything from produce production to farming practices until Wade politely excused himself to go back to his hotel.

The next afternoon, after touring another farm, Wade called Don Carlos to see if there was progress on the arrangements for Wade visiting the orphanage.

"Hello, Don Carlos. My tour today was interesting but I was not as inspired as I was seeing your operation," Wade opened the phone call.

"The farm you toured today is much smaller than mine, but he does a good job on cucumbers and red seedless grapes. They just have limited production," Don Carlos commented.

"I see that. Well it was good that I saw it for comparison. By the way did you have any luck with the orphanage I mentioned to you last evening?" Wade politely asked.

"Yes, it is run by the Sisters of the Adoration. I think the nuns have come on hard times recently. The head Proctor is Sister Sara Torrez. She is not a young woman, but was very receptive to my call. She knows our family name which is very important here. I have you set up for a meeting with her tomorrow at the orphanage at 3:00 p.m."

"That's wonderful, Don Carlos! I will be there," Wade replied.

"There is one other thing. I heard that the religious order may not own the facility any longer. I am still investigating that. I want to find out about who is behind that now."

"I understand. That information would be important to know if we decide to adopt a child from there. I hope there is no problem with me going there tomorrow," Wade replied.

With a chuckle Don Carlos said, "No, they know I gave you my introduction. There won't be any problems. I just want to make sure there are no undesirable political factions involved that might cause you problems with the adoption,"

Wade arrived at the Heritage Children's Home fifteen minutes before the scheduled meeting time and drove through the large arch and iron gate. The first thing he noticed was the absence of guards on the outside of the facility. Wade parked his car in one of the many parking slots outside the main office. The grounds seemed empty. He could see that two buildings extended back from the main building creating a large courtyard. A fence ran the entire distance between the two side buildings sealing off anyone who was inside the courtyard area.

In disguise, which included a hat, Wade grabbed his notebook and pen on the front seat and started walking to the office door. He immediately saw movement from the corner of his eye to his right. The man approaching wore a greenish-brown military uniform and carried an Uzi over one shoulder.

Wade turned his head acknowledging the man's presence and asked if he was in the right place to see Sister Sara Torrez. The guard understood Wade but barely spoke any English.

Facing Wade, he uttered some of the few words he had mastered, "Passport, please." Wade politely complied.

After reviewing and returning Wade's passport and patting him down, he said another word in limited English vocabulary, "security," as he extended his hand for Wade to pass to the office door. Wade entered the large, old, sparsely-populated principal's office.

A heavy wooden counter ran the length of the room to Wade's right. Behind the counter stood six unoccupied gray desks. Only two desks had a few papers on them. The room gave Wade an eerie feeling like everything had been frozen in time. He could almost hear the voices of children and their proctors in muted dialogue.

The empty desks spoke to Wade of administrative personnel banging messages on ghostly typewriters that lay silent now collecting dust. It was like everything in the principal's office came to a sudden traumatic halt in time and space. Wade's mind momentarily slipped to flashbacks of his own childhood principal's office and the yardstick whippings he received at the hands of well-meaning nuns. His visions were of a loud busy principal's office, not the lifeless space he found himself in.

The appearance of an elderly woman in the doorway at the end of the room broke his concentration. She was dressed in the older garments of her religious order, her face crisscrossed with deep lines of wisdom and grief. She spoke in broken English, "Mr. James, please come in."

Following the nun's directions, Wade slowly entered the smaller office and sat in the chair the nun had pointed to. "I am Sister Sara Torrez. I understand you are from North America?"

"Yes, actually the western part of Canada," Wade replied.

"Don Carlos speaks well of you. His family is known by almost everyone in the area. What brings you here to Realta?" Sister Sara asked.

"My wife and I are interested in adopting a child. My wife is unable to naturally conceive," Wade replied.

"Have you been to doctors who specialize in that problem?" Sister Sara asked.

"Yes, they say it is unlikely they will be able to help us," Wade replied.

Sister Sara paused in awkward silence, saying only, "I see."

Wade noticed a troubled look on Sister Sara's face. The meeting seemed awkward and tense for Sister Sara even though she tried to cover it up. Wade broke the silence.

"We were considering adoption of a child," Sister Sara remained silent with a blank troubled look. Wade continued, "I am new to this, but I was wondering if the orphanage had children they put up for adoption and what the procedures might be."

The troubled look returned to Sister Sara's face. This time she had an intense stare as if Wade had said something that upset her. Wade wasn't sure what her expression was communicating.

Without saying anything, she sat back in her chair and with a subtle extension of her left hand finger pointed in the direction of the corner of a bookcase sitting to the left and behind her. Wade instantly saw the small recording receiver mic and knew their conversation was being taped.

Wade looked back at Sister Sara and nodded letting her know that he had seen the device and slowly changed the direction of the conversation.

"My understanding is that Argentina has an agreement with Canada regarding adoption. Is that correct?"

"Yes, I think adoptions can be arranged through your country. The real spiritual question is why do you want to adopt a child?"

Wade saw an opportunity to speak while he could move about scanning other parts of the room. He started into a long-winded explanation of what brought him and his wife to the decision to adopt. He wanted to give himself enough time to search the room for more listening and camera devices.

"Well, that's a fair question, Sister. My wife and I both came from religious families and when we were dating we often spoke about having children, never believing that would be a problem after we were married."

Sister Sara could see what Wade was doing and was impressed with his technique. Her expression changed from being barely able to manage the uncontrolled stress to a more relaxed state. She watched with intense curiosity as Wade covered the room in search of devices with the expertise of a professional.

She felt Wade understood she was here against her will. Beyond the intrusion of the listening devices, Wade thought something was profoundly wrong with this picture. Sister Sara was a prisoner in her own sanctuary. Keeping his voice at the same tone and pace, Wade continued with his long adoption story to the point of rambling while Sister Sara sat quietly, but amused.

During a brief natural pause in his story, Wade put his finger to his lips indicating the "hush" position while he walked around the room looking for listening devices and cameras. By the time Wade returned to his seat and was ending

181

his story, the dark pupils of Sister Sara's eyes were deeply frozen in fear as sharply as if she had been crying out to him.

Her expression was not a fear for herself or the eighty-year-old wrinkled body she occupied. What Wade saw was a deeper fear, a fear for the children she had vowed to care for and protect. He reasoned that she was here against her will, but had gladly accepted her prisoner role to protect the children. As their eyes met Wade immediately understood her anguish as clearly as if she had confessed her feelings to the Archbishop.

Wade's presence both amused and gave a glimmer of hope to Sister Sara. She wasn't sure who he was or why he had come but she had a feeling of comfort that he was here to help. Sister Sara no longer believed he was just another distressed parent looking for a child to adopt.

The wrinkles above her eyebrows gave way to a smooth forehead as a quiet calmness ascended over their meeting. All the while Wade kept rambling on about his upbringing and the problems his wife had in conceiving. To provide a signal of good intentions to Sister Sara, he made a cross over his heart with his forefinger. Sister Sara acknowledged his signal with a slight bow of her head.

With her acknowledgement Wade sat back to focus on the right questions to ask that would give him much needed information while still maintaining the disguise of an interview that would not raise suspicions for those who were listening.

"Sister Sara, I've told you why my wife and I wish so much to adopt a child. Now may I ask you some questions about the orphanage?"

"Certainly."

"How many children are here at the orphanage?" Wade asked.

"We have forty-seven children now," Sister Sara responded.

"What is their age range?" Wade asked.

"They are from two to eleven years old," Sister Sara responded.

"Do you have any children younger than two years old?" Wade asked, showing some disappointment.

"No, not right now. We do get younger children, but we don't have any now," Sister Sara replied.

"Do you house and feed the children here in these buildings?" Wade asked.

"Yes, the boys on one side and the girls on the other. We also provide schooling here."

"Do you teach them only in their native language or other languages as well?" Wade asked.

"All the children are taught in both Spanish and English," Sister Sara replied.

"What about their medical care. Do you provide that here as well?" Wade inquired.

"No. There is a medical clinic in the next village not far from here. That is where we bring them for medical care," Sister Sara said.

"You know health is something my wife and I are really concerned about in adopting a child. We've read many unfortunate stories about adopted children with health care problems. Would it be possible to arrange for me to tour the medical facility? I just want to make sure it is maintained with high standards," Wade inquired.

"I think I can arrange that for you. I will have to call you if I can get approval," Sister Sara replied showing it was not her that approved access to the clinic.

"Certainly, I will give you my contact information. I'm only about a half hour drive away. As you know I'm working with Don Carlos," Wade replied bringing a partial smile to Sister Sara's face that acknowledged he made an important connection with her.

"I would, of course like to tour this facility as well. I am sure you keep it in excellent shape," Wade commented.

"We do what we can with the resources we have, but we can arrange a tour here perhaps when you see the medical clinic," Sister Sara suggested.

"That would be fine. I really appreciate your assistance," Wade acknowledged.

"It was my pleasure."

Wade provided Sister Sara his local phone number knowing it would be checked by the people in charge of this place.

"Thank you, again, Sister Sara, for your kind hospitality," Wade said in a gracious tone.

"You're welcome. Now go with God," she waved as he turned to leave the compound.

After leaving the orphanage, Wade noticed that he had the company of three cars behind him. From his side mirror the two men in the first car seemed to be in uniform. They were probably from the orphanage sent to tail him. His visit had attracted interest. He had to decide what he was going to do with his new guests.

Chapter 18

Wade slowed down, checking the names of the cross streets and appearing to be lost. He let the two cars between him and his followers pass. One car blew his horn seemingly irritated by the slow down and yelled something impolite in Spanish as he passed. That maneuver brought his followers closer to Wade, which is where he wanted them. His tail chose to stay back instead of passing Wade which would have put him in the following position. After jotting down the license plate numbers on his guests' car he picked up speed. His tail clumsily followed. They were not highly trained operatives, Wade concluded. Losing them would not be a problem, but Wade had other reasons he wanted them to remain close behind.

Figuring they already knew he was in town before today's meeting and concluding that they had not exposed his cover story, Wade drove to his hotel with his tail in tow and parked just outside the side entrance to his room. His two followers drove past the side entrance pretending they were going to another part of the hotel. Wade took the stairs quickly to his room on the second floor, which overlooked the parking lot. He needed only a few minutes to prepare a deadly welcome surprise if his guests followed and forced entry into his room.

With weapon in hand, Wade peeled back a thin portion of the curtain and looked out over the parking lot. As he suspected, the two men parked two spaces from Wade's car and sat quietly, showing no desire to follow him into his room. Wade concluded that their orders were to just follow and keep tabs on him. Having company like that actually played nicely into the next part of Wade's plan.

Wade fashioned details of his next steps around what was already playing into what he wanted to happen. He thought to himself, *I first want them to assure the controlling group at the orphanage that my interest in adopting a child was legitimate.* Secondly, he wanted these men to confirm to their operations headquarters that his cover story of being a produce buyer from Canada was legitimate. And finally he wanted them to advise their superiors that my relationship with Don Carlos was real. This was the only way he was going to achieve having a tour and getting through the front door of the medical clinic.

Wade knew his adversaries were already checking his background records in Canada. He felt comfortable those records would pass the scrutiny test. Now he wanted to reinforce that portion of his cover dealing with Don Carlos which would serve to enhance his local creditability. Wade didn't want his followers to get suspicious or to evade or take him out. Wade wanted these men following him to be messengers bringing back to their leaders confirming evidence that he was indeed the genuine article.

Turning on and off lights in different rooms gave his followers something to watch. Every few minutes Wade confirmed his follows were still settled into their comfortable surveillance positions talking to each other and smoking. Wade picked up the room phone and dialed Don Carlos.

"Don Carlos," the caller answered.

"This is Mr. James. I just wanted to call and thank you again. My meeting with Sister Sara at the orphanage went extremely well this afternoon," Wade explained.

"Good, I am pleased to hear that. If you are not doing anything this evening I would like you to join me for dinner. I want to hear all about your meeting," Don Carlos replied.

186

"Yes, I am free this evening, that would be very nice. What time would you like me there?"

"Eight o'clock would be perfect. That's when I normally have dinner in my country. Remember we have our two to three-hour siesta time in the afternoon that you don't normally take," Don Carlos laughingly commented.

"The dinner time is fine. I'll be there at 8:00 p.m.. I'm looking forward to telling you all about my visit."

"Great. See you later," Don Carlos ended the call.

Wade checked the window and seeing nothing had changed he went down the back stairs to the lobby. There he used the guest payphone which sat in a far corner. Yari always preferred Wade to use a payphone whenever he could because Yari could trace the call signal and determine if there were any listening devices on the line. With the NSA's security authority, Yari also had the ability to take that entire line off of the grid. International calls were more complex, but Yari had an uncanny command of security devices that included rerouting feeder lines with encryptions that always boggled Wade's mind.

"Yari here."

"It's Wade. I'm calling from a payphone in another country. I think we need to be careful."

"I see that. You're calling from somewhere in Argentina. I'm doing a backtracking analysis on all feeder lines now. It will only take a few minutes before I can reroute the line through a secure patch. In the meantime, how's the weather?"

"Sunny with patches of white cumulus clouds over the eastern mountain range. A five mile per hour breeze out of the southwest. Chance of afternoon light rain tomorrow and the next day; otherwise the day's high temperature is 68 degrees," Wade replied like a local meteorologist.

"I'm almost there. About twelve more seconds," Yari replied.

"I'm not going anywhere," Wade replied.

"I got it. We're okay now. I cut the transmission in two places then rerouted the call through some of our Intelligence feeder lines. I also put in two encryption patches on both ends of the feeder lines," Yari replied.

"I have a couple of things I want to go over now that you have my location. I have three taps that I need you to place on lines going in and out of the orphanage and what they refer to as the 'medical clinic' we discussed. Another one is on Don Carlos' ranch lines, and a final one on my hotel. I'm staying in Room 228. All these places are in close proximity to each other on the map. I'm not sure who is in control at the orphanage and medical clinic, but I assume they are using phone lines to communicate."

"Are you making any progress on the mission yet?" Yari asked.

"It's only been a few days since I've been in the country. What do you expect, man?" Wade replied showing some frustration.

"I'm only kidding, boss. I spoke to Max and he told me more about the Maryland mission. That was awesome," Yari replied.

"I can't chit chat right now. I was at the orphanage today and have two unfriendlies following me right now. I'm headed to the Don Carlos estate for dinner," Wade replied.

"Oh, my God. Sounds like you're going to need help getting rid of those unfriendlies. Can you handle them without help?" Yari inquired.

"The unfriendlies are not an immediate threat. In fact, I want them right where they are reporting back on my movements right now. When the time comes I'll handle them," Wade replied.

"I hear you, boss. I know you can handle things. Just wanted to know if you could use some help," Yari responded.

"Not now. Were you able to find out any more about the real group behind the orphanage and the medical clinic?" Wade asked.

"Still working on it, boss. I'm also doing a background check on that attorney nominee. Seems like he has some real questionable characters as clients. He had been under surveillance by our State Department and CIA boys for some time. I should have something in a few days," Yari pointed out.

"Looks like I may have to pay our attorney a visit before all this is over," Wade replied.

"In what capacity will you contact him?" Yari asked.

"As another nominee of course. Two can play that nominee game," Wade replied.

"I don't have a number to trace calls from the Don Carlos estate," Yari stated.

"I'm going to dinner there tonight. I'm sure I can use his phone," Wade replied.

"Instead of calling me at this number I'll give you a coded ID number to call. You just dial that number and when a buzz comes on just hang up. The program will automatically trace the number it is calling from and your calls will never be registered through the phone system," Yari instructed.

"I'm not even going to ask you how that works," Wade replied.

"Don't, because it's a complicated answer, but it works," Yari replied.

"When doing your research, include Don Carlos. I need to know his background and political connections," Wade replied.

"Will do. I'll add him to the list. Here is the ID number for Don Carlos' phone," Yari gave Wade the coded ID number to call when he was at Don Carlos's house before ending their call.

After completing his call, Wade moved around to a different window, peering out at his followers' parked car. He noticed that a side window from the lobby gave him a good view of the two men sitting inside the car. The idea of photos of his trail prompted him to quickly get his camera from his room and return to that window position. His telephoto lens provided the perfect magnification to give him several shots of the two men's faces as they sat chatting with each other. He moved to another window, which gave him a clean shot of the car's license plate. Wade would find a way to get the photographs developed and wired back to Yari so he could run background and ID checks.

Scheduled dinner time with Don Carlos was growing near. A quick shower and change and Wade left the hotel for his car, causing his followers who were dozing off to jerk to attention when they saw Wade pull out of the parking lot.

At one point Wade had to slow down for fear of accidently losing his followers. As his tail approached three cars behind, Wade turned off the highway at the exit, which led to Don Carlos' private road. Driving a short distance down the road, Wade saw the extravagant arched gates of the estate come into view. The gate was open and Wade turned left under the arch checking his rear-view mirror to see if his followers maintained their distance. Wade turned onto the long tree-lined estate road that led to the main house.

After making the turn, he checked his rear mirror again. To his welcome surprise his tail did not follow him into the estate property. Rather, his followers pulled aside and parked on the shoulder of the road just outside the estate gates and watched Wade traverse the tree lined entryway.

After parking Wade got out of the car and approached the grand, stone steps to the house. He looked back and saw that his followers had left their position and the area. Wade wondered what it meant that his followers were unwilling to tread on the Don Carlos estate.

Within seconds of pressing the doorbell, the butler opened the door and ushered Wade in with the subtle gesture of his white gloved hand. Before Wade took his third step into the marbled entryway, he saw the smiling face of Don Carlos with two large, open arms welcoming his arrival.

"My friend, it is good to see you again. You must be tired after your long journey today. Please, come in and have some refreshments," Don Carlos said in a gracious tone.

The two men sat in the same comfortable chairs they had occupied on their last meeting. After being seated one of the servants came and asked, "Can I get something for you?"

"I'll have a glass of that fine red wine we had last time I was here," Wade replied.

Don Carlos instructed the servant in Spanish.

Shortly after getting their cocktails Don Carlos turned to Wade, "So tell me all about your trip to the orphanage today."

"Well, at first I was searched by a guard, which I thought was strange, but then I met with Sister Sara who told me you had spoken with her. I could tell that meant a lot to her. Your reputation in this region made a big difference with her. We spoke for over an hour and I got a good sense of Sister Sara's philosophy. She is very committed to the children," Wade described.

"That is very important. You know even though I don't know their orphanage I give a lot of money to the church," Don Carlos exclaimed proudly.

"You know, that's interesting because I got a feeling this orphanage may have come under some difficult times. I don't know if it is about money or local politics or what, but just between us I felt Sister Sara was under considerable stress. Although let me say she tried very hard to keep that feeling from me. It was just instinct on my part," Wade explained.

"That is interesting. You know I have had those instinctive feelings myself in dealing with people. You can't put your finger on it exactly, you just know," Don Carlos replied.

"Yes, that's a perfect description of how I felt," Wade said.

"Let me do more investigation of the orphanage. Perhaps I can find out more. What else did you talk about?" Don Carlos asked.

"She wanted to know about my spiritual character and why we wanted to adopt. She asked all the right questions and I was very open to her about our desires and why we came to our conclusion," Wade replied.

"That is good. It sounds like you had a good meeting. How did you leave it with her?"

"We discussed the fact that I am very concerned about the health of children. My wife and I have read many articles about adopted children having disease problems because they were not vaccinated properly or didn't have good medical care when they were young. She said that the children have their healthcare provided by a medical clinic by the name of

Hospital General de Niños in the village near the orphanage. Do you know anything about that medical facility?" Wade inquired.

"I think I've have heard this name before but I don't know anything about this clinic. Let me investigate that for you as well," Don Carlos replied.

"Sister Sara was kind enough to invite me on a tour of the medical clinic, but she has to first get approval from them. She will be calling me directly or she may call here if she can obtain that permission," Wade replied.

"If she calls here I will be sure to let you know right away," Don Carlos assured Wade.

"After I tour the clinic I am supposed to tour the orphanage facilities and meet some of the children. I can then provide a complete report to my wife."

"That will be exciting," Don Carlos exclaimed.

The cocktail hour was politely interrupted by a waiter announcing that dinner was being served. Asking to be excused, Wade headed to the restroom knowing from his previous visit that it was just outside the library room, which had a phone. Wade freshened up and quickly dialed the coded exchanged numbers and hung up before joining Don Carlos and some family members in the well-appointed dining room.

After completing an exquisite meal of rack of lamb and fresh vegetables, all from the estate, Wade and Don Carlos bid each other farewell. Wade expected he would pick up his tail after he left the estate but no one followed. He was equally surprised not to find his followers waiting at his hotel when he returned that evening.

Looking forward to an uninterrupted good night of sleep, Wade set his alarm for 5:00 a.m. the next morning and his scheduled inspection of another produce packing operation not far from Don Carlos' estate. Having trouble sleeping was rarely a problem for Wade. For some unknown reason this night turned out to give him some problems.

Shortly after turning out the lights, Wade became increasingly worried about things he could not control. He had not heard back from Sister Sara about his tour of the medical clinic. His mind raced with Intel details he would have to know to ingress and egress the medical facility on a night excursion alone if Sister Sara's call didn't come soon. The rest of the night led to him tossing and turning over how he was going to singlehandedly take on the small army guarding the children, innocent nuns, and Megan. He kept telling himself that he first had to know what he was up against and that was all this part of his mission entailed.

The next morning, after his inspection of the produce packing plant and a large lunch with the packing house manager, Wade returned to his hotel for his own siesta. The uncertainty, his rigorous produce inspection, and a sleepless night were taking their toll. Throwing his tablet and jacket on the dining table, Wade checked the window overlooking the parking lot and confirmed his followers no longer had him under surveillance. As he sat on the bed to remove his shoes, he happened to glance across at the room phone and saw that the red light was on. Checking with the operator he pushed the two keys, which accessed the recording of Sister Sara's gentle voice telling him he had been approved for a tour of the medical clinic tomorrow morning at 10:00 a.m.

Wade collapsed back on his bed thinking about what he would encounter on tomorrow's tour and how he would get access to areas of the clinic they were not about to show him. With the good news from Sister Sara, Wade lay back and took a much needed two-hour siesta. He awoke suddenly thinking that he had wasted valuable time. His thoughts turned to questions he would ask and how he would handle tomorrow's event. One of those questions dealt with how he would react upon the unlikely event that he saw Megan, no matter how remote that possibility might be.

Chapter 19

The evening before the scheduled clinic tour, Wade pored over maps and his notes hoping to find clues on how clinical staff, nurses, and children were housed and transported under guard from the orphanage to the clinic. Workers, staff, children and even the guards had to be housed and fed at either the orphanage, medical clinic or some off-site location.

Wade kept asking himself what made the most sense from their perspective. *If the staff was housed in private off-site residences how would they be guarded?* For that, Wade realized that he hadn't estimated the number of guards at each facility or how they communicated.

The routine for shadow cell injections and experiments on the children was also unclear. He assumed that they took place at the clinic, but wasn't certain. Perhaps he could confirm those facts with tomorrow's visit. Wade concluded he had too many unknowns and he abhorred surprises. Chastising himself for not having done more, he decided going to tomorrow's meeting this unprepared was unacceptable. Despite the risk he devised a night surveillance mission to cure some of his deficiencies.

After darkness fell, Wade took the back hotel stairway down to his car. Dressed in a black combat outfit, Wade began his plan to find some basic answers about his adversaries. Leaving the hotel parking lot, he headed toward the Don Carlos estate, which happened to be in the opposite direction from the medical clinic. He purposefully took the wrong route to assess whether or not he was being followed.

Confirming that he had no tails, Wade doubled backed to the location where he kept a hidden trunk of weapons and equipment that he had shipped using a password code given to him by Yari. It was the same private carrier used by his own intelligence agency.

Going through his trunk with a small flashlight in his mouth, Wade selected the few items he needed including night vision binoculars, his silenced SIG Sauer semi-automatic weapon, fighting knife, climbing rope, and an assortment of lighter accessories. He put his items in a black lightweight backpack the same color as his outfit, keeping out the stick of black face paint in case he was stopped en route.

Heading for the area he spotted on the map behind the medical clinic, Wade's route brought him to a small sparsely-populated town on the hill above the clinic. He drove the outskirts of the town until he reached an unpaved road. Down that road, three blocks away, stood two old storage sheds that seemed vacant with collapsed roofs, broken windows, and damaged doors hanging from one hinge. Wade assessed the damage to the buildings as coming from a violent storm several years ago.

He turned around and drove back a quarter mile to a busy bar and restaurant he spotted. The place was packed with limited parking in the rear lot. Wade decided on one of the only two remaining parking spots. The space he selected was in the far corner. He slipped out of his car and down a narrow path between two buildings to the cross street. Since he didn't want to spend time finding a hide for his car, he used an old Intelligence practice: *If you can't find cover for your car park it in plain sight under watchful eyes.* In this case the watchful eyes were inebriated patrons coming out of a crowed bar trying to locate their own keys and vehicles.

Keeping off the main street, Wade found unlit footpaths behind the buildings that led him to the dirt road and abandoned storage sheds several blocks from where he parked.

Approaching the two derelict storage buildings, Wade easily gained access through the broken front doorway. He crouched down and settled among broken timbers with a clear view out of the rear window. Adjusting his night vision binoculars Wade had a good view of the clinic, which he estimated to be less than a hundred yards away. As he gazed Wade was surprised by what he saw.

At four stories the clinic was larger than he first imagined. Two of the upper three stories were dark. The front and rear iron gates to the clinic were locked and there was only one car within the locked yard premises. A thin line of light emerged from the base of the clinic. It appeared to be a basement.

There were no windows or doors visible to the basement. Each of two guards outside guarded the front and rear entrances with Uzi short barrel automatic weapons, which they carried over their shoulders.

Wade observed their patrol pattern noting that none followed a prescribed routine as they randomly went back and forth in a relaxed random walk, each covering approximately thirty feet before repeating their route.

By any account the level of security was low. The two guards would be easy to take out, but Wade wondered if there were more clinic personnel or guards in the basement of the building. Panning the rest of the building through his binoculars didn't reveal anything new. With his visit scheduled for the next morning Wade decided that he would wait to see what information he could gain from the interior of the clinic. He evacuated his position using the same entry route in reverse and headed for the orphanage.

The orphanage was located in the next village three miles east of the clinic. After remembering the maps and surroundings he studied on the day he visited Sister Sara,

Wade focused on the upslope hill at the rear of the orphanage. The moderately sloping hill started its incline after a hundred yards of clean-cut pasture, which ended at the rear gates. Wade remembered the hill was crisscrossed with narrow foot paths and fire breaks. The heavy natural vegetation halfway up the hill looked like a good place for a sniper's nest.

The peak of the hill gently curved onto a sparsely populated residential street. Homes on this street were older structures on large lots with wide spaces between each house. Wade took a back road behind the residential area until he emerged on the street above the hill.

He found a vacant lot surrounded by bushy plants. One spot seemed to have an opening on one side. Heading his car into the three-sided outcrop, Wade shut off his engine and lights and coasted the remaining few feet. Guiding the car further into the bush, Wade came to a quiet stop well surrounded by vegetation. The area around his car was littered with fallen branches which Wade collected and used to cover his car.

His position was approximately one mile east and above the orphanage. Gathering his backpack Wade started his approach, avoiding the street and hugging the edge of high growth shrubbery between the houses and a well-worn foot path. Wherever possible Wade kept to the narrow foot trails and fire cuts to maintain his silence. He moved down and across the hill following the lines of foot trails until soon they faded into darkness before him. Unsure of his footing Wade used quick bursts of his flashlight covered in red film to illuminate the ground.

Maintaining a slow but steady pace, Wade stopped every hundred yards and crouched to examine his target destination and surrounding area through his night vision binoculars.

Satisfied he wasn't being followed and there was no one waiting in front of him, Wade continued traversing the hill, cutting back and forth at roughly a forty-five-degree angle until he reached a dense growth area.

His location was now halfway down the hill and the area he liked was flat and surrounded by a few tall trees. A quick survey on all sides confirmed that he had good height, angle and distance to see the entire orphanage grounds. Grabbing a few branches from beneath his feet, Wade hung them naturally in the trees surrounding his position. This shielded three sides from any probing night vision binoculars that might be looking up from the orphanage. Pleased with his nest, Wade settled down for a detailed survey of his target.

Taking out his sketch pad and with a few quick bursts of his red film flashlight, Wade drew the outline and estimated the dimensions of the buildings in front of him. He recorded his estimate not only in overall size, but the distances between each of the buildings and noted all exit doors, windows, and counted the vehicles in the courtyard.

Systematically, Wade scanned from left to right and up and down in small increments, frequently labeling his sketch pad with the segment he was observing. He soon finished his building sketch and started a detailed scan of the left-side building which he labeled the *west wing*.

His scan included freezing on each window that emitted light. From behind the curtains he saw identifiable silhouettes he labeled by their shapes. Quickly Wade came up with a code system that allowed him to categorize the shapes of males, females and small, medium or large children. Sometimes the silhouettes revealed garment details and he was able to supplement his code by nun, nurse, or guard uniform. Each shape and window he observed was recorded along with the time the image appeared. By the time Wade completed scanning the third building, he had a long list of coded details he would analyze later.

During the day the high iron fence and gated courtyard served as a children's playground. At night it housed a variety of vehicles. Wade counted and noted the position of parked cars and small buses, answering one of his questions about transportation resources. His count included two half-size buses, nine sedans, plus the two additional sedans he observed parked at the clinic. From the count Wade quickly estimated he was up against an armed security force at both facilities numbering approximately fifteen.

Wade watched the orphanage for over an hour getting a sense of its nighttime rhythms. Soon the darkened areas overshadowed the lighted windows as people settled into bed. It was now well past midnight and even small reading lights were being turned off. There was little point in continuing observations and, after taking one last look to check his notes and comparing them to the orphanage images, Wade evacuated his position. He was pleased that he knew a lot more about where everyone resided.

As he traversed the hillside to his car Wade noted that the nest on the hill would provide a great sniper hide or location to cover an orphanage extraction. Before returning to his hotel Wade returned his equipment to its hidden location in case his room would be searched tomorrow while at the clinic. His sleep went well that night.

Wade was up early the next morning converting his diagrams and notes into codes only he could read. The complex code system he developed had been tested on missions with experienced Intelligence Officers and encryption specialists with great success. Once he completed his conversion, he lit a match to the originals and watched them burn, then flushed the ashes down the toilet in case he was captured.

As part of his clinic meeting countdown, Wade rigged his room with what he called (from his days in the swamp), *traps*-pieces of hair, folded cellophane tape, and piles of his own created "dust" were placed in strategic locations. His traps would tell him if anyone came into the room and where they looked. He dressed in the same disguise he wore for his visit with Sister Sara except for this occasion he wore a coat and tie.

As he left his room he hung the "Do Not Disturb" sign on the handle for the cleaning maid and gingerly placed a tiny piece of specially-folded cellophane tape in the door hinge. The tape was folded in a way that made it react like a spring. If the door moved even slightly it would eject from its location. He placed another small strip of clear cellophane on the upper side of the doorjamb. The small marker also had a special back fold. Depending on how that marker lay when Wade returned, it would tell him if anyone was still in the room.

On his way to the clinic Wade practiced an old intelligence trick of whistling and singing aloud to warm up his vocal chords to help avoid unwanted voice inflections if he asked or answered sensitive questions. He also practiced Megan's silent humming technique, which he had learned in Washington before taking his polygraph test just in case he was asked questions under duress.

Assuming he was being watched, Wade took the most obvious route from his hotel to the clinic. It was 9:00 a.m. and the mist was quickly burning off the pastures lining the road, yielding a clear beautiful day. Approaching the clinic Wade immediately noticed the absence of guards and their vehicles.

After parking his car, he grabbed his folder with a blank tablet from the front seat and headed calmly to the front door wearing a smile. Halfway up the stairs, two guards approached, one coming from each side. The right-side guard was a female and asked in broken but understandable English, "Your passport please."

Wade smiled while handing over his passport. He looked at the male guard on the other side. The guard's eyes ignored Wade's glance, remaining fixed on the female guard. Turning back to the female guard, Wade noticed that she was pausing as she looked at every page of his passport. It didn't seem normal that she would be trying to find something out of order for a clinic visitor. She handed Wade his passport and pointed to the folder under his arm.

"I need to see your tablet,"

Wade complied. She flipped through the pages confirming there was no writing and looked down the spine for hidden devices.

"Do you have an appointment?" she asked, knowing full well who he was and his expected arrival time.

Wade played along, "Yes, I am here to see the clinic director at 9:30 am. The appointment was set up by Sister Sara at the orphanage." He received a blank stare from both guards.

"Please wait here," the female guard instructed.

She proceeded through the clinic door leaving Wade and the male guard standing in silence.

A few minutes passed and the front door opened, "Please come in. Someone will be with you in a moment." The female guard gestured.

Wade stood in the hallway lined with two rows of chairs on each side. He decided to remain standing. Soon two men approached from an anteroom walking slowly toward him.

One was wearing a knee-length white physician's jacket and the other a brownish-green military uniform with two gold stars affixed to each lapel. He was carrying an officer's cap with a red band lined with gold trim wrapped just below the ornate center gold insignia.

As the men approached, the physician showed a slight smile but the military gentleman spoke first. "Hello, I am Captain Ruso and this is the clinic director, Dr. Alonso Kemp."

"I am Mr. James," Wade replied, offering his hand to shake. The two men responded with the Captain's hand coming out first.

Chapter 20

"Let's go to Dr. Kemp's office where we will be more comfortable," the Captain suggested after shaking hands. Wade nodded and the captain responded, "Please, follow me." Wade fell in line between the Captain and Dr. Kemp.

The captain took a seat to the side of Dr. Kemp's desk. The two men remained standing until Dr. Kemp was behind his desk, when they all sat.

The Captain spoke first again, "Dr. Kemp has asked me to join your meeting today. Perhaps questions will come up I can assist in answering."

Dr. Kemp gave a tentative nod to the Captain's statement, his eyes darting back and forth looking for the slightest instruction from the captain. The doctor spoke in a meek, barely audible voice, "I understand from Sister Sara you may be looking to adopt a child and wanted to visit the clinic."

Wade responded, "That is correct. My wife and I are from Canada and our doctors tell us she is having fertility problems. We are exploring adoption as an alternative while she is receiving fertility treatments in Canada."

"Is there something from the medical side you are looking for specifically that we can help you with?" Dr. Kemp asked.

"We've read a number of articles that discuss concerns about the medical care given in adoption cases, and since I understand you provide the medical care for the orphanage I wanted to learn more about your procedures." Wade paused before continuing, "As an example there are many stories of children coming down with diseases from not having the proper vaccinations and medical treatment when they are young. I just wanted to get a sense of what type of care is given to the children here," Wade inquired.

Dr. Kemp was about to respond to Wade's comment when the Captain jumped in and answered for him. Seeing the Captain's gesture, Dr. Kemp retreated from giving his response.

Using a sarcastic tone the Captain stated, "That is not a problem at our facility. We provide nothing but high-level care at this medical clinic. We practice state of the art medicine here,"

Quick to hear the annoyance in the Captain's voice, Wade responded, "Well that's good to hear." Wade turned his back to the Captain and faced Dr. Kemp, "Perhaps you can show me some of those outstanding medical practices, Dr. Kemp?"

The Captain looked at Wade, annoyed that he had turned his attention to Dr. Kemp.

"Are you by chance a medical professional, Mr. James?" the Captain asked before Dr. Kemp could respond to Wade's question.

"Not even close. I am a produce importer and stay as far away from the medical professionals as I can get. My wife and I have just read a lot about the health care of adopted children and there seem to be some major problems. We are just concerned if we decide to adopt."

"Other than telling you that we don't seem to have those problems here, what specific areas are you interested in knowing about?" the Captain asked, continuing his arrogant tone.

Detecting the potential for controversy, Dr. Kemp's eyes moved rapidly back and forth between the captain and Wade. He seemed to be looking for approval to speak. The Captain gave a slight nod to Dr. Kemp but he remained silent. Since there was an open unanswered question hanging in the room, Wade decided to fill the void.

Turning to Dr. Kemp, Wade responded, "Well, let's start with vaccinations for example. Please tell me what vaccinations you give the children and at what ages. I hope it is all right if I take some notes?"

Dr. Kemp looked over at the Captain who gave another nod before Dr. Kemp spoke. "Sure it's fine to take notes. I can also give you a list of the vaccine serums we use."

"That would be helpful," Wade replied. "Can you give me a little background on your medical training, Dr. Kemp?"

"After finishing high school I graduated in pre-med at the University of Buenos Aires. I then attended St. Andrews Medical School in the Falkland Islands. I also attended the University of Texas in San Antonio, Texas for specialty training and returned here to do my residency at Hospital Municipal General in Buenos Aires."

"You have an excellent medical educational background," Wade commented wondering, *Why would he take this position stuck in the middle of Realta under the control of the Captain?*

"Where did you practice before becoming director of this clinic?" Wade asked.

"For a private medical group in Buenos Aires," Kemp answered.

"Do you have your own laboratory here or do you send everything out for analysis?" Wade inquired.

"We have an extensive laboratory here. For specialized analysis we send some specimens out." Dr. Kemp answered, looking for approval from the Captain.

"Have you had any bacterial or strep outbreaks in the lab or facility here?" Wade asked.

"We had a little problem with strep infections several months ago," Dr. Kemp responded before looking over to Captain Ruso. After getting an expression of stiff objection from the Captain Dr. Kemp continued, "But it was only a very minor problem."

Wade no longer had any doubts that Dr. Kemp was here against his will and under the direct control of Captain Ruso. Wade watched carefully for a reaction before he asked his next question in a casual conversational manner.

"It must be nice running a large clinic. Is your wife and family here with you at the clinic?" Wade asked.

Dr. Kemp's eyes immediately moved to the Captain without responding. Wade saw tension in Dr. Kemp's face. It told him all he needed to know. The Captain ignored Dr. Kemp's look, maintaining his staunch expression. Dr. Kemp never answered the question. The tense expression on Dr. Kemp's face changed when Wade broke the silence in the room.

"Well, if it's okay with you and the Captain, I would like to see these fine facilities and some of the practices you described." Wade moved his hand to the armrest showing he was prepared to stand.

Dr. Kemp looked across to the Captain who gave a short nod. Immediately standing, Dr. Kemp said, "Certainly, please follow me."

The doctor led the way to the door as the captain brought up the rear so close to Wade he could hear him breathing. Turning left past the hall to the doctor's office, they made a right turn down the hallway to a large room with a sign that said *Admisión*. The men followed Dr. Kemp through the door facing a counter with three staff typing away at papers. There was a large padded bench lining one side that was empty of patients.

Dr. Kemp said with a smile, "This is admitting. We take the patients' basic information here and retrieve their medical file before admitting them to the clinic."

Wade commented, "It's interesting there's no one here waiting to be admitted."

"In addition to the children at the orphanage we get people from the nearby village. It just so happens this is not a busy day," Dr. Kemp responded.

Wade had never seen a medical admitting room so vacant of people. It wasn't clear what the three people behind the desk were typing since there were no patients. There didn't seem to be any piles of medical files or paperwork. The whole scene looked staged to Wade. After looking at the empty room for a while Wade suggested, "I'm interested in seeing your laboratory facility where you do your testing and analysis."

"I'm afraid that area is off limits today," the Captain replied.

"Oh, why is that Captain?" Wade responded.

"We are undergoing some renovations in those rooms and are concerned with maintaining a sterile environment. You can't be too careful about contamination," the Captain responded.

"Dr. Kemp, contamination must be a concern to you in particular," Wade redirected his question to Dr. Kemp.

"You can never be too careful when it comes to infectious contamination," Dr. Kemp replied.

They passed two more halls with large rooms behind closed doors. Suddenly one of the doors opened just as they approached another closed room. A short female dressed in white laboratory coat, mask, and covered shoes exited the room uttering in broken English, "Excuse me."

Wade got a quick look inside before the door closed. He saw a room full of females standing at chemical laboratory tables all dressed in similar white laboratory attire from head to foot. In a split second Wade's eyes focused on one female who looked like it could be Megan but he couldn't be sure. He asked in a curious tone, "What goes on in that room?" pointing to the door that just closed.

"That is a government-funded research project that is off limits," the Captain stated firmly.

Dr. Kemp didn't respond. Instead he turned down another hall to rooms that housed x-rays and other large equipment. Dr. Kemp opened the first door and exclaimed, "Here you see we have the latest in x-ray equipment."

"It is all state of the art equipment," Captain Ruso commented.

After looking for a while at the machines at rest Wade commented, "Very nice. It looks like your clinic is well financed."

"*Very* well-funded," replied Dr. Kemp

"May I ask where you treat the children when they come in with problems?" Wade asked.

Dr. Kemp pointed to another corridor twenty feet away that intersected their current position. "That whole wing is used for children," the doctor continued, "It is staffed with pediatricians and medically trained nuns who take care of this wing."

"Are there any children being treated now? It would be great to see how they are coming along," Wade asked.

"I am afraid that is off limits. We don't want to bring in any adult carried disease. Any adults coming into this area are quarantined except for the nuns who we test and monitor on a regular basis. So going into the children's ward I'm afraid won't be possible," the Captain answered.

"Are there other parts of the children's area that *are* accessible?" Wade inquired.

"What did you have in mind?" Dr. Kemp asked.

"Well, I was hoping to see your research facility in the children's ward."

The Captain interrupted Wade's sentence, "As we explained much of that is off limits for the reasons we gave you." Wade nodded, accepting the Captain's explanation and knowing he had no other choice but to continue with new questions that changed the subject.

"What is on the top floor of the clinic?"

"The top floor is used as offices for visiting doctors and researchers from the university. They are not being occupied now," Dr. Kemp responded.

"Is there any research going on in the basement?" Wade asked.

"The basement is used only for storage and has some electronic equipment there," the Captain responded before Dr. Kemp could answer. Standing between the two men and looking at his wrist watch, Captain Ruso continued, "I'm sorry but Dr. Kemp and I have a staff meeting to attend in just a few minutes. It has been a pleasure meeting with you. It is sometimes easy to get lost in this building so I have asked two of my staff members to escort you to the front door." The Captain gave a wave of his hand and two armed members of his staff approached, each standing to Wade's side.

"Well, it's been a real pleasure having this tour. Thank you for the courtesy and your time," Wade replied. The men shook hands and Wade started walking down the corridor with his escorts. Just before he turned, he saw Captain Ruso grab

Dr. Kemp's arm and escort him down an intersecting hall in the opposite direction.

As Wade walked down the hall a door to his right unexpectedly opened almost hitting his arm. Wade quickly reacted and grabbed the door. He got a good look inside the room. It was another large laboratory staffed by women clad in white laboratory uniforms.

The woman trying to exit the laboratory room said "Excuse me" as they exchanged eye contact. The two guards adjusted their position to let the woman pass. Wade turned again to look inside before feeling the resistance of the guard's hand pushing against the door and closing it.

Leaving the clinic parking lot, Wade felt frustrated that his visit had gained such little information. By the time he reached his hotel he tempered that frustration, believing that he may actually have more information than he first thought.

Wade came face to face with his hotel room door and checked his "traps." None had been sprung. He entered the room and sat at the desk to record notes and diagrams in his head to code. Concentrating on his sketching he overlooked the red light on the opposite bedside table until minutes later.

The message he retrieved was from Don Carlos expressing concern and urgency. Wade listened for a second time never hearing Don Carlos' voice with so much anguish. "Please contact me as soon as you get this message. It is something very important that cannot be discussed over the phone," Don Carlos exclaimed.

After trying to call first and getting a busy signal, Wade quickly put the receiver on the base, turned to set his traps, and sped off to the Don Carlos estate.

Manuel the butler answered the door quicker than normal. Even Manuel had the look of stress on his face. Before Wade got three steps into the foyer, Don Carlos greeted him with an expression of grave concern. Dispensing with his usual smile, hug and handshake Don Carlos said, "Let's go to the study. I have important information to tell you." The two men entered the library. Wade took his usual chair while Don Carlos ensured that the double doors to the room were securely closed.

Don Carlos looked Wade straight in the eye and started to explain. "Remember I told you I would do some investigating about your orphanage and medical clinic?"

"Yes, I remember," Wade replied.

"I just heard from my attorney in Buenos Aires doing the investigating and I have some terrible news to report," Don Carlos said in a worried voice.

"What's the problem?"

"My attorney has uncovered that some very dangerous people are involved in the orphanage and medical clinic," he paused, thinking of the best way to put the information in English.

"The person who is behind both the orphanage and clinic is Ocholo. He purchased both facilities under different entities he controls. This man is extremely dangerous in our country. How do you say in English? He is a gangster and very ruthless."

"Really, I had no idea, although I experienced a very strange reception when I visited the clinic this morning," Wade replied.

"There is more, my friend. My attorney has found out that the children of this orphanage are probably being used in some criminal manner, which he is still investigating. The sources my attorney uses are telling him Ocholo is dealing with these children in some various dangerous games with both the

213

Chinese and Russians. He is pitting one against the other in some kind of bidding game. He thinks the U.S. might also be involved somehow." Wade could see his friend's blood pressure was sky high. Sweat was running down Don Carlos' face.

"Isn't what he is doing *illegal* in your country?" Wade asked.

"Of course, but this man knows many people in our government who, for the right price, will look the other way. Do you understand what I mean?"

"Yes, of course," Wade replied.

"Does your attorney have more details on Ocholo and how he operates?" Wade asked.

"Yes, I am sure. Political and criminal investigations are his specialty," Don Carlos replied.

"I have to know more of these details. I may know some people in North America that may be able to help us. Is there any way I can meet with your attorney?"

Don Carlos thought for a moment before responding, "Of course. Take my plane to Buenos Aires. I have an excellent pilot, Guillermo. He can have the plane ready in a couple of hours. I will call my attorney and tell him to give you complete cooperation."

"I feel we have to do this. I am concerned about those children. Thank you for all your help, Don Carlos," Wade responded.

"I am the one who should be thankful that you uncovered all this. I should have done this investigation long ago. I hope we are not too late," Don Carlos exclaimed, feeling guilty that he did not act sooner.

"I'll go to my hotel to get a few things I need and come right back," Wade replied.

"I will have everything ready when you return," Don Carlos replied as Wade hurriedly walked toward the front door to leave.

Chapter 21
Buenos Aires, Argentina

Wade's stop included visiting his stash of equipment before proceeding to his hotel and quickly filling his backpack with overnight clothes and accessories. He made his return trip to Don Carlos' estate in record time. The front door was ajar with a bustle of activity by maids and the butler crossing the foyer in a hurry.

A ranch hand was waiting outside in a white truck partially covered in dirt. Don Carlos was moving quickly through the foyer and stopped when he saw Wade.

"I am glad you are back. I had my staff prepare an ice chest of drinks and sandwiches for your trip. My attorney is expecting you. Here is the name and address of his firm. Guillermo has the plane ready for you and my ranch hand will bring you to the airstrip."

"I'll transfer my things to the truck. I'm ready to go," Wade replied.

With a handshake Don Carlos wished Wade a good trip and instructed the driver to take good care of him. The airstrip was on the far end of the 36,000 hectare estate of Don Carlos. At times the ride got a little bumpy as the truck took on the gravel and dirt roads before reaching the paved two lane highway leading to the airstrip.

Wade's mind was on details of this upcoming trip and the driver offered little in the way of casual conversation. The metal hanger buildings of Don Carlos' airport and the shining reflection of the twin engine Cessna 421c Golden Eagle soon came into view. It was gassed up, cleaned up. and ready for flight. A uniformed pilot in aviator sunglasses was making a final walkthrough when they drove up. The truck pulled up parallel to the rear cargo hatch. Wade got out and introduced himself to Guillermo, who shook his hand and returned the smile. "Looks like a beautiful day to fly," Wade commented.

"Yes, let me check on the updated weather report and I will return shortly," Guillermo replied. Coming out of the hanger Guillermo smiled and gestured to the co-pilot's door. He helped Wade get buckled in and handed him the headset and wires which were already plugged into the console.

Shortly after the pilot was in his seat, the lights and gauges came alive just before the first engine prop turned. Guillermo's voice came into the headset. "We can speak through the headset, otherwise there will be too much noise."

Wade acknowledged by nodding, already forgetting they were connected by headset and microphone. The second engine revved with vibration assuring Wade that there was no shortage of power.

"Are you ready?" asked Guillermo.

"Whenever you are," replied Wade.

The plane's taxi seemed short and the runway long before Guillermo's hands moved both throttles forward. Wade seemed to feel each pebble of the runway as sound and vibration consumed the capsule. As they picked up speed Wade's foot drifted to the floorboard. His leg became a brace to which he applied increasing pressure.

Wade wasn't particularly fond of small aircraft or heights and this ride was no exception. Visions of how quickly a small plane fell from the sky became vivid when he downed the one in Belize with one sniper shot. That image had no business creeping into his mind at this particular time. Not being skilled in small craft aviation and based solely on his commercial flight experience, Wade wondered why they were still on the ground at this point on the runway. According to Wade's unprofessional calculation they should have been airborne a hundred feet back.

He looked over and saw Guillermo fighting the plane's steering wheel. "Is there a problem?" Wade asked showing his level of fear.

"No, I have to fight to keep the plane on the ground. It wants to lift," Guillermo replied.

"I thought the object here was to get lift," Wade replied.

"No, in this area of South America you have to build up ground speed because of the downdrafts coming off the mountains. You also need enough speed to overcome an engine failure," Guillermo said calmly. By the time Guillermo finished his explanation the plane not only lifted, but ascended at an angle that caused Wade's stomach to fly into his throat. Feeling a little ill, Wade said, "I see what you mean."

After leveling off, Guillermo turned north, set levers and frequencies, and the plane settled in for a smooth ride. Thinking it was a little late to be asking the question, Wade inquired, "Where did you learn to fly?"

"I got most of my training in the Argentina Air Force. I also flew commercial when I left the military and retired before coming to work for Don Carlos," Guillermo commented.

Wade felt more relaxed and trusting as the plane felt as steady as a rock.

"How long of a flight do we have?" Wade asked.

"Usually about two hours depending on the winds," Guillermo replied.

"This seems like a nice plane."

"Yes, the plane is almost new and top of the line for turbo prop. The next step higher is a jet engine," Guillermo replied.

"Does Don Carlos use the plane a lot?" Wade asked.

"Yes, he's always going to meetings all over the country. This plane also has a high weight capacity. It has also been modified so we can take out the seats for when I go pick up agricultural parts like pumps when they are needed on the farm," Guillermo replied.

There was a pause in their discussion as Wade looked out of the window and enjoyed the gorgeous view.

"Do you know Buenos Aires?" Guillermo asked.

"No. I've never been there before. I am always in the farming areas of a country."

"It is a beautiful city like New York. I grew up there," Guillermo replied.

"Really? You must know where the restaurants are and what hotels to stay in, you will have to give me some suggestions," Wade replied.

"Don Carlos has given me an envelope for you, which includes those places," Guillermo replied.

"He has been a very good man to deal with," Wade answered.

"He is a wonderful and honest man and that is why I work for him."

"That's nice," Wade replied.

Wade put his head back, feeling he was in safe hands with Guillermo in a Don Carlos plane. He helped himself to one of the sandwiches and passed one to Guillermo. After a smooth ride and a few short naps, they started their approach to Buenos Aires. Guillermo pointed out several historic sights.

"Are we going into the main airport in Buenos Aires?"

"No, it is much too crowded. We use a private airport on the outskirts of the city. It is much better. Don Carlos likes this little airport," Guillermo stated.

"That's good enough for me," Wade replied.

As they landed, a car approached the plane to pick up Wade's luggage. Wade inquired about his return trip. "Will you be heading back to the ranch this evening?" Wade asked.

"No, sir, my orders are to remain available for you until you are ready to return. I stay at my sister's house and see my nieces and nephews here in Buenos Aires," Guillermo replied.

Wade was impressed by Don Carlos' gesture of hospitality, but didn't want to abuse the privilege.

"I may be stuck here for more than a day. I'm just not sure," Wade replied.

"That's fine. I get to spend even more time with my sister and her family. I will give you her number. Just call me when you are ready to return."

Shaking Guillermo's hand, Wade said, "Thank you."

Turning to the car that just drove up Guillermo responded, "The driver will take you anywhere you need to go in the city."

"That's very kind. I need to find a hotel then I need to go to the attorney's office," Wade commented.

"It is not a problem. The driver will guide you," Guillermo replied.

Wade watched them put his luggage and equipment in the trunk and settled into the back seat. He waved as they drove past the plane toward the tall buildings making up the big city's skyline.

The downtown forty story modern chrome and glass office building could be located in any major city in the world. Wade approached the lobby feeling somewhat underdressed in ranch clothes surrounded by all the tailor-made suits going to and from the building.

Wade took the elevator to the thirty-sixth floor and entered a plush appointed reception area with the chrome letters of the named partners, Lorenzo, Rivas & Gallos suspended in chrome letters above the receptionist's desk.

"My name is Mr. James and I am here to see Mr. Roberto Gallos."

The multilingual speaking secretary took a call in a language other than Spanish or English that Wade didn't recognize. She answered him in perfect English without the hint of an accent. "Is Mr. Gallos expecting you?"

"I think so," Wade responded.

"Please have a seat and someone will be with you in a moment."

Wade's wait was less than ten minutes. "Hello, Mr. James, my name is Janet. I'm Mr. Gallos' assistant. He is tied up in a meeting right now, but asked that I seat you in his office and offer you something to drink. He will be along momentarily."

"That's great. I'll just follow you," Wade replied.

Wade had seen corporate executive offices in New York and law partners' offices in Los Angeles, but never anything quite like what he saw in Roberto Gallos' office.

It seemed half the size of a regulation basketball court. Wade put down his folder and wandered over to the wall. He admired the numerous degrees and awards. He was surprised to see among those a degree from Tulane University in New Orleans and one from Columbia Law School.

Looking at the hanging civil and law achievements, Wade brushed against Mr. Gallos' phone, accidently knocking the receiver off the base. Before putting the receiver back, he picked it up and heard a dial tone. A flash of numbers entered Wade's mind and he thought *what the hell* as he pressed in the seven digit tracing code Yari had provided. Wade quickly punched in the code and hung up the phone not having a clue if it would work on international phone lines.

Wade moved over to the window and was admiring the view when a voice from behind him said, "Mr. James, I am Roberto Gallos and I am so sorry to keep you waiting. Please have a seat," pointing at the round conference table near where he was standing. "Give me a second to get the files and I'll join you in a moment. Can my assistant get you anything?"

"No I'm fine, thank you," Wade replied.

Roberto came through the door with manila files stacked at least two feet thick and put them on the middle of the table.

"It's hard to know exactly where to start," Gallos commented as he continued. "Let me make a suggestion that you start by telling me how you became involved with the orphanage and medical clinic in Realta."

Wade told the story of his wife and how they were exploring the adoption alternative.

Gallos listened without a comment. After Wade finished his explanation, he waited for more questions or comments from the attorney. The response he got was a surprise and made him feel uncomfortable.

Grabbing a file from the top of the stack the attorney said, "Now let's see, you came here to develop sources to export produce into Canada. Is that right?"

"Yes," Wade replied.

The change in subject matter and tone was jarring as were the following questions.

"I see you graduated in Plant Science from the University of Vancouver, is that correct?"

"Yes."

"Before that you attended high school in Vancouver at St. Francis, is that correct?"

"Yes."

Wade was convinced he was being vetted from some investigation and wasn't going to receive any new information until he got through these questions. He hoped his Intelligence people in Canada had dotted all the I's and crossed all the T's. This was no time for a whoops!

After a brief pause, Gallos continued, "I see after college you were in the military."

"Yes, that's correct."

"In fact, you were part of what the Canadian Military today calls Special Forces?" Roberto asked.

Wade paused trying to remember details of his military cover story.

"Yes, but I'm not sure we were all that special back then. It seems like a long time ago," Wade smiled, dismissing attention to further military questions.

"Yes, I understand. After your military discharge you joined your uncle's produce company in Vancouver, which has been around for almost fifty years?" Roberto asked.

"That's correct. It was started by my two uncles before my father joined them," Wade responded.

The attorney seemed more relaxed and changed to a lighter topic.

"So how have your produce inspections gone with Don Carlos?" Gallos asked.

"Very well. I think he has one of the best farming operations I visited this trip," Wade replied.

"My apologies for all these questions. Don Carlos asked me to do some background investigation on you before your visit. You passed with flying colors. If you would like I can provide you a copy of our investigator's report," the attorney offered.

"That would be great."

Attorney Gallos placed Wade's file on the side of the table. He turned and faced Wade with a serious expression on his face.

"Now let's turn to our character in question. Ocholo's operations are definitely not clean and can be very difficult to uncover. In fact, nothing he does is what it appears," Gallos commented before he continued. "What do you know about Manuel Ocholo?"

"Nothing more then what Don Carlos told me just before I left for your office. Until that time I'd never heard his name," Wade replied.

Pointing to the two-foot high stack of files on the table Gallos commented, "These files represent about five years of investigations into Mr. Ocholo by my firm for various clients. Many of our clients are in politics or running for office. The orphanage and clinic are just the most recent part of our investigation."

"I had been wondering if that entire stack of files was about the orphanage and clinic," Wade responded.

"No, but it is safe to say that Mr. Ocholo has been involved in everything from murder, drugs, and rigging political elections to payoffs of government officials," Gallos commented.

"I'm surprised he's not in prison," Wade responded.

"He manages to stay just outside the reaches of the law. Many of his henchmen are guests in our prisons. With his own personal army of attorneys they always seem to be short of some important piece of evidence or witness. Make no mistake about it: Ocholo is very smart and dangerous criminal and the fact that you have run up against one of his operations puts you potentially in his sights," Roberto commented.

"That's unnerving. I see now why Don Carlos was so concerned," Wade replied.

"Rather than discussing all of Ocholo's misdeeds, let me focus on what we found out about the orphanage and medical clinic."

"That sounds good to me," Wade replied.

Grabbing a stack of five files from the pile, Roberto Gallos took a moment to scan the contents before he began. "As far as my investigators can tell Ocholo's involvement starts back some years ago with his father."

"His father?" Wade asked.

"Yes, Ocholo's father was as much a gangster as his son is today. His father was actually killed in a shootout with authorities six years ago. Back when World War II was ending there were a number of Nazi military officers looking to escape Germany. Many had their eyes set on Argentina, which had already given a number of German citizens asylum. They saw our country as a safe haven to escape the allies."

"Yes, I've heard stories about that migration," Wade replied.

"Feeling pressure from their allied friends in the world, Argentina put restrictions on granting asylum requiring that among other things, anyone wishing asylum needed to have an Argentina *sponsor*. In addition to paying for their asylum in the country this 'sponsor' was to be responsible for the good conduct of the immigrants they sponsored. In fact there were laws on the books here that said a 'sponsor' could be imprisoned if the person they sponsored committed unlawful acts."

"I assume that gave the country some assurance that someone besides the government was assuming responsibility for these new German immigrants," Wade confirmed.

"That's correct. Well, Ocholo's father sponsored a German military officer by the name of Dr. Schultz. Schultz was a physician in Germany before the war and was wanted by the allies and others for conducting horrible experiments on children in the concentration camps. Apparently Dr. Schultz's research found a way to have children become a carrier of a disease that infect others without becoming infected themselves. When Dr. Schultz escaped and came to this country he had all the paperwork documenting his experiments and findings with him."

"So what happened to Dr. Schultz and his documentation?" Wade asked.

"Well, the simple answer is that Dr. Schultz died of natural causes two years after Ocholo's father died. As far as we can tell, Dr. Schultz never engaged in any experiments in this country before he died. After his father's death we believe Ocholo's son came into possession of Dr. Schultz's documentation, through his father, and saw the potential for exploitation. We have not been able to track down exactly what or how Ocholo is using this information for or how the clinic and orphanage fit into his plans exactly but my investigators feel there is definitely a connection there."

"That's so scary it's almost unbelievable that Ocholo is backing some kind of mad scientist project that involves those same experiments on children!" Wade exclaimed showing his expression of shock.

"I agree. That is why your piece of the puzzle fits. It seems you have stumbled quite by accident on how he is using the Schultz experiments," Roberto explained.

"Did your investigators run across a Dr. Kemp by chance? He is the director of the medical clinic. I met him yesterday and he seems very strange," Wade commented.

"Let me take a look at the files for a moment," The attorney paused to look through several investigators files. As he read the file he replied, "Yes, we do have a Dr. Kemp here. It seems he just recently came to work as clinical director. It says here Ocholo was Dr. Kemp's sponsor through medical school. In other words, if you do not have the money for medical school in Argentina you can find a sponsor who either loans you the money or just funds your medical education. It seems Ocholo has provided all the funding for Dr. Kemp's education."

"There is something else in this investigator's report."

"What do you mean?" Wade asked.

"It seems that Dr. Kemp is married with two children. His wife's name is Kimberly."

"That doesn't seem strange by itself," Wade commented.

Reading the file the attorney looked up at Wade, "It does if your wife and two children have been missing for two months."

"What?" Wade's mind was already focused on the worst. "That's why Dr. Kemp acted so strange."

"What do you mean?"

"When I asked him a question, he couldn't look me in the eye. I got the feeling he was there against his will. He was totally under the control of a Captain Ruso during our meeting," Wade explained.

Gallos grabbed another two files and started to review them, knowing that he had heard that name before.

"And here is your Captain Ruso. It seems he was formally a captain in the Argentina army before joining Ocholo. He had problems in the Army and was investigated several times for using excessive force. In several cases the suspects died in prison under strange circumstances."

"Can we come back to your file on Dr. Kemp's wife?" Wade asked.

Reviewing the file again, attorney Gallos asked, "What exactly are you looking for?"

"I am wondering if the investigator has any suspicions about where Dr. Kemp's wife and children might be. I think Dr. Kemp might be a key in this puzzle and it explains the fear that I saw in his face when I toured the facility."

The attorney read what appeared to an extensive segment of the investigator's report. "Yes, it says here the investigator believes the wife and children are being held by Ocholo under what he calls 'house arrest'," Roberto commented.

"Does he say where?" Wade asked the attorney, who didn't look up from reading the report.

"His best guess is they are being held at one of Ocholo's estates."

"Does he say which one?" Wade asks curiously.

"Ocholo has many estates throughout the country." Pointing his finger as he scanned the investigator's report, he continued, "He feels it might be his estate in the mountains called Monte Lamar. He goes on to say it would require additional investigation," Wade was already formulating a plan but didn't wish to provide any of those details at this meeting. He was curious how long the attorney was willing to spend time with him.

"I don't suppose you could allow me to study those investigation reports? I think the details could be important," Wade asked hoping for a favorable response.

"Unless you read Spanish they won't do you much good," replied Gallos.

Wade's face took a dive as his expression changed to discouragement.

The attorney's face remained stern and calculating when he looked up and said, "I'll do you one better. How about if I have the Ocholo files translated into English and give you a copy along with an office here to analyze them?"

Wade's face instantly lit up with joy. "That would be outstanding. I can't thank you enough."

"Don't thank me… thank Don Carlos. We are on the same team and anything you come up with on Ocholo can only help me and my other clients." Wade loved the attorney's offer. That's what he needed to hear.

The two men continued to meet for another half hour before Janet came in reminding Gallos that he had a conference call waiting. Wade knew enough Spanish to make notes from the files while the attorney was deep in discussion using the phone at his desk. Wade waved as he headed for the door and his hotel room. He passed Janet in the hallway who said someone was on their way to pick up the files for translation and copying that evening.

Chapter 22

After a light supper near his hotel, Wade settled down to an evening of work. He didn't want to get behind on coding his observations of the clinic so his first task was to integrate his layout sketches with his detailed notes on what took place in each window of the medical clinic before they passed from memory.

As he noted, coded and reflected, his mind wandered to the meeting he just had with attorney Gallos. The more he understood about Ocholo's history and operations, the clearer his orphanage and clinic operation became. He even had the basic outline for an interdiction and extraction plan forming in his mind, but it was too premature to put on paper. He needed more of Ocholo's operating details and research which he hoped lay among the stacks of investigative reports he would receive the next morning.

For his next step this evening, Wade needed information and help from Yari. He thought better than to call from his room phone and left to find a payphone on the crowded street in front of his hotel. Asking several shopkeepers along the way led him two blocks away to a department store where the basement level housed restrooms and a bank of payphones. After dialing the secure number it was comforting to hear Yari's voice.

"It's me, Wade."

"Where the hell have you been? I was worried crazy trying to figure out where you were!" Yari exclaimed.

"I'm here in Buenos Aires, man. Where did you think I was?" Wade replied.

"Do they have farming in Buenos Aires?" Yari asked.

"No. I just flew in on private plane from the farming area," Wade answered.

"I have lots of stuff to go over with you," Yari responded.

"I have a lot more stuff to give you," Wade replied.

"Tell me what you have, then I'll go over my list," Yari said.

"Just so you know I will be getting my hands on a lot of the information I asked you to find out about. This information is coming to me out of a very unexpected source so don't take it the wrong way that it may be a duplicate the research you did. I'm very appreciative of that, but sometimes things move on the ground a lot faster than expected," Wade explained as he didn't want Yari to feel left out.

"That's not a problem. Sometimes it's good to have information from multiple sources," Yari commented.

"I'm here in Bueno Aires at an attorney's office who is translating and copying a lot of investigative files on the guy behind the orphanage and medical clinic. His name is Manuel Ocholo... a real bad character. I need to know what you can find out on him. Even though I will have those files I still want you to find out what you can on Ocholo. Two important things I'm looking for are where his estates are located and which one Ocholo is currently staying on. I also need to know about any U.S. current intelligence mission on or off the books," Wade summarized.

"I'll get on that right away," Yari responded.

"My most immediate need is knowing about the Ocholo estates. I need to know where they are, where he is, and anything about his security on those estates."

"I take it he has more than one?" Yari asked.

"He owns lots of them but I am particularly interested in the one at Monte Lamar and the one where he is currently living," Wade said.

"Got it. I'll get on that one first," Yari replied.

"I have another person of interest by the name of Dr. Alonso Kemp. He is a physician in Buenos Aires. I need to know if he is having any financial problems or is in any other kind of trouble," Wade asked.

"Got it," Yari replied.

"Last thing. I pinged your tracer number here into the law firm this afternoon having no idea of whether it works on international phone line or not. Did you get the tracer?" Wade asked.

"Yeah, I got it, but I'm still working through some international phone line issues so I can get a clean tap. I should know in a day or so," Yari responded.

"The phone number I dialed in on is the attorney I am working with here. He deals with a lot of investigators. It would be good to know if they are providing him any current information on the orphanage, clinic, or Ocholo's current whereabouts. Let me know if you get that tap set up," Wade asked.

"I have a question for you. Actually I have several questions," Yari asked.

"Shoot."

"On the estate questions, are you planning on paying this Ocholo character a visit?" Yari asked.

"You never know. I hear he throws wild parties," Wade responded, not answering Yari's question.

"Do you need help down there? I've been talking to Max. He is chomping at the bit to be down there with you," Yari commented.

"Tell Max to hold off right now. I'm facing a small private army of around fifteen right now and think I'm going to need more resources. Tell Max I appreciate his offer and will reach out to him when I know more about the situation here," Wade replied.

"I'll convey that to Max," Yari replied.

"I have to run now. Can you leave a secure patch on this line for another call? We'll talk soon, partner," Wade responded.

"You're secure. Look forward to your next call," Yari replied, ending the call.

Wade debated with himself before making his next call. He didn't want his plan to come across to Leo like it was half-baked, yet he needed to know Leo's position on reinforcements in case he needed them. Deciding that disclosure at this point might be the better part of valor Wade dialed the convoluted set of digits through Yari's patch believing he could at least leave a message. Wade was shocked what came next after a long set of rings.

"Leo here," the voice answered.

"Hi, it's Wade Hanna. I didn't think you would pick up. I was ready to leave a message," Wade explained.

"What's your message?" Leo replied always choosing to use the least amount of words.

"The message was just to ask you to call me. I know you don't like receiving long messages," Wade responded.

"Now I'm here so what's the message kiddo? I'm real busy," Leo said.

"I'm calling you from my mission here in Argentina. The mission I previously told you about. I've run into a name here and wondered if you knew the name or had any interest in this individual," Wade asked.

"It looks like you're calling from Buenos Aires. What's the name?" Leo abruptly answered.

"The name is Manuel Ocholo," Wade responded, but heard nothing in return. He thought they might have been disconnected. "Are you there?" Wade asked.

"I'm here. How is that name connected with your mission?" Leo asked.

"It looks like Ocholo is behind the medical clinic experiments on the children at the orphanage. Those are the experiments spreading diseases in the U.S." Wade explained in case Leo forgot about his prior explanation. There was another long pause. This time Wade waited patiently.

"I may have interest in this suspect," Leo replied.

"I mean do you know this person? Is he involved in any of your missions?" Wade asked in rapid succession. Getting information out of Leo was like pulling teeth.

"He is a person of interest to me. I can't confirm or deny how he is of interest. You ask too many damn questions, kiddo." Leo responded.

"Okay if he is a person of interest to you I need to know if we can work together on a mission that would remove or capture him and shut down his orphanage and medical operations," Wade asked.

"That depends," Leo replied.

"On what?" Wade responded.

"On what you have in mind," Leo answered.

"I'm in the middle of formulating a plan now and will probably have it completed in the next day or two," Wade replied.

"Call me when you think you have a plan," Leo responded.

"Is there some way we can speak more directly on this?" Wade responded, feeling the plan may have a lot of details and moving parts.

"I can hear you fine," Leo commented, frustrating Wade by his process.

"That's not what I mean. I am referring to resources and physically communicating on the ground here," Wade clarified

"How do you know I'm not already there?" Leo responded.

"Are you saying you are in this country now?" Wade asked.

"I'm everywhere. You should know that by now. You ask too many questions, kiddo. You don't need to know where I am at any given moment," Leo replied.

"Okay, forget where you are now. What I'm talking about is do you have resources here on the ground. I'm talking about dealing with a militia army of around fifteen," Wade emphasized.

"That's not a problem, kiddo," Leo responded.

"Do you need anything from me at this point?" Wade asked.

"Yeah, a plan and where are you staying?" Leo asked.

Wade confirmed to Leo that he would have an operational plan in place in the next couple of days and where he was staying. They ended the call but not without Wade feeling frustrated, like he always felt when he worked with Leo. It was Leo's way of operating, never letting anyone know where he was or what was on his mind , and that often got to Wade. He knew the reason why Leo operated this way but it didn't make it easy to work with him as part of a team. Wade also knew that there was no better operative he would risk his life for in the field.

Having a chauffeured car was nice but inhibiting to Wade. He checked the phone book under the telephone stand in front of him and took a cab to a nearby car rental agency. They were kind enough to supply maps of the city and surrounding countryside. He asked the attendant to show him where he might find an area they called Monte Lamar.

Early the next morning, Wade was performing rigorous exercises in his room to keep in shape. He showered, had breakfast and was in the lobby of the law firm minutes before they opened. Janet had already reserved an office for him and upon opening the office door found a stack of files almost a foot high on his desk. Asking if he could use the copy room, Janet showed him the code for operating the machines and got him a glass of water which Wade, consistent with his compulsive habit, covered with a napkin.

The rest of the morning hours were spent pouring over investigative file details, understanding how Ocholo thought and finding pieces of the puzzle which fit or didn't fit his operating plan. After skipping lunch Wade emerged mid-afternoon to an empty hallway with a smile on his face. He looked like the cat that just swallowed the yellow canary. Now he had to take his plan apart finding every possible loose end and weakness before presenting it to Leo.

As the afternoon wore on Wade called Janet to see if he could meet with Mr. Gallos. She said he would be in a meeting for another hour but could squeeze him in after that. Wade confirmed, thinking now about what he would say to the attorney to put into motion one part of his plan. Janet rang on the intercom and said, "Mr. Gallos can see you now."

Wade approached Gallo's desk and they exchanged smiles. The two seemed to have established a team spirit and cordiality which Wade thought would be helpful.

"Please have a seat," Roberto responded, pointing to the familiar round conference table in his office.

"Thank you," Wade replied as he placed several files on the table.

"Well, how is your research coming? I think you agree now he is quite a dangerous character," the attorney commented.

"Yes, I feel I'm getting to know his ruthless ways. As I go through this I've come up with a couple of ideas I wanted to pass by you," Wade responded.

"Certainly," said Gallos.

"In looking at all the relationship between all the moving parts it seems to me we have to keep one thing in mind and that is the safety of the children and for that matter the safety of the nuns who care for them."

"I agree wholeheartedly," Roberto responded.

"We have to find some way of getting the children and nuns temporarily removed from the orphanage. Tied to that we need to establish a permanent location for the children," Wade commented.

"What do you mean? I'm not sure I understand,"

"Well the idea I am thinking about is perhaps a religious festival where the children of the orphanage could be featured by the archdiocese. The event should be out of the area that would require the children and nuns to be picked up by buses and removed from Realta," Wade speculated.

"Okay I see. That gets them out of the area temporarily but then what?" the attorney asked.

"I'm still working on that part. I've reached out to some of my former military contacts in Canada. They are arranging for me to speak to some intelligence operatives about the situation. Perhaps they have some ideas. I'm not sure who can be trusted in the Argentina intelligence so I thought I would get a reaction from some people out of the country," Wade explained.

"You are correct about trusting anyone in our government right now. Except for a very few who are my clients, I know Ocholo's tentacles reach far and wide in our government and he would hear of any plan involving our government very quickly. I am interested in your plan so far, please continue."

"After the temporary evacuation we have to find a new home for these children. Perhaps some other orphanage could take them and the sisters. I figure that will require the church's involvement," Wade said, looking at Roberto who was rubbing his temple in concentrated thought.

"You are correct. The permanent placement of the children would best be handled by the church. I have a few ideas about that and I also want to speak to Don Carlos. You know he is a large patron of the church and has many connections. Let me work on that angle," Gallos commented making a few notes on his pad.

"Until I speak with my military contact that's as far as I have gotten with my ideas," Wade replied.

"I assume once the children are removed, you are proposing some kind of military interdiction of the orphanage?" Gallos questioned speculating.

"And the medical clinic," Wade responded.

"And how would that be accomplished?"

"I don't have any answers yet but that part of the interdiction would have to include removing the Ocholo guards, protecting the innocent workers, and destroying any evidence of the Dr. Schultz experiments," Wade replied.

"Those are all good ideas, but you don't sound like a produce man by the way you have approached this," Gallos responded.

Wade realized that he might be showing too much of his real self and tried to defuse the attorney's thoughts as he ducked back under cover.

"Oh, thank you, but this whole thing with the children I guess did bring out some former military in me I hadn't felt in a long time. When I think about it, planning is planning even when you are involved in a farming operation. I am sure Don Carlos thinks the same way," Wade commented

"Perhaps you are right. I have my assignment which I will get to work on right away. What is the next step for you?" Roberto replied.

"I still have lots more to review in the file and speak with my military contacts. I should know more at that time in a few days. Remember when you come up with the religious festival it has to be real and believable so Ocholo will approve the children's participation or the rest of this doesn't work. I'm hoping Argentina has lots of those types of festivals going on," Wade added.

"We are celebrating something religious almost every week here. I don't think that will be a problem. I will discuss the options there and let you know," Gallos responded.

The two men shook hands as Wade went back to his office to work on his plan. Behind his closed office door, Wade's plan started to take shape. He knew the level of detail Leo would require and anticipated his comments as he broke out various elements of position, ingress, egress, evacuation, equipment, vehicles, maps, weapons, number and position of men and timing. When Wade looked up Janet was standing in his doorway letting him know the law offices were closing. Wade took the papers he needed and headed to his hotel room for another several hours of work.

Chapter 23

Wade worked on his operational plan through much of the night and reviewed it again in the morning making a few changes here and there. An early morning call to Yari gave Wade an update on Ocholo. Yari's information confirmed but didn't add anything to what Wade already had, except Ocholo's current location and more information about the location and structure of his estate at Monte Lamar.

"Were you able to get a tap on Ocholo's phone lines?" Wade asked.

"Already done," Yari replied.

"Good. I need you to watch them closely," Wade responded.

"Everything's being recorded," Yari said.

"Yeah but that still needs to be translated and listened to," Wade replied.

"I have that covered too. I pulled in two guys to help me with that," Yari replied.

"Great. I'll get back to you soon," Wade replied as he ended the call.

The next call Wade made would be to Leo and he decided to make that call on a payphone at a drug store a few doors from the hotel. He felt awkward standing on the corner at the drugstore payphone with papers under his arm hoping Leo wasn't going to ask for a lot of detail about the operational plans. After obtaining a secure line from Yari he dialed the extended fifteen digit number and listened to four unanswered rings. He was preparing to leave a message when the receiver picked up.

"Leo here."

"I was getting ready to leave you a message again," Wade replied.

"Don't tell me what your message was going to say, just tell me what you have," Leo retorted.

"I have prepared the operational plan. It has several phases and a lot of details. Where would you like me to start?" Wade asked.

"Is the plan written or in your head?" Leo asked.

"It's written and very detailed with maps, men, equipment, and timing just like you like them," Wade exclaimed.

"Good. I'll be the judge whether it's any good or not," Leo replied.

"How do you want me to get it to you?" Wade asked.

"Can you have a copy made?" Leo asked.

"Yes," Wade replied.

"Leave it in an envelope on your desk," Leo replied.

"You mean on the desk in my hotel room?" Wade responded.

"Do you have any other desks?" Leo asked sarcastically.

"As a matter of fact I do. I also have one at the law office," Wade replied.

"Well, excuse me. I mean the one in your hotel room," Leo replied.

"Don't you want to go over it with me?" Wade asked.

"Not now. I'll ask questions after I review it," Leo responded.

"Do you want me to leave a key at the front desk?' Wade asked.

"Nope. Don't need one," Leo replied.

"I'll have it copied and on my desk in an hour," Wade responded.

"Good. I have to run," Leo replied.

"See you," Wade replied hearing Leo's receiver disconnect.

Wade immediately copied the operational plan documents and returned to his hotel room. He left the copy on the desk and hid the originals because he didn't want them lying around the law office. Returning to his office at the law firm Wade dug back into reviewing the investigation reports for some minor detail that might give his plan an edge.

Buried in his work, Wade didn't even look up until lunch time when he saw Roberto Gallos standing at the glass panel in his door. Wade was shocked to see a named partner of the firm at his meager office door. "Come in. I'm still just reviewing the files."

Gallos came in and took a seat opposite Wade in a space with barely enough room for a chair. His knees were crowded under the desk overhang and his whole body seemed wedged against the wall in the tiny office. Seeing the space problem Wade rose and pulled back his desk. "Let me get you some more space."

"Don't bother, I remember these offices. I started with this firm in one." They both smiled.

The attorney quickly came to the point of why he came down to Wade's office. "I have an update on your plan we discussed yesterday," Roberto said.

"That's great. Where do we stand?" Wade replied.

"I spoke with Don Carlos at length later yesterday afternoon. He likes the plan and immediately has gone into action. He called his good friend the Cardinal who approved the plan and has asked one of his Bishops to set up a task force to work with Don Carlos. The Cardinal believes everything should move very quickly on this matter."

Wade listened in utter amazement. "What kind of team?" Wade asked.

"It's going to involve some priests and nuns. The Cardinal likes the idea of getting the children out of there and thinks participation in a religious festival is excellent."

"That's great. Have they picked a festival yet?" Wade asked.

"No, but that won't be a problem because they have some festival going on in this country almost every week." Gallos replied.

"What about the transportation of the children and nuns?" Wade asked.

"The Cardinal suggested a patron of the church who owns a tour bus company. Getting a bus won't be a problem. They have to house the children and nuns for some period and they are working on that issue. There is however one potential major problem," the attorney replied.

"What's that?"

"The Cardinal feels it will be a delicate maneuver to get Ocholo's permission. It's just that the Cardinal wants to think about it and discuss it with his team," Gallos replied.

"Why is that a problem?" Wade asked.

"You see Ocholo and his family are big contributors to the church with powerful political allies. If Ocholo becomes suspicious it might put the church at risk," Roberto explained.

A disturbed look came over Wade face. "What do we do now?"

"I'm afraid all we can do is wait until the Cardinal decides how he wants to handle this. All I can tell you is the Cardinal is very smart and he didn't get to the position he holds being naive about Ocholo. He just has to be very careful," Gallos explained.

"I see. I guess that means we just wait. I would like to let the Bishop's team know a few things that I discovered."

"Sure I can get that to them," Roberto replied

"First, I think Sister Sara is aware that we are trying to help them."

"How do you know that?"

"In my meeting with her she is the one who pointed out the recording device in her office. I simply acknowledged her using sign language that I think she understood I was trying to help," Wade explained.

The attorney grabbed a piece of blank paper on Wade's desk and made a note. "The second thing is I am pretty sure that Dr. Kemp is there against his will and could be helpful."

After making another note the attorney asked, "How do you know that?"

"Nothing more than reading his expression in my meeting with him and the Captain," Wade explained.

"How does that help the Bishop's team?"

"Only that I don't think Dr. Kemp is going to stand in the way of them leaving the area. He's one less person we'll have to deal with if they get Ocholo's consent," Wade explained.

"Interesting observation. I'll let them know although I don't understand how the clinic will be involved," Gallos questioned.

"Only if they want to leave in the middle of one of the planned treatment sessions," Wade advised.

"I see. Good point. Is there anything else you have that might help the team?" Roberto asked.

"I think it would be good somehow to let Sister Sara what the plan is. I think that should be done in person. Perhaps a nun can visit her where they can take a walk away from the recording devices," Wade suggested.

"Another good suggestion. I'll pass it on," attorney Gallos replied as he squirmed to free his knees from under the top of Wade's desk and got up and headed toward the door. He turned back. "Let me know if you have some time. I'd like to take you to lunch one of these days."

"Sure thing. Thanks. Today I have to get back to the hotel for a conference call on some produce," Wade replied.

Wade did return to his hotel but not for a produce conference call. He wanted to see if his operational plan had been picked up. Standing over his hotel room desk, the envelope with his operational plans was gone and in its place was a green drab military two-way radio receiver based on the military AN/PRC 77 model which used encrypted signaling. The unit looked familiar to Wade, just like the one he had used in his operation in Morocco. He immediately knew it was Leo's calling card. The frequency settings were preset but he decided not to press the transmit button until after he spoke with Leo that afternoon.

Grabbing a sandwich at an open street vendor's cart, Wade headed for the drug store payphone and called Yari to report on what he had just learned from attorney Gallos. He needed Yari to be on his toes.

"Yari here."

"I have an update on our discussion of this morning," Wade advised.

"I'm ready," Yari replied.

"You did tell me you had the Ocholo main residence tapped?" Wade asked.

"Already done and recording," Yari replied.

"Good. I'm looking now for an important call to Ocholo requesting the orphanage's participation in some religious festival. It's a very important call," Wade explained.

"I hear you. Everything is being recorded from all of his residences we could find."

"That's great but those calls still have to be translated and listened to," Wade said bluntly.

"That's right and I have two guys helping me on that."

"Good. I just need to know when that particular call comes in, how Ocholo responds and if he makes a call to his people at the orphanage or medical clinic. The call will probably go to a Captain Ruso."

"I hear you. I'll set our translation and review crew up to check more frequently right away," Yari said.

"How frequently?" Wade asked.

"How about every hour, boss?" Yari replied.

"That should work."

"How do you want me to get ahold of you if I find something?" Yari asked.

"Leave a message at my hotel room phone. I'll call you back on a payphone from the drug store," Wade replied.

"You use that drugstore phone a lot, don't you?"

"Yeah, too much; they look at me funny when I come in," Wade responded.

"See you," Wade replied as he ended the call.

After finishing up at the law firm and a light dinner, Wade sat in his room looking at the military receiver Leo's person left for him debating with himself when he could call Leo. "The hell with it," Wade said to himself as he left the room for the basement of the department store.

When he called Yari to set up the patch he asked if there was any news of the call he was looking for to Ocholo. Yari replied, "Not yet. We're checking every hour."

Leo answered this time on the first ring.

"Wade here, I take it you got the plan?" Wade asked.

"Yes, I've made a few tweaks here and there," Leo responded.

"Are you going to tell me what those are or do I have to guess?" Wade responded.

"The tweaks don't concern you," Leo replied.

"Okay, so other than the tweaks you feel the plan is good?" Wade inquired.

"It's ambitious but deals with the problem." Wade took that as the closest thing to a compliment he would ever receive from Leo.

"I'll take that as a compliment," Wade answered.

"It's not about compliments. It's a paper plan. It all depends on how it is implemented. You know this is not some classroom, kiddo. I'm not going to give you a grade until I see it implemented. There are lots of things that can go wrong. Like most plans it's an outline to be adjusted as you meet opposition. You should know that, school boy," Leo explained.

"Okay, I know the plan has to have a lot of room to wobble if it's going to work. I just wanted to know if you were comfortable enough with what I sent to support me," Wade asked. There was a pause which made Wade feel uncomfortable thinking "here we go."

"Yeah, I'm good," Leo replied and Wade exhaled a breath of relief.

"Thanks," Wade replied.

"No thanks necessary. Are you ready to execute?" Leo got immediately to the point. Wade hesitated and gave an uncomfortable response which brought the ire of Leo.

"Yes and no," was Wade's reply.

"What do you mean? You can't run an operation on that," Leo criticized Wade.

"What I mean is I am waiting for a call from the church to Ocholo to get his buy-in on the children participating in the religious festival," Wade explained.

"That's in your plan. Are you ready to execute?" Leo asked annoyed.

"I don't have an answer on that call but I expect it shortly in a day or so." Wade tried to explain.

There was a pause. Wade wasn't sure why. It seemed he had explained the problem as best he could.

"Tomorrow I want you to have dinner with one of my men," Leo said, surprising Wade.

"Okay, do I meet him here at the hotel?" Wade asked.

"No!" Leo said emphatically, "Hold on a minute." Leo came back on the line. "Meet him at the Ambrosia Restaurant at 7:00 p.m. It's about two blocks from your hotel."

"How will I know him?" Wade asked.

"You won't. But he knows you. Just get a table. He'll introduce himself when he arrives. He goes by the name of Mario," Leo replied.

Wade was a little bewildered by the typical Leo call, but spent the next day refining operational details of the plan while awaiting word from either the attorney or Yari that the Bishop's call had been made to Ocholo. As 6:30 p.m. approached he hadn't heard from either source so he left the law offices just before they closed. Wade was early for his meeting with the operative at the restaurant and decided to walk a few blocks wondering what this guy that worked for Leo must be like who went by the name of Mario.

Chapter 24

Fifteen minutes after he had taken a seat in the Ambrosia Restaurant a gentleman in a suit roughly Wade's size approached him from behind.

"Hello, my name is Mario. I work for Mr. Leopold." The soft spoken voice said with the hint of an accent. Wade rose, shook his hand and pointed to one of the empty chairs, inviting him to sit.

Glancing at the operative from the side, Wade sized him up, trying not to be obvious. The well-tailored suit hung on his well-conditioned body. He stood an inch shorter than Wade but the slightly smaller frame was more compact and muscular. Small scars on his face and hands told of a boxer or contact sport athlete. High cheek bones and the way he held his chiseled jaw suggested stern military training. He took his seat with erect posture but was comfortable in his own skin. The soft tone of his speech didn't seem to fit the rest of Wade's assessment.

"Mr. Leopold sends his regards," Mario exclaimed softly.

"I trust he is doing well?" Wade responded.

"He is, yes," Mario replied as he picked up the menu.

"Do you get to see him often?" Wade asked hoping to get some insight on Leo's whereabouts.

"You never know when you are going to see Mr. Leopold," Mario replied.

Realizing he wasn't going to get anywhere with that line of questioning Wade quickly changed direction. "Where are you from?" Wade asked, hoping the change in direction might ease the conversation.

"I grew up here in Argentina," Mario responded.

"It must be great living here," Wade commented.

"I grew up here and was in the Argentine military but left to work many years in Europe. I returned here six years ago," Mario explained.

"I bet I can guess that Europe is where you met Mr. Leopold?" Wade asked.

"You are correct but I worked for several agencies before we met," Mario responded

"What other agencies did you work for?" Wade asked.

"Perhaps we should consider ordering," Mario answered.

"Certainly, I don't know this restaurant but the menu looks interesting," Wade commented as the waiter came over and the two men ordered, then looked at each other not sure of who was supposed to open the discussion.

Wade started, "Leo wasn't specific when he suggested we meet so I wasn't sure exactly what he had in mind."

"I think he wants us to discuss your operational plan," Mario commented.

"Oh, has Leo shared some of the plan with you or did he have specific questions?" Wade asked.

"He shared the plan with me and some other operatives and gave us a few of the changes he wanted. I was told to commit the entire plan to memory so there would be no copies around," Mario revealed.

Wade was momentarily caught off guard. It was just yesterday when he gave Leo the plan. He decided to test Mario's knowledge of the plan.

"What aspect of the plan do you think you will be involved with?" Wade asked.

"All of it, but that has not been determined yet," Mario responded.

"Can you share with me some of those changes to the plan Leo has made?" Wade asked.

"I can't really speak of those but I think the changes have been relatively minor."

"And can you tell me what those are? I'm in the dark here," Wade pushed.

"I'm not at liberty to discuss those. Mr. Leopold says those are on a 'need to know' basis and you would understand that," Mario conveyed.

"It sounds like Leo but I think we are going to go around like a merry-go round if we can't get specific about the plan," Wade exclaimed, not really sure how much Mario understood or was told to reveal.

"I believe we should get specific. For example, in your Phase 1 what Intel do you need to know from the Monte Lamar house?" Mario asked.

Wade's head jerked back from Mario's directness. All of a sudden Mario had gotten real specific. Wade remained silent, pausing to allow the waiter to serve an appetizer of fresh shrimp. "For starters, I need to know for sure where Ocholo is keeping Mrs. Kemp and the children in that house. I also need to know the number and placement of guards at the estate," Wade explained in a low voice.

"Anything else?" Mario calmly asked.

"There are lots of details like how old the children are? How are we going to evacuate them? And where will they be up at a safe house?" Wade said, maintaining his low voice.

There was a pause as Mario swallowed. He looked at Wade and calmly said "Consider that information will be in your hands tomorrow." Mario said in a calm demeanor.

Taken aback by the response, Wade wanted more details about how they were going to get that information. "That was a surprise response I wasn't expecting," Wade exclaimed.

"Your Intel request is perfectly normal. I will gather the information myself and will also have an ingress layout, security force survey and if possible a report on the hostages physical condition," Mario replied.

"I was planning to participate on that mission," Wade replied.

"You are welcome to but it won't be necessary. Mr. Leopold felt that you would be more valuable being more visible here with the attorney," Mario shared.

"I'm not with the attorney during the evening," Wade commented.

"I am going to conduct my observations in both daylight and nighttime to insure there are no variations in their security," Mario replied.

Wade pondered Mario's response as he consumed another shrimp. "In that case perhaps it would be best if I remain here until we have the 'Go Signal' on the rest of the operation. After that I definitely will participate in obtaining the hostages," Wade said emphatically.

"But of course, it is you operation." Mario calmly replied.

After the waiter came with the main meal of local seafood delicacies the men continued their discussion of operational details. Wade suddenly looked up at Mario with an annoyed expression. "What else did Mr. Leopold tell you he wanted to control in this operation?" Wade asked directly.

Mario looked up seemingly caught off-guard by the harshness of the question. "I don't think there was anything Mr. Leopold wants to control. He made it clear this is your operation. There are just certain things Mr. Leopold wants from the operation. I thought he would have told you these," Mario responded.

"And what might those things be as you understand them," Wade asked.

"I know he wants the suspect alive, after you are of course done with him in Phase II," Mario said almost apologetically.

"I don't have a problem with turning over Ocholo when I am done with him," Wade said.

"Alive," Mario added as a reminder.

"Yes, of course," Wade replied.

"He suggested you might need to be alone with him for a half hour to an hour according to your plan," Mario said.

"Yes, that's what the plan calls for," Wade confirmed.

The men continued their discussion through the remainder of dinner. By the time the plates were cleared, Wade was convinced Mario understood the operational plan forward and backward including the important detail of timing.

The waiter approached asking if they wanted desert or coffee. Both men declined. Mario quickly said, "Bring me the check, please."

Wade replied, "I thought I could take care of this."

Mario insisted, "Mr. Leopold gave me strict instructions that he was treating."

As the meeting ended and they waited for the check, Wade's mind raced through small details he hadn't remembered to ask Mario.

"How do I communicate with you?" Wade asked.

"I believe you received our communication device. I use frequency number two settings and Mr. Leopold works off of frequency one settings. Otherwise you can always leave a message for me through Mr. Leopold's encrypted telephone line," Mario said.

Wade left the restaurant and stopped at a payphone to call Yari for updates. Yari had just checked the recorded taps and no calls of interest had come into Ocholo's line. That evening Wade had trouble sleeping, knowing that everything depended on the call to Ocholo. He worried about Megan and the interdiction of the children. The positive attitude he had developed toward Mario and his capabilities was the only thing that seemed to hold promise during that evening's sleepless night.

The next morning Wade rose early for his exercise. There were details about something else he wanted to discuss with the attorney. His instincts were telling him that something was about to happen as he walked the few blocks to the law office.

Mid-morning Wade knocked on Gallos' door after clearing it with Janet.

"Janet told me you might have a spare moment?" Wade politely said.

"Sure. Come in. Would you like some coffee?" Gallos asked.

"No thanks, I'm fine," Wade replied.

"What's on your mind?" The attorney asked

"I've spent a little time in your law library in the last couple of days and have a legal question," Wade commented.

"What is it? I'll try to answer."

"While we wait for a response from the Bishop's team I am wondering, speaking hypothetically of course, assuming Mr. Ocholo got religious all of a sudden and wanted to turn over the orphanage and the medical clinic back to the church, what document would he execute to do that?"

The attorney smiled. "It is very unlikely that Ocholo would see such spiritual light but sticking with your hypothetical question he could transfer it through either an assignment of his interest or by executing a deed to the property in favor of the church. Either form of conveyance would be acceptable in our country," the attorney replied.

"I was reading in the legal file that Ocholo owns those properties through corporations as nominee. Can you explain that?" Wade asked.

"The process would be the same for the transfer. You would still need an assignment and deed convenience. Our investigator knows the nominee Ocholo uses. We have our ways of finding how the nominee attorney holds the deeds in Ocholo's name through his entities. But I don't understand; where you are going with your question?" the attorney responded.

"In speaking with my Intelligence contact in Canada it appears they may have some leverage with Ocholo through some U.K. dealings he is involved with. It just occurred to me that if they could exert that leverage Ocholo might be persuaded to turn over those assets," Wade explained.

"That's an interesting concept. Preparing the documents is straight forward; the problem will be getting Ocholo to sign them," the attorney responded.

"I'm not sure that is possible either but I thought out of caution that it would be good to have those documents ready, just in case my contacts tell me he is agreeable to sign them. All this may come about very quickly," Wade replied.

"That's not a problem. I will have an associate prepare the documents and leave them on your desk," Gallos replied.

"I'll get them off to my Canadian contacts right away. I don't guess you've heard anything about the call to Ocholo on the festival?" Wade asked.

"No, as a matter of fact if I haven't heard by this afternoon I will call the Bishop," Gallos said.

"As soon as we hear the children will be safe I will be leaving. In case I don't get to formally say goodbye I just wanted to thank you for all your help," Wade said extending his hand to shake.

The attorney responded by standing up and shaking Wade's hand. "Are you leaving to Canada from here?" Roberto asked.

"No, I actually have to hitch a ride back to Realta on Don Carlos' plane to gather a few things before I leave for Canada in a day or two."

Chapter 25

That afternoon Wade was in his law firm office reviewing investigative reports, waiting to hear word on the Ocholo call and anxious to get back to his hotel room for word from Mario. Three soft knocks on his door and it began to open. Roberto Gallos was standing in the doorway with an envelope in his hand.

"Here are the assignment and transfer documents to the property we discussed this morning." Wade smiled and said thanks as he took the envelope from his hand.

With a smile on his face Roberto continued, "More importantly I just got news from the Bishop's office that Ocholo approved the orphanage's participation in the Festival of the Holy Lights. In fact, according to the Bishop's office Ocholo was delighted."

"That's great news!" Wade exclaimed. As he looked up the attorney's face seemed troubled. He was about to ask what was bothersome after such good news but the attorney spoke before Wade got the first word out.

"I'm not sure exactly what happens after the festival is over. Those children will have to return to the same place and will be under Ocholo's men," the attorney exclaimed.

"I'm still working on that part. What the good news tells me is I have to get my act in gear. I know we will need the help of Don Carlos and the church to find those children another more permanent home before they get back. I will discuss that problem with Don Carlos as soon as I get back to the estate," Wade explained.

"Please give him my regards," Roberto replied.

"I certainly will," Wade replied as he shook his hand.

Wade immediately turned to get his files and belongings. Before exiting the floor he took one last detour to Janet's desk to thank her before heading to the elevator. Janet was thankful that Wade stopped by. They agreed to stay in touch.

His mind racing with details all the way back to his hotel room, Wade had to be certain he informed the right people in the right order. He stopped at the department store basement to call Yari for a confirmation of the phone call. Yari picked up on the second ring.

"It's me, Wade. I heard we may have news," Wade asked.

"How did you find out? I was hoping to be the first to give you the surprise with details," Yari replied.

"The attorney told me the call was made but I still don't have any details," Wade responded.

"Good," Yari replied.

"So what are the details on the call? This is no time for playing guessing games," Wade asked.

"The call came to Ocholo from Bishop Senica at 1:42 p.m. your time. The call seemed cheerful enough they just chit chatted about the church at first. The Bishop then told him about the festival and that the orphanage has been selected to participate in singing and some other ceremonies. The Bishop said the orphanage school was also going to receive an award." Yari continued, "Ocholo was all over it. He thought it was great and felt honored,"

"And then what?" Wade asked.

"The Bishop told him all the arrangements had been made for room and board for the children and the nuns for three days," Yari explained.

"Great. Did they talk about transportation?" Wade asked.

"Yes, the Bishop said he had made all those transportation arrangements," Yari replied and continued, "Ocholo asked if he could pay for any of the expenses."

"What did the Bishop say?" Wade asked.

"That payment of expenses won't be necessary. Everything is being donated. His festival team has everything under control," Yari explained before continuing. "The Bishop added at the end that God always appreciates a small donation to the festival fund."

"Then what?" Wade asked.

"Ocholo said he would take care of a donation right away," Yari replied.

"Now I need to know if Ocholo made any other calls after that," Wade inquired.

"Yes, an hour later he made a call to a Captain Ruso at the medical clinic."

"He told the captain about the festival. The captain didn't like the idea at first. Ocholo overruled him and said he had given the Bishop his word. That was the end of the conversation," Yari explained.

"What exactly what did Captain Ruso say? It may be important." Wade wanted the answer.

"Nothing, he just accepted Ocholo's order saying, 'Si comandante'," Yari concluded.

Wade confirmed the dates and times the two buses would arrive and signed off with Yari. He hurried back to his room. There were no messages waiting so he picked up the receiver mic, switched to frequency segment II frequency and radioed Mario.

"Base 2 to Rover 2. Do you read?" Wade asked.

"Rover 2 to Base 2. I read loud and clear," Mario responded.

"Do you have status update?" Wade asked.

"I am Evac en route to the city. Will meet at Three Carrera at 1700. Over," Mario replied.

"Say location again? Over," Wade asked not having a clue what the code meant.

"Three Carrera. Over."

"Copy and out," Wade replied, feeling frustrated he was left out of the loop on the code but knowing the two way frequency was no place to discuss it.

In fact, Wade didn't want to use the radio or the room phone for his next call. That meant another trip to the department store basement. This time he smiled when he recognized another shopper from his many other trips. He wondered if they thought he was some pervert hanging out around the restrooms.

After checking in with Yari and getting a secure patch, Wade made his next call to Leo.

"Leo here." His voice came across on the second ring.

"It's Wade. We have a Green on the festival. Ocholo has agreed," Wade confirmed.

"Good. My men are ready," Leo replied.

"What the hell is 'Three Carrera'?" Wade asked not knowing why he was out of the loop.

"It's one of our safe houses in Bueno Aires," Leo replied.

"How the hell am I supposed to know what it is or where it is?" Wade asked.

"Didn't you discuss everything with Mario?" Leo replied.

"We didn't discuss anything about safe houses," Wade exclaimed before continuing. "Anyway, I'm supposed to meet Mario at Three Carrera at 7:00 pm. tonight."

261

Leo replied, "Let me get my list." After a short pause Leo returned to the phone and gave Wade the address of Three Carrera.

"I am assuming he is going to give me an update on Monte Lamar?" Wade asked.

"I'm not sure." Leo paused. "It's your operation. Whatever you guys decide," Leo replied.

"Okay, I should know more after I meet with him tonight," Wade answered.

"I sure hope so," Leo replied in a somewhat sarcastic tone.

Ending the call, Wade considered what equipment he wanted in the back of his car in case anything went wrong at the safe house. After checking city maps for directions to the Three Carrera address and packing his night vision binoculars and sidearm with silencer Wade headed to meet Mario at the designated time.

He drove slowly, intentionally passing the safe house enough times to get a good look at the property. The large three-story house was set back from the curb streetlight and mostly in dark shadows. Surrounded on all sides with a ring of high shrubbery Wade saw the obvious two entrances. The house was dark inside and looked empty from the street.

Wade parked and approached the front door. He saw two silhouette shadows approaching him in black combat gear from each side of the porch. The men were expecting his arrival and gestured him to the front door.

As Wade turned to face the wood-grain door the two men on both sides disappeared. He gently knocked three times. After a short pause he heard the sound of not one but two electronic solenoids unlock two different mechanisms in succession. The door came loose from the jamb. Wade grasped the side of the door so he could control the speed at which it opened. He instantly knew he wasn't holding a wooden door. The simulated wood-grain finish matching the era of the house decorated a heavy steel door that moved smoothly on ball-bearing hinges.

Pushing the door open slowly and not being sure of what to expect, he entered a strange living room. Just in front of him hung heavy black curtains from floor to ceiling which ran the width of the room. He stood in the dark four foot space between the front wall and the curtain, trying to understand the purpose of the funeral décor. To Wade's right the curtains suddenly parted outlining Mario's silhouette in front of a strong back light. Mario greeted Wade with a contrived smile and proceeded past him to reset the metal locking mechanisms on the front door.

"Follow me," Mario said, returning through the curtain passage he just created. Wade followed to a small room with a wooden table and four chairs.

"Can I get you anything?" Mario asked.

"I'll have some water. The entrance procedure made me a little thirsty," Wade replied.

Mario asked someone outside the room to get Wade's water. Mario opened a thick folder and proceeded to put documents on the table.

"If you don't mind me asking, what's the deal with all the black funeral curtains?" Wade asked.

"It keeps a light barrier from the street," Mario replied.

"The front door seems to have some weight to it," Wade replied

"It's made of layers of armor plated high carbon steel. It can take a 50 caliber round at less than thirty yards," Mario exclaimed as he organized the paperwork on the table.

"Did Leo have any input in the design?" Wade inquired.

"This was all designed by Mr. Leopold," Mario replied.

Wade could see Mario was now ready for serious discussion about Monte Lamar when he asked. "How did your surveillance go?"

"Fine. Let me go over everything then I'll answer any questions you have," Mario replied as he laid out a map in front of Wade.

"Please. I'm anxious to hear what you found," Wade replied.

Mario began with a detailed description of the property's location and various routes which intersected ingress and egress to the general area. He proceeded to explain the orientation of the structures on the property.

"The property is approximately twenty acres. The main house sits at a slight fifteen degree angle running southeast to southwest from the main street. There are three levels to the grounds which from top to bottom are approximately 100 feet."

"The three areas look like terraces cut into the hillside," Wade observed.

"That's correct. Each terrace runs almost the entire width of the property. The main house is on the second level and the guest cottage is on the third level."

"What's on the first level?" Wade inquired.

"That's a fruit tree orchard and garden. The driveway winds through the second and third level in an 'S' shape," Mario replied.

"What's the security situation?" Wade asked.

"There were two Ocholo uniform guards when I was there. One was stationed at the front of the main house on the second level and the second guard behind the main house and in front of the guest cottage," Mario explained.

"How were the guards armed?" Wade inquired.

"Each carried an Uzi over their shoulder and a side arm. They also had two-way radios with speakers clipped to their shoulder epaulets," Mario replied.

"That creates a problem for us. Those radios might also be tied to home base," Wade responded.

"That's correct. It is unfortunate for us but that is their equipment," Mario replied.

Wade immediately knew the impact of Mario's comment that these men couldn't just be immobilized but had to be eliminated to ensure an alarm was not sent to the main office.

"What about the hostages?" Wade asked.

"Ms. Kemp and her two daughters, ages approximately eleven and thirteen, live in the guest cottage and come to the main house for their meals," Mario replied.

"What about their condition?" Wade asked.

"They appear to be stressed but otherwise physically fine but we have another problem," Mario replied.

"What is it?" Wade asked.

"There is a fourth person staying with Ms. Kemp and the children. She is a housekeeper or nanny. She stays in the guest cottage all the time," Mario replied.

"What's the background on the housekeeper?" Wade inquired.

"We are still checking but I think she is just one of Ocholo's employees there to help Mrs. Kemp but also to keep an eye on them," Mario explained.

"I see that as a problem as well," Wade exclaimed thinking about alternatives.

"She is an innocent bystander but we can't risk bringing her to the safe house," Mario explained.

"In fact we can't let her out of our sight for fear she will alert the main guard," Wade said.

"I know. That is a problem," Mario commented before continuing. "With your permission I would like to consult Mr. Leopold on that issue."

"Sure, but I have another thought we can discuss with him," Wade replied.

"What's that?" Mario replied.

"We may need a sub-cover story that could involve the housekeeper to our advantage," Wade said with his face showing he was in deep thought.

"I don't understand," Mario exclaimed.

"The idea just struck me. What if when we rescue the family we stage a fake robbery of the main house and involve the housekeeper like a hostage forcing her to show us where all the valuables are kept. We separate the family from the housekeeper keeping her on ice for several days. When she is released she reports to the authorities or to Ocholo's men about the robbery," Wade explained.

"I like the idea. That way we don't have to eliminate the housekeeper."

"Not only that, but is gives the entire takedown a good cover story," Wade replied.

"I still think we should see what Mr. Leopold thinks of the plan," Mario replied

"Let's consider a few more details before we call him," Wade commented.

"I agree," Mario replied.

After completing their discussion on how to handle the housekeeper they called Leo on the speakerphone. He gave his endorsement, adding a few suggestions. Following the call the men focused their discussion on the sniper positions to be taken and weapons. Mario used photos to provide a real sense of location and relative distances between positions and targets.

"These photos seem wet," Wade commented.

"I just got them from the laboratory less than an hour ago," Mario replied

"Do you have a lab nearby?" Wade asked.

"We have a complete photography lab in the basement here," Mario replied.

Wade was now at a point of needing closure on the timing so he could consider other pending dates, the orphanage festival pick-up and other phases of the operation plan.

"Based on the information we went over do you have a sense for a date and time we might engage?" Wade wanted Mario's opinion.

"I think we should execute tonight," Mario exclaimed.

Wade was shocked at his response.

Chapter 26

Mario made his arguments on why the hostage take down needed to happen soon regardless of what other moving parts and uncertainties Wade was dealing with on other phases of the operation. After giving Mario's position more thought Wade agreed, telling himself, *The stars may never be aligned as perfectly as you would like them but failing to act now may have far greater consequences.*

"Okay, let's execute tonight," Wade responded without further consideration.

"Good. I think the decision is right. We have everything we will need right here," Mario replied.

"I want to make a call. Can I have a room with a phone?" Wade asked.

"Certainly, I will arrange for that and while you're on the phone I'll assemble the equipment we need," Mario replied.

The call Wade made was to Yari's secure line.

"Yari here."

"I need our conversation encrypted," Wade replied.

"Give me fifteen seconds while I reroute the call through the encryption device," Yari responded.

After the brief pause Yari came back on the line. "We're good."

"I'm calling you from a friendly safe house. We are starting to execute my operational plan tonight," Wade related.

"Okay, what's the plan?" Yari naively asked.

"Never mind the plan. I need several things from you over the next two days that are very critical," Wade replied.

"I'm ready," Yari replied.

"I need tight monitoring on several tapped lines," Wade stressed.

"Which lines?" Yari asked.

"First is Ocholo's main residence and any branches to those lines. In other words, any communication coming into or going out of his main command post," Wade indicated.

"I got it. What else?" Yari asked.

"Any call going into or out of the Monte Lamar residence," Wade asked.

"Anything else?" Yari asked.

"That's it for now," Wade replied but stressed, "I really need those checked very frequently."

"How about every fifteen minutes?" Yari asked.

"That's fine. I'll call you when the interdiction is over," Wade said.

"I don't guess you can tell me who you are interdicting?" Yari asked

"You should know better than to ask," Wade responded.

"I hear you. Good luck, partner," Yari responded.

"Thanks, we'll talk soon." Wade replied as he ended the call.

Mario summoned Wade to a staging room that looked more like a gym locker room than a conference room. Laid out on the table were a change of clothes, climbing shoes, weapons, a red gel flashlight, communication radio and receivers, and maps in a protected plastic sealed wrapper. The outfits were black and tight fitting with a hood and mask more like a ninja outfit than a military combat field outfit.

Wade was surprised that the shoes and clothes provided were his exact size. There was little conversation between him and Mario and the other men assisting. Everyone seemed to have their pregame introspective face on. After getting dressed, Mario and Wade checked their weapons and ammunition, ensuring that everything was operational. Mario asked Wade to go into the other room so they could check their communication radios. Unlike the bulky military radio receiver these units were compact, each having an earpiece and miniature clip-on mic.

After checking com gear and setting watches, Mario instructed four other men in Spanish and told Wade in English to use Base and he would use Rover code as their call signs. The other men were instructed to use the Sparrow as code and each were given a number by Mario.

Little time was wasted loading the single car Wade and Mario would use for the mission, and the two departed on the two-hour drive to the mountains.

The men were mostly quiet during the drive out of the city. Each knew his assignment and had conducted this type of operation in training many times.

Wade broke the silence when he asked Mario, "What do you think about right before a mission?"

"I try not to think. That is what I was trained to do," Mario replied.

"I know. I am the same way but we both know thoughts creep in no matter how much we try to follow protocol," Wade replied.

"I think about my mother and family back home mostly. What do you think about?" Mario asked.

"I mainly think about my girlfriend which got me into the mission in the first place," Wade replied.

"I thought she was just another operative," Mario exclaimed.

"She is an operative and a good one risking her life for those children. There is also a personal side to our relationship," Wade replied but quickly added, "That last part

270

is not for public consumption including anything to Leo my friend."

"I understand. That information is on a need to know basis and doesn't affect anything having to do with your operations," Mario replied.

"Thank you. That's the way I feel as well," Wade replied.

More than an hour passed before the road started to climb to the resort area known as Monte Lamar. Even under the dim light of a quarter-moon and overcast sky the merging sides of the two smaller mountains started look familiar to Wade. He recognized the distinctive shape and angle of the two opposing mountains from all the time he spent studying the maps.

"I recognize these shapes of the two mountains," Wade stated.

"We're not far from our destination now, another ten miles of the twisting roads," Mario replied.

"I'm glad to see there have not been many cars coming down since we started turned off," Wade commented.

"I counted only three cars coming down and two pretty far behind us. I've been tracking them all and don't see anything suspicious," Mario replied.

"I've been watching them too," Wade commented.

Ten minutes passed and Mario pulled into a turnout and stopped the car. Wade checked the side-view mirror and wondered what he had in mind.

"We are about ten minutes away from your drop-off. I'm going to let these two cars following pass me. I'll pretend to be reading a map with the cabin light on so I can get a good look when they pass. You might want to jump in the back seat staying low with your weapon ready just in case," Mario suggested.

Wade was quick to leave the passenger seat and entered the back seat, cocking his weapon as he lay below the window. "I'm ready," he stated.

"They're still pretty far behind. I'll keep you posted as they approach," Mario replied.

"The two cars are fairly close together now. It looks like the second car behind us is trying to find space to pass," Mario updated as the two cars passed the bend in the road before his turnout.

"They're not slowing down," Mario updated Wade

Wade soon heard the noise of the two cars passing at high speed.

"Not a problem, two couples trying to get a start on an early weekend," Mario said.

"Good. Do you want me to remain here for the drop off?" Wade asked

"Only if you are comfortable," Mario replied.

"I've actually gotten a chance to stretch out my legs back here," Wade replied.

"Good, because they won't be getting much rest until our mission is over," Mario commented.

Wade's drop off went smoothly and he headed by compass almost two miles into dense forest to the other side of a tree line that should give him sight of Ocholo's mountain estate. He was to hold up at the tree line until he received word that Mario was in position on the opposite side of the estate.

After twenty minutes of slow travel through thick underbrush, Wade found the tree line he was searching for. His spot was higher and to the north of where he thought he should have been. Making his way down the slope over some tricky footing caused a few small slips, one that landed him squarely on his butt.

He found the trunk of a fallen tree at just the right angle for a back rest and sat down to scan the outreaches of terrain which lay in front of him. Aside from two rabbits and a squirrel in the near foreground there was little movement of anything except tree limbs blowing in the night air. He was still too far from the estate to see anything meaningful. Wade checked his radio and confirmed it was operational remembering that Mario trekked to his hide from where he hid the car twice as far as Wade was from his drop. Taking a deep breath of the night air Wade told himself, *Patience. Enjoy the calm before the storm.*

"Rover to Base. Do you read? Over," Mario's voice came through.

"I read. Clear to Position 1, over," Wade replied.

"Clear to Position 1, over," Mario replied.

"Proceed to Position 2. Over,"

"I copy. Proceeding now on countdown. Over," Mario replied.

"Proceeding now on countdown to Position 2. Out," Wade confirmed.

The next approach included navigating the open fields of underbrush to a position of less than a hundred yards from the edge of the estate property. A key to this approach was minimizing any sounds as he approached the estate. After trying several frontal and side moves with his body Wade found that traveling sideways between the thick brush pants caused the least amount of sound. By reversing his stance and leading with his other foot every fifty feet it balanced the stress to one side of his body. Mario had different challenges with the terrain but both found their way to their next destination at roughly the same time.

"Rover to Base. Do you read? Over," Mario transmitted.

"I read loud and clear. Are you on Position 2?" Wade asked.

"Rover to Base. On Position 2 clear. Over. Are you in position? Over," Mario asked.

There was a pause before Wade answered. "Base to Rover. I feel like I've been square dancing all night but now in position. Over." The joke about square dancing confused Mario.

"Rover to Base. Please repeat. Are you clear Base? Over."

"Base in Position 2 clear. Over," Wade replied.

"You should have vision of hide. Over," Mario was seeking confirmation.

Wade checked his binoculars to locate the hide Mario had prepared earlier that day. He also got a good look at the side of the main house and guest cottage and saw movement by one of the guards.

"Base to Rover. I have clear vision of hide and target. Ready to proceed on signal," Wade replied.

"Rover to Base. I confirm same. Proceed to hide when ready and report when in place," Mario responded.

The two men had another fifty yards to travel before reaching their respective hides. Wade had good cover most of the way but thought he would crawl the last thirty feet after cover ended. Mario was able to reach his hide using a small trail that allowed him to keep trees between his position and the target.

"Base to Rover. I am in position 3 with eyes on target," Wade reported.

"Rover to Base. I am in position 3 with eyes on target ready to fire on your command. Over," Mario reported.

Wade's instincts were speaking to him. He didn't know why he hesitated but he surprised Mario by his next command.

"Base to Rover. Hold your fire. I want to watch these guys for a while. I think we might be early for the party. Over,"

"Rover to Base. I copy. Do you see a problem? Over," Mario asked.

"Base to Rover. Negative. Call it instinct. We are seven minutes to the hour. Just watch targets until a minute after the hour," Wade instructed to Mario who didn't understand why additional time was necessary. They both had a clear shot now.

"Rover to Base. I copy but don't understand order. I have a clean shot," Mario explained.

"Base to Rover. I know. It's just a hunch but security details are often required to check in with command on the hour. Over," Wade responded.

Both men watched their targets. It was Mario's target that on the hour turned to his shoulder mic and made a call.

"Rover to Base. East target just made radio call on the hour. Good call, Base. Do I have a 'Green' now? Over," Mario asked.

"Base to Rover. Negative. Hold for another two minutes. Guards usually check in with each other after they call command. Over," Wade replied.

"Rover to Base. Both targets are in conversation. You called it again. Over," Mario reported.

"Base to Rover. Hold until they break communication on my countdown," Wade replied.

The guards finished their conversation, performing their last duties as Ocholo's security.

"Base to Rover. You are 'Green' on my command, seventeen seconds on my countdown. Be sure your shot is clean. Those receivers may have alarm buttons and their mics are only inches away. Over," Wade reminded his partner.

"Rover to Base I copy. Waiting for your countdown," Mario replied.

"Base to Rover. You have my 'Go'. Seventeen seconds starting now," Wade replied looking at the second hand on his watch.

At seventeen seconds silenced shots fired from both rifles into the night air and within a fraction of a second both guards dropped dead where they stood. Neither guard heard the shot or knew the direction from which it came.

"Rover to Base. East target down and silent. Over," Mario reported.

"Base to Rover. South target down and silent. Scan perimeter and report back before approaching wall. Over," Wade replied.

"Rover to Base. East perimeter clear. Over," Mario reported.

"Base to Rover. South and west perimeter clear. Over," Wade responded.

The two men met at a predesignated point just outside the estate wall. Both men put their masks on as they entered the estate through a side door gate which Mario had already pried open. Masks were required to insured they were not identified by the hostages. Both men had to be ready just in case the disturbance woke the Kemp family and housekeeper causing them to run out of the guest cottage.

"We need to confirm those bodies are dead and move them out of sight before we approach the family," Wade stated as they walked to the first body. Each man grabbed an arm and moved the two bodies behind large planters so they were out of sight in case the children came running out of the cottage.

"Approaching the cottage in masks will scare the hell out of them but I don't know any other way," Wade stated.

"I agree. I've already called up my clean-up and Evac teams waiting down the hill. They will be here in ten minutes," Mario replied.

"We have to get the housekeeper separated from the family if we are going to save her," Wade replied.

"Yes and we need her for the staged robbery as well," Mario commented.

"I want you to do the talking with the housekeeper. I don't want her picking up on my accent," Wade replied.

"We'd better separate her immediately then," Mario concluded.

"Look, that main house has alarms and cameras. Please have your men disarm the alarm and cameras and get the doors open when they get here," Wade requested.

"Sure," Mario responded. "I think those are my men pulling into the driveway now."

"Let's hope it's not somebody else at this hour. We need to get rid of these sniper rifles as well. Let's just use side arms," Wade commented.

"Let me have yours. I'll go meet the men and have them take care of these rifles," Mario responded.

Wade marveled at the efficiency of Mario's team. In a matter of minutes they had deactivated the main alarm and opened the doors, and removed the bodies as well as any traces of blood. As one of bodies was being brought past Wade he told them to stop. He waved Mario over. "Let's remove the receiver and speaker from this man." Mario gave the instruction in Spanish to the team.

"What are you thinking about?" Mario asked

"We have another call to make to command at the next hour. I think it is best for you to make that call in Spanish using a low raspy voice with lots of static and background noise," Wade suggested.

"I get it," Mario replied as a smile came over his face.

"Why not make the call-in every hour. Who knows how much time we can buy? They aren't scheduled for another guard change for five hours," Mario commented.

"I like that and in fact I may have someone back in our national intelligence office who is a communications expert and may be able to help with those calls," Wade offered.

Wade and Mario approached the guest cottage door. Mario knocked, hoping he would not wake up everyone. No one responded. He knocked again, this time louder. A rustling inside soon became a frustrated voice in Spanish cursing the person who disturbed her restful sleep. Mario turned and whispered to Wade, "It's the housekeeper." Half asleep she opened the door still rambling away until she saw the two masked men then started to scream.

Mario immediately grabbed her as she was kicking and trying to bite his gloved hand and pushing herself away from the front door of the cottage. He signaled another masked team member to take her away towards the main house.

Wade entered the cottage first, ready for the unlikely event that Mrs. Kemp was armed with a gun.

She opened the bedroom door in her robe awakened from the commotion. She saw the masked men and pulled back with her hand over her mouth gasping for air, too terrified to scream. Wade grabbed her and spoke in a calm voice.

"We are not here to harm you Ms. Kemp. We are here to rescue you and your daughters. Our masks are being worn only because we can't identify ourselves. Do you understand?"

Kimberly Kemp stood with her hand over her mouth too terrified to speak. She was crying but also nodding that she understood what Wade was saying.

He continued. "Ocholo's guards have been removed. Do you understand?" Wade said Mrs. Kemp was speechless but continued to nod that she understood.

"We are here on behalf of the police and we want to take you and your daughters to a safe house and then free your husband. He will join you and the girls shortly. Do you understand me?" Wade asked.

Kimberly remained in her same frozen position. She was crying but appeared a little less terrified, managing to give an affirmative nod to Wade's last question.

"What we would like you to do now is quietly wake the children and get everyone dressed. We will have one of our female task force members come in and help you get the children ready and gather your belongings. Once we get you and the family out of here you will never have to face the likes of Ocholo or his men again. Do you understand me?"

Her hand came down from her face. She managed to squeak out a "thank you" while still crying and nodding.

"Your terrible ordeal is almost over," Wade assured her, giving Mario the signal to wave over the female team member. They introduced the team member to Mrs. Kemp and left her being consoled in the calming arms of the female officer.

The two men walked from the cottage to the main house. Mario looked at Wade and said, "That went better than I expected."

Wade changed the subject. "Let's see what goodies Ocholo keeps in the main house."

"I can't wait," Mario replied.

"Remember, you do the talking to the housekeeper. Impress upon her that we are robbers and do not wish to harm her if she cooperates by telling us where Ocholo keeps his valuables. We need to make this look good," Wade stated.

Looking back at Wade, Mario asked, "Were you ever an actor?"

"No. Why do you ask?" Wade replied with a surprised look on his face.

Chapter 27

Wade spent the night at the safe house separated from the Kemp family, now cared for by Mario's staff. Rolling out of bed Wade felt stiffness in his legs and hips from his two-step, hip swinging square dance take-down routines of the night before.

There was much to do. Now that Phase 1 was complete, Phase 2 of the operational plan called for the interdiction and capturing of Ocholo himself. It was only days before buses would pick up the children at the orphanage and Wade would be responsible for Phases 3, 4 and 5 of the operation which included the freeing of Megan.

As planned, the Kemp housekeeper had been taken blindfolded to another safe house after showing Mario's men where all the valuables in the house were kept. She would be released near Ocholo's command center sometime that afternoon.

Ironically, one room in the main house holding Ocholo's valuables was a collection of church relics and art work dating back to the twelfth century. Wade thought it was most appropriate that those items be removed and eventually returned to the church. Mario assured Wade that this could be handled through appropriate channels without attracting attention.

Before implementing Phase 2 Wade had to be certain that there were no unforeseen adverse repercussions from last night's raid. He needed current information from wiretaps of Ocholo and his command center. There had to be line chatter of the break-in since the guard change of that morning occurred at 6:30 a.m. Wade grabbed a cup of coffee and used the safe house office to call Yari.

"Yari here."

"Good morning from my end of the world," Wade replied.

"I guess you're calling wanting an update on phone calls," Yari stated.

"How did you guess? Last night was busy here," Wade replied.

"I thought so. Here's what I've got. Command center is all over some break-in and robbery from last night at the Monte Lamar residence. It seems the thieves not only stole a lot of things but also took hostages."

"Did they say who?" Wade asked.

"Seems like some family members staying at the estate as guests of Mr. Ocholo," Yari exclaimed.

"That's an interesting way of putting it. Anything else?" Wade replied.

"Yes, two of Ocholo's guards are missing. They think the guards were either taken as hostages or were in on the robbery. They're starting to investigate now," Yari confirmed.

"What else?" Wade asked.

"One of the hostages, a housekeeper managed to escape from the robbers. She is where they are getting most of their information," Yari replied.

"Have they gone to the police?" Wade asked.

"No. These guys don't seem to want any part of the police. They say they are handling it internally," Yari responded.

"Any suspects talked about?" Wade asked.

"The head commander thinks this is the work of one of their rival drug gangs. He's already talking about a retribution strike," Yari replied.

"Where is Ocholo in all these discussions?" Wade asked.

"That's the problem. He's MIA," Yari exclaimed.

"What do you mean?" Wade nervously asked.

"I've got no calls into or out of his estate. I picked up one long distance call from his command center to Paraguay involving travel arrangements. I think our man has left Argentina," Yari replied.

"What! That completely screws up my plan," Wade replied, annoyed at the news.

"I checked Buenos Aires airport flight schedules and seems like Ocholo's pilot filed a flight plan for his jet to land in Paraguay yesterday. His command is placing a call trying to reach him Paraguay now," Yari reported.

"Damn it. I'm screwed. What the hell does he have in Paraguay?" Wade asked hurriedly.

"I'm researching that now. It's hard to know but remember this guy has illegal operations all over the world," Yari responded.

There was stressful silence while Wade thought about the consequences of the news. Yari broke in.

"It's none of my business but I thought it might be a good thing that Ocholo is out of your way for a while," Yari commented.

"You don't understand. His presence here was absolutely critical for the next phase of my operation. This changes everything," Wade said, sounding very worried.

"Maybe you can track him down in Paraguay?" Yari suggested.

"I've got to run now. This news really screws up everything," Wade exclaimed.

"Sorry about that," Yari replied as they ended the call.

Wade called Mario and told him the news. They bounced alternatives back and forth both knowing that the operating plan as currently designed was not going to work.

"As I see it we have three alternatives," Wade explained.

"I think I know them but tell me what you see." Mario replied.

"If we try a take-down in Paraguay that would mean bringing Ocholo back here. It's very risky for a lot of reasons. We can do a night raid on his estate without him there and hope we find where he's hiding the 'shadow cell' papers. Or we can skip this phase of the operation and come back to him. Depending on when he returns it might work before he knows everything about the mission, but," Wade added, "I can tell you already I don't like any of these alternatives."

"I'm not wild about them either. You also have one other thing to consider," Mario answered emphasizing his warning.

"What's that?" Wade replied.

"I think you're going to have to get Mr. Leopold's buy-in on this because the only reason we are involved is he wants Ocholo as part of the deal," Mario replied.

The silence that followed was deafening.

"You're right and I'm not looking forward to that conversation," Wade replied, already thinking he may have to accomplish the rest of the mission alone.

Shortly after their meeting Wade returned to his hotel. He pulled out all of his operational documents and once again anguished over the details of phases, maps, timing, manpower, procedures, and weapons before he called Leo. No matter how many times he studied the details his problem kept appearing before him like a big white elephant that he couldn't remove from the table. The pick-up of the children was already set and couldn't be moved. That meant his three day window to act remained fixed no matter what other changes he made to anything else. His task of getting to Megan who was behind a fifteen person private security force without help from Leo's men was a suicide mission.

He ran through scenarios of how Leo would response before making the call. Dialing the fifteen digit code to Leo's secure number, Wade counted four rings before he heard the receiver click, then delay and finally a voice.

"Leo." His voice came across in a serious tone.

"It's Wade. I wanted to give you an updated report," Wade replied.

"Clean operation last evening," Leo responded letting Wade know he had already been updated on last night's events.

"Thanks, I was pleased how everything worked out," Wade responded.

"How did you like working with Mario?" Leo asked.

"Outstanding. Top-of-the-line operative. I would work with him anytime," Wade replied.

"Where do we stand on Phase 2?" Leo asked.

"That's one of the reasons I'm calling. We have a problem there," Wade responded.

"What problem?" Leo asked.

"It seems Ocholo has left Buenos Aires and is now in Paraguay," Wade replied.

"Do you know why he's there and how long he's staying?" Leo asked.

"No. I haven't been able to get any Intel on that yet," Wade answered.

There was a pause. Leo had either gone into one of his deep thought modes or was preoccupied with something else.

"Sounds like you have a problem." Leo emphasized the "you" in his comment.

"I agree," Wade responded.

"What's the solution, kiddo?" Leo asked putting everything back on Wade.

"Let me tell you what I consider our alternatives to be before I tell you my decision," Wade answered.

"Okay," Leo responded.

Wade went through all the operation options and scenario details with Leo and told him that his recommended option was to skip the Ocholo step in the plan for now and move on to the other phases. When they were complete they could come back to Ocholo. Clenching his jaw, Wade waited silently for Leo's response.

"The only problem I see is you don't know how long the man is going to be out of the country and what state of readiness he will have his troops in when he hears about what has happened," Leo commented.

"That is true for now but I hope to have Intel on him before he finds out," Wade responded.

"That's iffy reasoning. Let me see what I can find out about our man and his operations in Paraguay," Leo responded.

"My plans are to get back to the orphanage and medical clinic so I have eyes on everything. Do you have a problem with that decision?" Wade asked.

"It's your operation, kiddo. You might want to keep Mario informed," Leo replied.

"Of course," Wade replied as they ended the call.

The next call from the department store basement was to Guillermo.

"Hi Guillermo, I know this is short notice but I need to get back to Don Carlos' farm as soon as possible. When can you have the plane ready?" Wade asked.

"Give me two hours and we will be ready to go," Guillermo replied.

"I'll just take a cab and meet you at the private airport," Wade responded, soon ending the call.

He dialed several times before he got an open international line to Yari's secure phone. While he waited for a clear line he smiled at the familiar faces of men and women going to the restroom all seeming to recognize Wade as a telephone fixture. He thought to himself *I've got to stop using this phone.*

"Yari here."

"It's Wade. In two hours I'm returning to my hotel in Realta. Do you have any last minute updates?" Wade asked.

"Yes. Ocholo's head man at command reached him in Paraguay and told him about the robbery and hostages at Monte Lamar," Yari replied.

"What did Ocholo say?" Wade asked.

"He went ballistic. He couldn't believe anyone would have the guts to rob him. Ocholo wanted no stone unturned. He cursed out his command for allowing it to happen and said he would deal with them on his return. The other thing he asked was if anyone told Dr. Kemp about the kidnapping," Yari explained.

"How did his man respond?" Wade asked.

"He said no. Ocholo said 'good'. He wanted to keep it that way. He also said he didn't want his security men at the clinic to know anything about the robbery and hostages either. Ocholo ranted on about how he was going to supervise the investigation himself when he returned," Yari answered.

287

"Did Ocholo say anything about when he was returning to Buenos Aires?" Wade asked.

"No, but they did talk about the robbery and hostages as retaliation from the Santinas gang," Yari explained.

"Why were they focused on that particular gang?" Wade asked.

"I don't know but the timing may have something to do with Ocholo's trip to Paraguay," Yari replied.

"Why do you believe that?" Wade asked.

"Ocholo said he would make some inquiries with others during his meetings," Yari replied.

"Sounds like Ocholo's meetings in Paraguay may be related to consolidating power with others at the exclusion of this Santinas group," Wade reasoned.

"I don't know, but at one point Ocholo said he received confirmation that if this gang was involved he wanted his command to prepare for war," Yari said.

"That's heavy," Wade replied as they soon ended the call.

Wade returned to his hotel room, quickly packed and checked out. He drove to the safe house and met with Mario. He wanted Mario to know his side of the story and where everything stood, still uncertain if they would be working together again on this mission. After explaining his Intel on what was said between command and Ocholo but not giving him his source, he then briefed Mario on his conversation with Leo.

"So I had my call with Leo and told him everything straight as it was," Wade stated.

"What did Mr. Leopold say?" Mario asked.

"I think he was upset that I didn't already know why Ocholo was in Paraguay and how long he would be gone. He said he was going to make his own inquiries," Wade replied.

"Where does that leave us on other phases of the operation?" Mario asked.

"I'm not sure. All I know is those buses are arriving for the kids and I've got to get my other operative out of there or die trying. I'm heading back to get eyes on the orphanage and clinic in case Leo decides we are moving forward with the rest of the operation."

"I want you to know if it were only up to me I would be there with you brother all the way but I work for Mr. Leopold and he calls the shots," Mario explained.

"I know you would man. I understand. Maybe this works out and maybe it doesn't. Either way we are brothers in arms," Wade said solemnly.

"Can I get you any equipment or weapons for your trip back?" Mario asked.

"No thanks, I think I have everything I need at the ranch," Wade said then added "But if we get the 'green' on this I'll need everything you've got."

"I'll be there for you," Mario responded.

Shaking hands, Mario insisted that one of his men drive him to the airport and return his rental car instead of Wade taking a cab. During the ride to the airport Wade got updated that the Kemp family was adapting well to life in the safe house and the children were taking regular tutored lessons.

The plane ride back to the Don Carlos ranch seemed shorter than their ride to Buenos Aires. Wade looked back on the buzzing metropolis below, recalling in the afternoon city reflections everything his trip had entailed.

Waiting when they landed was the same ranch hand and white truck that had brought Wade to the airport. The ride to the estate was just as bumpy and silent as the former ride with Miguel at the wheel trying to keep the tires away from the large muddy ruts. His car was still parked in the same spot he left it and Miguel had his gear ready to transfer before Wade got his trunk opened. After a 'thank you' was exchanged Wade approached the large familiar hand-carved doors. The door opened and the butler showed Wade past the foyer into the library room where he and Don Carlos had met so many times in the past.

Don Carlos came through the double library doors with outstretched arms and a smile.

"It is so good to see you my friend. I have so much to tell you but first we must have a glass of fine wine to toast," Don Carlos said. The butler was back with a wine carafe and two glasses on a silver tray.

"To you my friend, who has made all of this possible," Don Carlos extended the toast. They touched glasses and drank. Wade could see Don Carlos had his story of everything and it would be good to sit back and let him tell the story his way. There would be time to cover some remaining delicate points later in the evening.

"It is you my friend who did all the heavy lifting here to make everything work. I just merely stumbled on a need that wasn't being handled properly," Wade replied.

"You are far too modest. My attorney has already acknowledged how clever your mind was in this matter," Don Carlos replied.

"I merely gave your honorable attorney a few suggestions which he implemented with great skill," Wade replied.

"All of the buses have been arranged for the pick-up the day after tomorrow. I know the owner of the bus company who is supplying the buses and I told him I wanted new, very clean buses," Don Carlos said.

"That's wonderful. I am certain the children will get a great deal out of the festival," Wade replied.

"I am told the children are singing their recitals every day. I even saw it through my church channels that the children have new clothes to wear," Don Carlos explained.

"That's wonderful," Wade replied.

Don Carlos insisted that Wade stay for dinner as he continued to describe the details of what he had done behind the scenes with the church. The two retired back to the library for an after dinner drink. When the level of discourse slowed to a quieter pace, Wade broached the topics he felt he needed Don Carlos' involvement.

"May I share with you a few concerns I still have?" Wade asked respectfully.

"But of course," Don Carlos responded.

"My concern is what happens to these children after the festival. They are going back into the same dirty hands," Wade asked implying Ocholo but without raising the offensive name in his house.

"I have been thinking about that as well my son. In fact the Cardinal has given me assurance he is looking into a new permanent home for them," Don Carlos answered.

"Good. I also raised this concern with Roberto, your attorney. In fact he even prepared some documents for the transfer of those two facilities," Wade explained.

"Yes, he told me about it but I don't know what would make the current owner make such a decision. He is very greedy and difficult to deal with," Don Carlos responded.

"I know. It will only come if enough pressure can be exerted on the current owner. Toward that end I have contacted friends in my country's intelligence services. They are analyzing it now. In either case we still have to find a solution for the children."

"I agree. Let me work on this from the church side. Please continue your efforts. Perhaps God has a solution," Don Carlos said.

"I am sure he does," Wade replied.

After the meeting ended Wade didn't return directly to his hotel room. Instead he took an observation position on the side of the hill behind the orphanage counting room lights and silhouettes to compare with his prior counts in order to be prepared for the next morning's activities.

Chapter 28
Realta, Argentina

In the absence of certainty, Wade did the only thing he knew how to do, which was stay prepared for the moment his number would be called. Assuming the worst would only demoralize him causing a flawed plan, more risk to Megan, and his own death.

Among Wade's list of uncompleted tasks was to find where Dr. Kemp was being housed and how he was guarded. Despite his long hours at the clinic, at some point in the day or evening Dr. Kemp would leave or be escorted to where he would sleep. It was possible that he resided in the clinic, but Wade's night surveillance of the clinic caused him to think that was not the case.

At 5:30 the next morning Wade was in his clinic hide observing the changing of the guard. Surprisingly, Dr. Kemp was already in his clinic office and making hospital rounds. He watched the guard change and confirmed that neither of the two night guards was responsible for Dr. Kemp.

Diligently Wade stood watch over the clinic most of the day. He took breaks only to call in for status reports, keeping his military radio at his side all the time. Wade's sniper training taught him it was necessary to sometimes wait in narrow confines for days just for one shot. He didn't have days to wait in this case and he knew that at some point Dr. Kemp would grow tired but he also knew that during their internship physicians learned to take small cat naps just to keep going.

Late in the afternoon a tan security car pulled up with a guard Wade had never seen before. The guard armed with only a side arm, went into the clinic. Minutes later the guard and Dr. Kemp came out. They got into the tan sedan and turned

293

down one of the roads leading away and to the west of clinic. Wade got a good fix on their direction and soon followed at a safe distance behind.

The guard and Dr. Kemp pulled into the driveway of a single story house. Wade found a good observation spot partially covered in shrubbery across the street and a block away from his target. His angle with binoculars gave him a good view of the targets. He observed that both men were now inside the house. After a five minute discussion in the living room the doctor retired to one of the bedrooms. The guard came out with a cup of coffee and reclined in a rocker. An hour later the doctor's light turned off and the area around the house became cloaked in dark silence except for two disgruntled cats in dispute.

Wade left the post and headed for his favorite payphone near his hotel to call Yari.

"Yari here."

"It's Wade. I'm getting real nervous here. The buses come tomorrow and I really don't have confirmation of anything," he said in frustration.

"I'm sorry I can't help boss. There's no chatter on the taps. What about your other resources?" Yari replied.

"Still unconfirmed. Everybody is waiting for someone else to make a move," Wade responded.

"What do you do if your troops don't arrive?" Yari asked.

"My three-day window is closing and I don't have a Plan B in place. I don't like the odds but I'm going to have to go in and try the rescue myself," said Wade.

"That's suicide man. What about getting Max down there to help?" Yari asked.

"One man isn't going to help. He has a family and I'm not going to put him against those odds," Wade replied.

"What if I came down with Max?" Yari asked, knowing he wouldn't be much help in the field.

"Thanks man. I appreciate that but I need you where you are. Those com lines mean everything to the mission and me," Wade replied, suggesting they sign off for the next few hours.

Wade tried to sleep that night but was haunted by his uncertain predicament. Yari was right about the slim odds of a mission succeeding without Leo's resources. If this had been any other mission Wade would have objectively assessed the odds and backed down to fight another day. But this was about Megan and Wade felt he could not do that even if it meant his life. She would have done the same for him.

It was three in the morning and Wade gave up on trying to go back to sleep. It was either the restless night or some strong instinct that was calling him to the hill behind the orphanage now. He rarely disobeyed that feeling. Intending to be there anyway in a few hours when the buses arrived he couldn't understand why the call to be there now was so strong.

Wade quickly dressed in his black combat coveralls and gathered his binoculars, military radio receiver and other equipment and headed for the empty lot on the other side of the hill. After concealing his car Wade settled in his covered hillside nest long before sunrise.

His first observation was that the security vehicles normally parked behind the locked gate of the orphanage courtyard were not there. Someone had made a conscious decision to have the vehicles removed for appearance purposes. Wade waited patiently for the morning cadence of the orphanage routines to begin, usually with the nuns going to prayer before dawn. A silhouette headcount served no purpose at this hour of the morning. Moving a few branches and leaves around his hide to prop up his back, Wade settled in for the long wait, leaned back and closed his eyes.

No sooner did his eyes shut than a crackle came across his military receiver. Jolting to an upright position Wade quickly turned down the volume and positioned the antenna for better reception. Another crackle followed by a raspy voice speaking through static. He put the radio to his ear. Even with all the static Wade positively identified the voice as Leo.

"Sparrow to Command do you read, over?"

"Command to Sparrow. I read but you are breaking up, over," Wade replied, pressing the radio firmer against his ear.

"Sparrow to Command. You have Green on Phase 3. Rover proceeding to your location. Do you read?" Leo replied.

"Command to Sparrow. I read, affirmative on Phase 3. Confirming Rover en route to my location. Over," Wade responded.

"Meet Rover at G-7 coordinates at 1700 hours, do you read? Over," Leo replied.

"Command to Sparrow. I read. Confirming meet. Over," Wade replied.

"Sparrow to Command. After meet confirm on secure frequency. Over," Leo replied.

"Command to Sparrow. Confirm and out."

Wade's heart was pounding. In that short radio exchange Wade's life changed. He now had troops on the way and they were back on schedule. His body was flooded with relief. Operation details started filling in those empty spaces he had when he thought his plan had been scratched.

Thinking his plan was going forward at the time, he and Mario had worked out several possible meeting places and coded them before he left Buenos Aires. With the emotion of the moment Wade couldn't remember where the G-7 location was without consulting his notes. Details started racing through Wade's mind. Quickly calculating the driving time to his location, Wade estimated Mario must have left Buenos Aires two hours before Leo's radio call. Wade's relief was short lived. Questions and uncertainty followed. He didn't know how many men Mario was bringing, weapons, equipment or vehicles. Wade didn't know where his men would be staying or if their presence would call unwelcomed attention in the small village. Finally, Wade didn't know if Mario's late arrival would cause him to change the operation plan. Wade's face showed the frustration from having to wait to meet Mario to get answers to his questions.

Above all, Wade knew that Mario's presence would bring some level of competent backup that he didn't have ten minutes ago. He was thrilled at the prospect that he might just come out of this alive. For now Wade turned back to his observation which took on more intensity as a few lights came on to begin the morning prayer ritual in the nun's rectory.

The G-7 coordinates on Wade's coded map were two road crossings three miles outside of town. One road led directly into town, the other headed north and bypassed the larger town where they were staying. There was a service station on one side of the road. Wade arrived a few minutes before 1700. Mario soon arrived and the two men shook hands and gave each other a shoulder hug.

"Man, I'm glad to see you, brother," Wade exclaimed.

"It's a long story. Instead of standing out here, why don't you follow me to our encampment? I'll fill you in," Mario replied.

"Sure," Wade replied.

Mario took the road north away from town. A few miles out of town Mario turned left on a dirt road Wade hadn't known was there. He followed Mario along a dirt road which eventually ran parallel to a small stream bordered on both sides by trees. The trees ended in a cluster which hid a large barn behind them. Mario took a right down another dirt road that led to a large barn. The area surrounding the barn looked empty. Wade noticed one of Mario's men come out from behind a haystack on the side of the barn. He parked his car alongside Mario's vehicle.

The two men smiled and walked towards the entrance to the barn. Wade nodded and smiled to several of Mario's men whom he recognized as they approached.

"Let me show you around," Mario said.

Pointing to a section of the large barn Mario commented, "We turned this section into a command center. The barracks are in the center and we park all the cars inside at the other end so as not to attract attention." Wade was in awe at the completeness of the facility's conversion. Each section included neatly arranged equipment including communication equipment, weapons storage and even a free standing tack board already with maps of the local area attached.

"How in the hell did you ever find this place?" Wade asked.

"Mr. Leopold has his resources," Mario replied, gesturing to two empty chairs to the side of a large table.

"Okay, I really need to know what's going on. When I left Buenos Aires Ocholo had gone to Paraguay and the whole operation was in suspense," Wade summarized, asking to be updated.

"That's true. It turns out that Ocholo is still in Paraguay and his meetings there have to do with consolidating several competing factors in the drug trade from three different countries. It also turns out that Ocholo's presence in the Paraguay meetings is of great interest to Mr. Leopold. He credits you for uncovering those secret meetings," Mario explained.

"He actually told you that?" Wade asked.

"Yes, but he didn't discover it until after you left Buenos Aires," Mario clarified.

"Do the meetings in Paraguay have anything to do with our operation here?" Wade asked.

"No. The meetings in Paraguay have to do with other reasons and operations Mr. Leopold is involved in with Ocholo. Your project simply fell into place as a convenient way for Mr. Leopold to get to Ocholo," Mario replied.

"So Leo was just riding on my project to get to his own end with Ocholo?" Wade asked.

"Well, that's partially correct. You see, Mr. Leopold also sees you in a very favorable light and wanted to help you. At the same time I think he was watching your covert skills carefully in heading this operation," Mario explained.

"Why was he evaluating my skills?" Wade asked with some annoyance.

"He didn't say anything to me. Perhaps he has you in line to head future operations. I don't know," Mario speculated before continuing. "He also found that it was a way to get at Ocholo who has been his target for some time," Mario explained.

"But with Ocholo out of the country Phase 2 of my plan fell apart," Wade replied.

"Initially that is true. But the more Mr. Leopold learned of Ocholo's dealing in Paraguay the better he liked the idea that it came in the middle of your operation," Mario explained.

"I don't get it," Wade replied.

"You see, Mr. Leopold has been able to plant some recording devices in Ocholo's Paraguay meetings and from those recordings and his Paraguay informants Mr. Leopold has learned a great deal about Ocholo's operations," Mario explained.

"Are you involved in the Paraguay operations?" Wade asked.

"No. Mr. Leopold has other operatives who handle that operation. I don't even know who the other operatives are. He tells me very little," Mario responded.

"So now how does Ocholo being in Paraguay affect our operation here?" Wade asked.

"Our operation has the green light to go forward as planned just without Phase Two. We are to make any adjustments here that are needed because of the timing of the children's bus schedule. We are behind in that schedule right now," Mario said.

"I'm not understanding. What do you mean we just skip Phase two and make adjustments to other phases?" Wade asked.

"Yes, it is confusing. Let me explain why he had to make the changes. Mr. Leopold has never had a problem with taking out Ocholo any time he wants. What Mr. Leopold wants is Ocholo alive in order to interrogate him. You see Mr. Leopold's assignment with Ocholo has to do with much larger matters than your operation. He wants information on Ocholo's operations all over the world and he is now getting a lot of that information from the Paraguay meetings," Mario commented before pausing then continued. "He still wants you to come back and complete Phase 2 after Ocholo returns. All I meant about changing our operation here is we have less time to complete Phase 3 and 4. I have a few ideas to discuss with you about how we might change a few things that would allow us to take advantage of the reduced time frame."

"We are in a time bind and I needed eyes two days ago in several places. The buses picked up the children and nuns on schedule this morning. I have located Dr. Kemp's residence. He only has one guard watching him. Most of the security vehicles have been moved away from the orphanage and clinic, I assume for appearance. We need to find out where those vehicles are and what complements of security are still in place," Wade responded.

"My men and I are at your disposal and ready to go into action," Mario replied.

"I need to hear your ideas on any changes. We really need to get to work. There is little time," Wade said with urgency in his voice.

The two men exchanged ideas for almost an hour before Wade decided to stop talking and showed Mario and one of his men to his observation points thinking that actually seeing them was far better than looking at maps, diagrams and notes.

As the sun set that afternoon the men met at the barn to discuss what they saw at Wade's two hides. Mario gave instructions to his crew in Spanish as Wade went over operational details in preparation for the interdiction of Dr. Kemp as called for in Phase 3 of the plan.

At 10:00 p.m. Mario appeared from the barracks in the black, hooded ninja outfit he had worn at Monte Lamar. He handed Wade similar clothing and jokingly commented that they had been cleaned following the prior operation. As Wade changed, Mario gave instructions to his team on various evening surveillance goals and assignments. The group dispersed in different directions as Wade and Mario headed for the car they would use with weapons in hand. Both men knew their assignments, each checking the other to ensure that they had not forgotten anything.

"Is Comset on the right frequency?" Wade asked.

Checking the dial on the two-way Mario replied, "Affirmative."

"Do we have the ties and restraints?" Wade asked.

Mario replied, "Affirmative."

"Are silencers affixed?" Wade asked.

Mario replied, "Affirmative."

"Is your radio patch in place?" Mario asked.

"Affirmative," Wade replied followed by, "Let's go."

They approached the Kemp residence on foot, having parked in an empty lot two blocks away. The house was dark except for the porch light. Under that light sat the armed security guard in his rocking chair. A cup of coffee rested on one arm of the rocker barely being held by the guard. His Uzi rested across his chest. The guard was not asleep but in a very relaxed state.

Using only hand signals Mario and Wade split up. Wade took the back of the house near Dr. Kemp's bedroom, crouching behind the rear screen door waiting for Mario's signal.

Mario approached the guard from the side of the house closest to his rocker. Suddenly a dog barked on an adjacent property causing the guard to turn his head. In two quick movements Mario leaped to the porch level and cleared the railing, placing a strap around the guard's neck from behind. With his free hand he locked the safety of the Uzi and blocked the trigger housing with his fingers before the guard could respond. The strap tightened until the guard's body fell limp from lack of oxygen. Mario released the body to the floor making as little noise as possible. He turned to his shoulder mic stating, "Position 1 secure."

On signal Wade picked the rear door lock and entered turning right from the kitchen to Dr. Kemp's bedroom. Mario dragged the body of the guard inside and joined Wade in the hallway. They signaled each other to enter in low profile just in case Dr. Kemp had awakened and was armed. Mario quietly twisted the handle.

Wade entered low, ready to fire if he had to. Dr. Kemp was dead asleep. Wade waved Mario to enter. After checking bedside tables for arms the two masked men stood over Dr. Kemp.

"Dr. Kemp, we need you to wake up slowly," Wade said in a calm voice.

Kemp didn't move. Wade bent down and put his hand on Dr. Kemp's shoulder and gently shook it several times repeating, "Dr. Kemp, we need you to wake up slowly please." Kemp awoke from a deep sleep. When his mind and eyes cleared from his dream he immediately lunged upright in the bed.

"Do not be concerned about these masks Dr. Kemp. They are for our own security. We are here to rescue you from Ocholo. Your wife and children have been rescued and are waiting to see you."

Chapter 29

Dr. Kemp sat up in bed gathering his thoughts. He started asking questions in rapid succession.

"Where did you say you were from?" Kemp asked indignantly.

"We are an intelligence security force working for the Argentina government but cannot disclose anything further than that," Wade responded.

"Do you have some form of identification?" Dr. Kemp asked.

"We are part of a secret intelligence force and don't carry formal identification," Wade replied.

"You claim to have my wife and children. Where are they?" Dr. Kemp asked.

"Your wife and children are now at our safe house in Buenos Aires. They were rescued from Ocholo's estate in Monte Lamar," Wade replied, seeing that the reference to the Monte Lamar location helped.

"If you have my wife what is her name and the name of my children?" Dr. Kemp demanded.

"Your wife's name is Kimberly and your two daughters are Clara and Sofia," Wade continued. "Rather than you asking me these questions I think it would be best that you speak with them. We have arranged for a secure telephone call so you can do that. You will know her voice and if we are telling you the truth." Wade replied and signaled Mario to dial in the number. He waited until the call went through Yari's international patch to the safe house. He handed the phone to Mario who spoke to his man that answered and gave him a code in Spanish, then handed the phone back to Wade.

304

"Ms. Kemp, I am the gentleman who rescued you at Monte Lamar. I am here with your husband who we just rescued. I would like to put him on the line," Wade heard Kimberly starting to cry. He handed the phone to Dr. Kemp.

"Are you all right, honey?" Dr. Kemp asked.

"Where are you?"

"How are the children?"

The call lasted for five minutes and served its purpose. Dr. Kemp consoled his wife and spoke to each of his children. As the call ended Dr. Kemp handed the radio back to Wade, visibly moved by the experience.

He turned to look at Wade and Mario and said, "Thank you. You have no idea how much this means to me."

"You're welcome, Dr. Kemp, but now we have to move," Wade replied.

"What do you want me to do?" Dr. Kemp asked.

"We need you to get dressed and come with us. We will be happy to assist you gather your belongings while you're getting dressed. Just tell us what you need. You won't be coming back here," Wade replied.

The doctor hurriedly pulled out clothes he was going to wear and pointed to a suitcase in the closet. He gave general instructions as to where to find his belongings while he went into the bathroom to change.

Wade and Mario went through drawers and closets throwing everything they found into the suitcase and plastic bags. Mario radioed for a clean-up team for the body and car removal.

As they left the bedroom Dr. Kemp saw the body of his former guard. He turned to Wade and said, "I hated that pig."

Mario was pulling up with the car as Wade and Dr. Kemp left through the rear door carrying the suitcase and bags of belongings. As the car headed away from his residence, joy and anticipation started to emerge from Dr. Kemp. He was more talkative wanting to know more details about everything. Wade and Mario kept speaking in a moderate calming tone.

"I assume the drive will be taking a few hours to Buenos Aires?" Dr. Kemp exclaimed.

"You will be going to Buenos Aires tomorrow. Right now we are headed for the clinic," Wade explained.

"What? You didn't tell me anything about that. What are you guys up to?" Dr. Kemp asked.

"There is a matter of some documentation and files that need to be handled. It won't take very long," Wade replied.

"There are guards at the clinic twenty four hours a day. You're going to get us killed," Dr. Kemp responded.

"By the time we get there those guards will have been neutralized," Wade replied.

"You mean just like my guard?" Dr. Kemp responded.

"That's right. Just like your guard," Mario replied, causing Dr. Kemp to sit back in his seat with most of his excitement gone. He held his hand to his chin in deep thought, staring out into the night sky without making a sound.

Mario pulled over to the side of the road and used the two-way radio on the front seat. In seconds he got a coded reply. "We are clear to approach," Mario stated. He pulled up to the front door of the clinic. One of his men had already unlocked it from the inside and turned on the lights. The two guards had been neutralized. One was lying on the ground crossways as Wade led the way to Dr. Kemp's office.

"Here's what I need Dr. Kemp. I'll say it once and I want you to take my words very seriously if you want to see your wife and kids again," Wade explained as he watched Dr. Kemp's face turn from apprehension to fear.

"We know that you are conducting shadow cell experiments here on these children." Dr. Kemp started to interrupt but Wade put his hand up silencing him. "I don't need you to talk, just listen right now."

"What I want is all of your documentation on those studies and any information you have on the original studies from the German scientist Dr. Schultz. I want every bit of the documentation in this clinic. Do you understand?" Dr. Kemp started to speak. Wade interrupted, "Answer my question. Do you understand?" Wade asked with emphasis.

"Yes," Kemp replied immediately. "May I explain?" Dr. Kemp followed. "I have been trying to explain that I did everything in my power to try to slow down those experiments. I did so risking my own life. I want you to understand I was here against my will. Ocholo threatened my wife and children. He is a murderer and would kill them if I didn't comply," Dr. Kemp pleaded.

"Dr. Kemp, I understand all of that and in fact am sympathetic to your cause. If I didn't believe that, you would not be alive. I am not the person to judge your actions. I am here to collect the documents and specimen samples and to get you back to your wife and children. Do you understand?"

"Yes," Dr. Kemp exclaimed.

"Then where are the documents?" Wade demanded.

Dr. Kemp immediately turned to the credenza behind his desk and unlocked it. "Here are the most recent progress reports on the current experiments." Dr. Kemp started to lift out a single report.

Wade motioned to Mario and said, "We need everything." Mario's man pushed Dr. Kemp back and unloaded his entire credenza on top of the desk.

"If this is the documentation on the current studies, where is the documentation on the past studies?" Wade demanded.

"They are kept in the file room," Dr. Kemp responded.

"Show us," Wade instructed. Dr. Kemp led them to the file room.

Mario instructed his men to clean out the several five-drawer metal filing cabinets saying, "Keep them in order and box them."

"Now where are Dr. Shultz's original formulations and studies?" Wade asked.

"They are kept in the safe in the basement. I have one copy here and Mr. Ocholo has the originals in his home safe." Wade and Mario followed Dr. Kemp to the basement. On the way down Mario motioned two of his men to follow. They approached the basement door and Dr. Kemp took out a key and inserted it. Wade signaled Mario to be ready.

"Is there anyone in this room?" Wade asked.

"There shouldn't be at this hour," Dr. Kemp replied.

With Wade and Mario on each side of the door Wade instructed Dr. Kemp, "When it is unlocked open it wide and look inside before you enter."

Dr. Kemp complied and stood in the doorway looking in. "I told you there is no one here," Dr. Kemp replied.

"Are the lights always on in this room?" Wade asked knowing the answer from his previous observations.

"Yes," Dr. Kemp replied.

"Why?" Wade asked.

"Some staff have injured themselves tripping over things in the dark. So we keep the lights on all the time."

"Where is the safe?" Wade asked.

"In that corner," Dr. Kemp responded, pointing to a location on the other side of the room.

Mario stepped out to see around the corner and confirmed to Wade that it was clear. "Proceed to the safe," Wade instructed as the two men followed, doing their own surveillance of the room behind their sidearms.

"Do you know the combination?" Wade asked.

"Yes, of course," Dr. Kemp replied.

"Mario, please write those numbers down as he turns," Wade instructed.

"What else is in this safe?" Wade asked as Dr. Kemp turned the knob on the large black state of the art safe.

"We have some salary information and personnel records on our staff." As Dr. Kemp answered as he pulled back one of the heavy doors.

"What else?" Wade asked.

"I have some of my notes on Professor Shultz's experiment that I thought were in error," Dr. Kemp replied.

"I want everything," Wade replied, turning to Mario who instructed his men.

"You said the original set of these were in Mr. Ocholo's safe. Is that correct?" Wade asked. "Where exactly is that safe?"

"He has a fake panel behind his desk that slides into the wall when the button is pushed," Dr. Kemp responded.

"Where is the button for the sliding wall?" Wade asked.

"I think he has one under his desk and another one on hidden in a side wall to the right of his desk," Dr. Kemp responded.

"How do you know he keeps the originals in the safe?" Wade asked.

"Because I was there. When he first hired me he showed me the originals and I told him I would need to have a copy if I was going to replicate the experiments," Dr. Kemp explained.

"Go on," Wade replied.

"I spent about an hour with the originals in his office. He said he would have copies made and send them to me here but I was to keep them in the safe at all times," Dr. Kemp replied.

"As far as you know there were a total of just two copies?" Wade asked

"That is my understanding," Dr. Kemp replied.

"Do you happen to know the combination of Ocholo's safe?" Wade asked.

"No sir, I do not," Dr. Kemp replied.

As they walked up from the basement Wade asked Dr. Kemp general questions about what went on in various rooms of the clinic. Mario's men soon finished boxing up all the documents and left through the back door. He instructed one man to stay behind and make sure nothing was out of place before he turned out the lights and left.

Walking to the car Dr. Kemp turned to Wade and asked, "I've given you everything you asked. What happens to me now?"

"We will blindfold you for a short trip to our safe house here. You will then go with one of the men to your wife and children at the safe house in Bueno Aires, just like I told you," Wade replied.

Dr. Kemp let out a sigh of relief. "Thank you," he said.

Wade turned and said, "You're welcome."

"Can you tell me what happens to my family after I get back?" Dr. Kemp asked.

"That may take some time and it depends on what happens to Ocholo. You may have to answer questions with authorities about your role here. That's when you can explain your actions. You will be given instructions when it is safe to return to a normal life," Wade answered.

"That is still much better than the life I was leading here," Dr. Kemp responded.

Mario and Wade took their masks off and watched a blindfolded Dr. Kemp get in the passenger seat and leave the barn with a driver back to the safe house in Buenos Aires. They went in and sat down to a meal at the barn, both a little worn from the night's mission.

As they ate Mario asked, "I wonder what will happen to Dr. Kemp?"

"If this experience has taught him anything he might want to go work in a clinic helping children," Wade replied.

"That would be a nice ending for his family and his life," Mario commented.

"Things don't always work out that way but sometimes they do," Wade replied.

Getting up from the table Mario stated, "We'd better get some shut eye. We've got a big day tomorrow."

Wade replied, "I'm already asleep."

Chapter 30

Members of various assault teams stirred in the operations barn early the next morning. Wade greeted Mario on the way to mess. The short line ended with a plate of scrambled eggs, toast and coffee. The two men sat together.

"You know last night might really work well with the changes we have planned for today," Mario commented.

"Are you holding out on me or am I just slow? What changes?" Wade asked.

"I just took a page from your book," Mario replied.

"What the hell are you talking about?" Wade asked annoyed by the game Mario seemed to be playing.

"The book on acting. You know the act you pulled on me at Monte Lamar with the robbery idea," Mario replied.

"Are you playing some kind of game here?"

"No. I'm dead serious," Mario replied.

"Well you'd better start telling me what you have in mind. We're about to leave on this mission," Wade said, somewhat annoyed.

"Look, I was sharing this idea with Mr. Leopold and he said he liked the idea of Dr. Kemp being part of why we are showing up at the clinic," Mario explained.

"You mind telling me what this idea is all about?" Wade asked, frustrated.

"It's better if I show you. Let's go to my bunk," Mario replied.

The two men put their trays back and Wade followed Mario to his blanket-enclosed chamber. He bent over at the trunk and pulled out two official officer's uniforms of the Argentina Army, medals and all.

Staring at the uniforms Wade replied, "That's nice but I

don't get it."

"They're authentic down to the last thread," Mario said.

"Okay, so they are authentic. I still don't see where they come in." Wade replied.

"Look. The most difficult problem we have today is getting through the front door of the clinic. The current plan calls for us to shoot our way in. I think with a little acting and these uniforms I can get us inside, in fact, through the entire facility," Mario replied.

"We have to talk. I think you've been hitting the booze or something. You don't modify an operational plan at the last minute unless you absolutely have to," Wade said.

"This is just a slight modification of the plan. We can still shoot our way in if it doesn't work," Mario reasoned.

Wade turned away, shaking his head in disbelief. "You don't just spring this on me minutes before we execute," he stated emphatically.

"If you don't like my idea we'll do it your way. It's your operation," Mario responded

"Give me a minute to think." Wade tried to visualize the scene. He ran through multiple possible responses from Captain Ruso and his men. If they responded negatively there would be a blood bath on the steps of the clinic. If Mario pulled it off they would be inside and in control.

"You'll have to do all the talking. He'll pick up immediately on my accent," Wade commented.

"That's not a problem. Look I had six years in the Argentine military taking orders from colonels. I know how they think, act and order subordinates around," Mario commented.

"I'm going to have to be in additional disguise. Remember Captain Ruso saw me on the tour," Wade explained.

"You would look good with a mustache. Keep your brim down over your eyebrows, he won't recognize you," Mario commented. "If the ruse works I'm going to need you to provide directions. I've never been inside the clinic but you have. Just don't speak." Mario insisted. "We can use hand signals.

"I'll try to stay behind the captain," Wade replied, getting more comfortable with the approach.

"So do you want to get into uniform or try it your way?" Mario asked.

"Okay. Let's try it your way," Wade replied.

"I think it's worth the risk," Mario stated.

"I hope so for the sake of you and your men," Wade replied as the two men started to change into their military uniforms.

Two Argentine army military staff cars decked out with appropriate stickers followed Mario's car which had a blue starred colonel's flag on the bumper. The convoy proceeded down a dusty road from the barn headquarters to the two lane highway leading to the medical clinic. The cars boldly parked in front of the clinic in formation behind the colonel's vehicle. Wade and the men exited their vehicles first and formed a regimental platoon standing shoulder to shoulder in the parking lot.

Slowly the driver of the colonel's car came around and opened Mario's door. Mario's pressed uniform and insignias shimmered in the sun. He turned to his platoon and ordered the men to parade rest. He did a formal about-face and headed firmly to the front clinic door. As he approached the two Ruso guards came to attention and saluted with guns at their side. The colonel saluted in reply. Mario turned to his squad and signaled. Wade and one other man broke rank and double timed it near the colonel and stood at attention.

Colonel Mario approached the Ruso men with a commander's firmness in his eyes. "We are here on official business to see a Dr. Kemp," Mario ordered.

Without hesitation the higher ranking Ruso guard replied "Yes sir," and immediately turned to go inside the clinic. Mario stared down the second guard showing his annoyance of being inconvenienced by even a moment of wait. The guard inside returned and reported, "Sir, I am advised that Dr. Kemp is not at the clinic."

"How long has the clinic been open?" Mario asked.

"The clinic is open at 8:00 a.m., sir," the guard replied.

"And it is now two hours past that time, sergeant," Mario responded.

"Yes sir, but that is what I was told," the guard answered.

"That is unacceptable Sergeant. Who is in charge here?" Mario barked out.

"My commander. Captain Ruso, sir," the guard replied.

"I want to see your Captain Ruso immediately," the Colonel ordered.

"Yes sir," the guard replied and turned back through the clinic door.

The colonel paced in front of the door showing increasing annoyance as the second guard avoided eye contact. Soon the door opened. Standing in the doorway, in his brown khaki uniform and officer's hat was the robust frame of Captain Ruso.

"Colonel, welcome to the Realta Medical Clinic. I am Captain Umberto Ruso at your service, sir," the Captain said showing a welcoming smile.

"I am here on official business to see Dr. Kemp," Colonel Mario replied.

"But of course. I have sent one of my men to find him. Would you please come in? Can I get you and your men some refreshments?" Captain Ruso replied, gesturing for the Colonel and his two men to follow him into the clinic.

"Please come into my office. We should not have a long wait," Ruso replied.

Mario and his two soldiers entered the large office of Captain Ruso. The captain closed the door behind them for privacy.

"Please have a seat," Captain Ruso offered.

"We can stand, it has been a long trip from Buenos Aires," Colonel Mario responded.

Ruso tried to lighten the wait by bringing up his background in the same military.

"I was with the army for many years before my retirement, Colonel. If you don't mind me saying it was rare in my time for anyone to make Colonel at such a young age. Your achievements must have been great," Ruso commented.

"In the new Army the focus is on merit and not on political connections," Mario snapped back.

"But of course, Colonel. That is the way it should be," Ruso replied.

"Why is Dr. Kemp not at the clinic, Captain?" the colonel asked firmly.

"Well, I am as surprised as you are Colonel. He is usually one of the first people here and the last to leave," Ruso replied and continued, "If you don't mind me asking Colonel, what is your business with Dr. Kemp? Perhaps I can help." There was a pause as the Colonel stiffened his expression.

"I am here to arrest him," the colonel replied, as Ruso pulled his head back in surprise.

"Arrest him? I do not understand, sir?" Ruso pleaded, hoping for some explanation.

Mario slowly reached into his coat pocket and pulled out an official document which he began to slowly unfold under Ruso's view. The document was an official military ARREST WARRANT. The document was legal size parchment with all the official government stamps affixed.

Ruso's expression changed to very serious concern. Mario allowed him to briefly glance at the numerous charges which continued for several pages before folding it back into his coat pocket.

"These are very serious charges, sir. Let me go out and see if my man is back with any news of Dr. Kemp," Ruso volunteered.

"One of my men will go with you." Mario nodded for his man to accompany Ruso. The two men soon returned to the room.

"Colonel sir, my man reports that Dr. Kemp is not at his residence and one of my men who is usually with him and our vehicle is not there either. It is possible they are out running errands and will be here shortly," Captain Ruso reported to the colonel.

"That is not an acceptable story Captain. You are in charge of this facility and I cannot be certain you are not hiding him here," the colonel exclaimed in a stern voice.

"But Colonel, that is not possible."

Colonel Mario interrupted. "I have heard enough. Captain Ruso you are under arrest. We will search this facility and if we find Dr. Kemp you will be brought up on charges for hiding a federally-accused suspect." Turning to his men Mario ordered, "Take his weapon and bind him."

The barrel of Wade's weapon pressed into Captain Ruso's back as the other soldier cuffed him. When the captain was secure they turned to walk out his office door.

Mario then commented firmly, "I suggest you tell your men to stand down or I will bring in the rest of my troops who are just outside these premises. If there is any trouble with your men I will tell my men to make sure you are the first to fall."

"Yes sir," the Captain replied.

As the men walked down the hallway with the captain bound between them, Ruso's men reacted in surprise and uncertainty not knowing if they should come to his defense. As they turned down the hallway in search of Dr. Kemp a few of the guards assembled in a group at the cross section of two hallways. The group blocked the hallway to the right brandishing their submachine guns in the ready position. Mario's procession moved to within fifteen feet of the gathered men and came to a stop.

"This would be a good time to speak," Mario advised Ruso as Wade pressed his weapon firmly in Ruso's back.

Ruso exclaimed in a strong authoritative voice, "You are not to take any action these military men or you will pay a severe penalty if you do. This is an official investigation dealing with Dr. Kemp. Stand down and lower your weapons. Do you understand me?" the captain exclaimed.

Ruso's men obeyed and quickly backed down. A few quietly turned and left the building through a side door.

Mario turned to Wade for directions. Wade nodded to a direction behind Ruso's back. Mario followed Wade's direction.

"Let's go this way," the colonel ordered.

As they proceeded Wade and Mario saw more of Ruso's troops moving down the hallways away from the procession. Several doors were opened and Captain Ruso's torso was pushed through first in case of return fire. The rooms were either empty or occupied by administrative personnel who shuddered at the sight of Captain Ruso in custody. Wade signaled a different direction to Mario. He had mistaken the hallway with the laboratory rooms and where he might find Megan. They had to backtrack and go down another corridor.

Just as they approached the hallway where the labs were housed, gun shots rang out nearby.

Mario handed the captain to Wade and pointed to a corner out of earshot. Wade took the captain and pushed him to his knees, keeping his semi-automatic near his temple. Mario instructed his other team member to have the platoon disperse to both sides of the building and return fire.

"Yes sir," the team member replied and turned to run to the front door to give the order.

Submachine gun fire at the back of the building increased. Mario turned to the captain and said "Your men have committed a grave error by not following your orders, Captain. I will hold you personally responsible for these acts." Pulling the captain to his feet the colonel asked affirmatively, "Where is the closest rear door to the building?"

The Captain nodded to the next hallway indicating to the right when they reached that point.

Grabbing each of the captain's arms Mario and Wade hurriedly pushed the captain down the hallway to the large doorway at the back of the building. When several rounds hit the door they all fell to their knees on the side of the doorframe, listening to the rapid fire firefight on the other side of the door.

Mario could feel the captain trembling.

"My men are stupid for not following my orders," the captain said.

"This will be you chance to test your training skills," Mario replied.

"You cannot open that door Colonel. I will be killed," Captain Ruso replied.

"Only if you fail to be convincing," the Colonel replied.

Mario nodded to Wade to open the door. Wade gingerly slipped his hand up the door frame reaching to pull down the silver handle. The door released its grip on the frame. Lying flat on the floor Wade edged the door to a slight crack getting a partial glimpse of the scene before him.

Chapter 31

Ruso's men had taken cover behind vehicles and large drainage pipes stacked at the rear of the lot. Mario's men were split holding positions against both sides of the building. Wade described the scene and positions of men to Mario using sign language while Captain Ruso looked on. Mario acknowledged that he understood with a nod.

The rear door was four feet above the surface of the parking lot grade and opened on to a concrete landing with side stairs. A pipe railing surrounded the landing. Huddled near the doorjamb the three men listened as the firefight went back and forth with rapid bursts coming from both sides. Several rounds pinged the door edge and concrete block building.

"Your men are pinned against the rear lot and my men will soon be receiving reinforcements," Mario said describing what he hoped would appear as a hopeless situation to the Captain.

"I told you they were stupid," the captain explained.

"They are either stupid or untrained under your command," Mario replied. "When the fire pauses you will have a chance to stand out there and train them," Mario commented.

The Captain recoiled with fear. "You cannot do that to me. You see they don't follow my orders," he exclaimed.

"You will stand there trying to convince your troops to lay down their arms or die right here. Do you understand that?" the colonel explained.

"Yes sir, I will do my best," the captain replied.

"Good. Concentrate on what you are going to be saying," Colonel Mario instructed.

"Yes sir," the captain exclaimed trying to collect his thoughts.

The next five minutes seemed like an eternity for the captain as short bursts of fire from both directions continued. Overall the fire fight seemed to be cooling off. During one of the pauses Mario and Wade brought the captain to his feet each holding one of his trembling arms.

Wade gave a sign to Mario that he would hold the captain's cuffed hands crouched behind him while Mario tried to assess the field of battle looking out from inside the door frame. Mario nodded in agreement.

During a pause in fire Wade pushed open the door to an avalanche of sunlight filling the hallway. As the Captain offered moderate resistance. Wade pushed from the back until the Captain stood waist high at the railing exposed to his men and the military units on each side of the building.

"Attention! Attention!" the Captain spoke in a loud commanding voice.

Mario jumped back and forth to both sides of the door frame. He saw four dead bodies of the captain's men lying on the ground and one of his own men wounded and bleeding badly.

The Captain who saw the same scene exclaimed, "I am ordering you men to cease fire and come forward with your weapons opened," the Captain continued, "Our facility is being inspected by the Argentine military. Any men resisting my orders will be severely punished by me and then turned over to the military for prosecution." He paused, and there was no fire but none of his men were coming forward.

"Attention! This is Captain Ruso and this order applies to all of my men. Immediately come forward and turn yourselves over to the Colonel's men. You will not be harmed if you obey my orders now," the Captain ordered.

There was a pause and awkward moment of silence over the back parking lot. Several of the captain's men were seen whispering among themselves trying to decide. The Captain remained calm but nervous. If a fire fight broke out now he would be the first shot. Wade could feel his legs almost giving away at the knees.

Both sides held their ready positions for what seemed like an eternity. One of Ruso's men who had taken cover behind a drainage culvert was the first to show himself with his hands raised above his head. He started walking forward to the open area between the two opposing forces, stepping over the bodies of his own fallen men.

A second man in Ruso's troop followed. A third then a fourth man followed suit. Mario's men relaxed and took the weapons from Ruso's men as they approached the deadman space between the two positions, stepping over the lifeless bodies of their fellow guards. The colonel's men set up a guarded circular perimeter on the side of the building placing Ruso's men inside as they surrendered.

Wade walked the captain backward from the platform through the door and allowed him to sit, collapsing as he hit the floor. Mario assumed the captain's position on the platform ordering medical attention for his wounded man. Two men lifted the wounded man, moving him to the front of the clinic where nurses treated his wounds on a gurney. Mario ordered his man Miguel in through the rear door to assist with the Captain, giving him instructions to follow behind him and Wade as they secured the interior of the clinic. Miguel lifted the weakened Captain Ruso as Mario moved forward to join

323

Wade, who was already at the cross section of the next hallway.

As Mario approached, Wade turned and said pointing to the hallway, "Down this hallway are the labs where I think they are holding Megan."

"I'll follow you," Mario replied.

Before they took their second step submachine gun fire broke out in the area Wade had just designated. Wade kept low and quickly moved down the hallway to the two doors he suspected where they would find the medical technicians. He wasn't sure which door to open first. A mistake could be costly. His mind jumped back and forth trying to remember what he had seen in a brief glimpse during his inspections while Mario looked at Wade's puzzled face.

Wade gave signals using hand sign codes saying both should enter low. Mario was to roll right first and Wade was to follow rolling left. Both would have to shoot upward from an awkward prone position. Mario nodded in agreement. Slipping his fingers up to the handle and being uncertain if the door was locked from the inside. Wade quietly turned the silver knob until he could hear it release from the door guard. He nodded to Mario that it was unlocked. Mario returned the nod. Wade silently counted mouthing each number 3, 2, 1.

The door opened and Mario did a fast even roll to the right followed by Wade to the left of the room. Their first sight was of two dead bodies of Captain Ruso's guards, one female and one male lying permanently silent on the floor beside them. Wade turned and saw the white feet and pants of five women standing in the far corner.

"We are friendly," shouted Wade. "Megan, are you there? This is Wade Hanna."

There was no response. Wade looked up between the supports of the laboratory table. He got a better view but all of the technicians were dressed in white-clad medical garments with mask over their faces. One was holding a semi-automatic weapon. Mario lay in a prone position on the opposite side of the room behind one of the dead guard bodies. His gun was pointed toward the indistinguishable group of women.

"Megan, this is Wade Hanna. You and the women are safe now."

Realizing he had his disguise mustache on, Wade immediately ripped it off.

"I'm going to stand up now with my hands in the air without my weapon. Please let me know that you understand what I just said."

He turned to look at Mario, who was shaking his head back and forth, "No".

The whimper of a response came back, "Okay". Wade took the chance and slowly got to his knees then to his feet without lowering his hands.

After all this time Wade finally set eyes on Megan who stood protective in front of the other women ready for another firefight. She turned to the other women giving them the okay to relax. Wade walked around the lab table to Megan's side.

"You okay?" Wade asked.

"We're fine now," Megan responded, then smiled.

One of the other techs said, "She saved us", pointing to Megan. "The guards were going to kill us."

Mario soon joined the group and Wade introduced him.

"Our men have all of Ruso's men contained and are now sweeping the clinic for any holdouts," Mario explained. "You may want to join the rest of the clinic employees who are being guarded by my men."

The women acknowledged and were proceeding to the door when Wade turned to Megan. "It's not quite over. We still have the orphanage to clear," Wade commented.

Shaking her head in understanding she responded, "Do you need me to help clear the orphanage?"

"I think we are fine. Just not sure how many men Ruso has there now," Wade responded.

"Thank you for being here. It was getting real bad," Megan replied as Wade turned to leave the room. "Wait, there is a sick boy on the second floor of the orphanage," Megan said in anguish.

"I'll remember. Thanks," Wade replied as he left to join Mario.

Mario ordered six men to follow with Captain Ruso in tow. Three cars left the clinic for the orphanage. Wade asked Mario, "Do you have a sniper in that hide I showed you?"

"I have two snipers in the hide you showed me already in place," Mario replied.

"I think we should go through the rear fence into the courtyard and let the captain issue another set of orders," Wade suggested.

"Yes, but we need to cover the side and front entrances," Mario replied.

"I agree."

Mario had his man keep Captain Ruso at the car as he huddled his men close to the orphanage side entrance. He dispersed his men to cover the various entrances, telling them of the sick child on the second floor. He radioed his two snipers on the hill at the back of the orphanage and called them to ready position explaining how they should cover. Mario walked over to Captain Ruso as Wade joined them.

"How many men do you have at the orphanage?" Mario asked the captain.

"I do not know now with all of the confusion at the clinic. Some of the men have come back here," Ruso replied.

"That may be unfortunate for you, Captain," Mario responded.

"But Colonel, how can you expect me to keep track of my men when I am in your custody?" the captain pleaded.

"Very simple, you know how many men are dead or captured at the clinic and you know how many total men you have. It should be a simple matter for you to estimate how many men are left here," Mario replied.

The Captain shrugged his shoulders. "Perhaps five or six men here," the captain replied.

"Let's hope you have estimated correctly because here is what is going to happen," Mario stated. The Captain was already developing his fearful expression.

Mario continued, "You will be driven to the center of the courtyard and let out of the car. There you will deliver a command performance asking your men to surrender. If they resist or they don't come out you will suffer the consequences. You see that clump of trees on the hill just outside the orphanage?" Mario pointed and the captain acknowledged with a nod. "One of my snipers is there and the other one is also hidden. They will both have the crosshairs of their scopes trained on you the entire time you are in the courtyard. If your men don't surrender in three minutes from the time you give them the order or they provide resistance my men have their orders that you will be the first shot in the hope that your men know we are serious. Do you understand?" Mario explained.

"Yes sir," Captain Ruso acknowledged.

"Make your speech a good one," Mario encouraged.

The car sped off, turning quickly in a semi-circle to the center of the courtyard. Mario and Wade assumed their positions at the east side entrance of the orphanage to listen to Captain Ruso's command performance. As his handcuffed passenger stepped out of the car and walked to the center of the courtyard his delivery vehicle spun around and left through the gates of the courtyard. Captain Ruso walked a bit to one side then the other clearing his throat. He spoke in a loud theatrical voice so that all three sides of his audience would be able to hear.

"Attention! Attention! This is Captain Ruso speaking. Under my approval we are undergoing an inspection of the orphanage and medical clinic by the Argentine Military. I am giving you orders which must be followed or there will be severe penalties. All of my men come forward in the courtyard with your hands up and surrender your weapons. Do not offer resistance of any kind to these Army personnel." Ruso ordered, "Come to the courtyard now."

The Captain's order produced no visible signs of compliance. The Captain turned and faced the opposing building and restated his orders. Still no one responded. He turned to face the front of the building and repeated his orders. Wade and Mario had no other choice but to ready themselves and their men for a room to room search. They removed the safeties on their weapons. Wade's instincts said to give them another minute which Mario quickly agreed to.

Almost on queue when the minute expired, a single door opened on the opposite side of building and one of the Captain's men appeared in the courtyard with hands above his head. Soon a second man followed and just like the clinic, within minutes the six remaining men surrendered. After the men were searched and cuffed, the caravan left to join the men at the clinic.

When Wade's car stopped at the clinic, he raced to Megan's side telling her that the orphanage had been cleared and the sick boy on the second floor was under a nun's care and doing fine. Megan acknowledged her appreciation and turned to rejoin the clinic staff caring for the wounded. Wade gently grabbed her arm in mid-turn.

"Now that this is almost over I have a nice hotel room in town if you would like to stay there," Wade offered.

"Thanks, but I feel I need to be here with the staff. I hope you understand. It's been a long day," Megan replied.

"Of course I understand. I just thought I would ask," Wade said with a smile.

"Thanks for understanding," Megan replied as she answered a question from one of the staff looking for guidance. When she turned back Wade was already attending to some other matter. Wade lost sight of Mario during all the myriad of details of stabilizing the clinic site. Wade turned back and caught a glimpse of Megan helping others and thought he could be of better use at barn headquarters.

Chapter 32

Back at the barn Wade kept to himself making the assignment list for the men's night guard duty. Mario was busy giving directions to the body clean-up detail and explaining to other men how he wanted the weapons they had just collected disarmed and what they were going to do to quarter the prisoners for the evening. Crossing the room Mario stopped to give instructions to one of his men boxing clinical documents. Wade and Mario met near the center of the barn on their way to separate locations in different directions.

"You want to debrief?" Mario turned to Wade and asked.

"Sure," Wade replied.

"Let's meet in the planning room in fifteen minutes," Mario replied.

"See you in fifteen," Wade confirmed.

The men sat at the table in the makeshift planning room whose walls were blankets hanging from ropes supported by tent posts.

"So what's your take on the day's work?" Mario asked.

"All the innocents are safe, one wounded on our side and five dead on their side. Captain Ruso and his men are in our custody. I would say that qualifies as success by any operational standard," Wade replied.

"Anything you feel we should have been done differently?" Mario asked.

"I wish we would have gotten to the women in the lab sooner. It all turned out okay, but it could have been a disaster," Wade replied.

"I agree. Thanks to your operative friend. Man, she must be something, disarming and eliminating both of the guards singlehandedly," Mario commented.

"Yeah. She's like fifth black belt competitive champion and special ops, hand-to-hand combat instructor," Wade replied.

"Don't ever get her pissed off," Mario warned.

"I try not to," Wade responded.

"Say man, I know you too well and we've been through a lot together. I know when something is bothering you. If you want to talk about it let me know," Mario volunteered as a friend.

Wade responded by changing the subject. "Are you going to give Leo a detailed report?"

"I sure am. I know he'll want details so I'm waiting for my men to give me weapons and document counts. I'll make notes and call him. You want to be part of that call?" Mario asked.

"No, he doesn't need both of us telling him what happened. It sounds better coming from you. He'll call me if he has any questions." Wade paused then continued, "It probably won't come up on your call but I know I still owe him Ocholo. I just want him to know I'm not done until he gets his man."

"My guess is that won't come up on my call but I'll let you know if it does. Is that by chance what's been bothering you?" Mario asked.

"A lot of things are bothering me but I wasn't thinking about Ocholo until just now. I don't want to let Leo down. I'd probably be dead now if you guys weren't here," Wade replied still showing his distant mood.

"Are you going to stay to have chow with us? I assume at some point you're going to spend the night at your nice hotel, hopefully with your girlfriend?" Mario asked.

Wade's head popped up. He turned giving Mario a penetrating stare and snapped "For your information I'll be spending the night alone." Wade left the table disgruntled and headed out of the barn back to his hotel.

Mario thought, *I hit a nerve.*

The next morning Wade found himself driving toward the orphanage instead of the clinic where he intended to make his first stop. His mind was still elsewhere. Reversing direction he headed back to the clinic. Two staff cars were parked in the clinic's front parking lot. Wade could see Mario's men posted on the front, on the sides and at the rear of the building. He parked and got out of the car greeting the duty watch who promptly told him the women technicians were already working in the laboratory.

Wade proceeded to the lab door knowing to knock before he entered. Megan's voice answered. "Who is it?"

"It's me, Wade, can I come in?" Wade asked.

"Are you dressed in sterile operating room scrubs?" Megan asked.

"No, but I did put on clean clothes this morning," Wade answered.

"We're in the middle of sensitive lab procedures. If you want to come in you'll have to put on sterile operating scrubs," Megan said firmly.

"Where do I get operating scrubs?" Wade replied, annoyed.

"Three rooms down on the left there is garment storage and changing room. Just make sure you are completely covered. You're welcome to come in if you're dressed properly," Megan replied.

After going up and down the hallway opening doors Wade finally found the surgical garment room. He followed the instructions on the wall with diagrams on how to properly dress in operating room garb. Soon Wade emerged covered in baby blue hospital scrubs from head to booties.

Walking down the hall he passed three of Mario's men coming the other way. Seeing their fearless operative leader dressed in baby blue scrubs brought smiles to their faces. Wade sneered back at them in response. Complying with instructions, Wade placed a pair of blue covers over his blue stocking feet and knocked. Megan confirmed his dress before opening the door.

Approaching the laboratory table in the center of the room Wade was subjected to more giggles and smiles from the other women. Megan came around to his side and in a more serious tone described the procedures being undertaken.

"We're removing stem cells from the growing test media. That's the white gelatinous material in the petri dish," Megan stated.

"It looks important," Wade replied, not having a clue what he was observing.

"It's very important. With those cells plus the addition of other proteins we can grow shadow cells," Megan explained.

"How do we get that material out of here?" Wade asked thinking pragmatically.

"My team has come up with a way to suspend the sensitive material in a frozen substrate for transportation. I asked the guards to see if they could find us dry ice. They found an ice cream plant in town and brought back chunks of dry ice," she replied, pointing to the box on the floor with a vapor trail coming out of the top.

"We'll line that box with a sterile material then pack the petri dishes inside surrounded by the dry ice," Megan continued.

"Then what?" Wade asked.

"The box will then have to be flown to Atlanta. That's where I am hoping you come in my dear," Megan responded.

"I can check on flight availability," Wade volunteered.

"I can also contact my intelligence handler here. They supposedly have a military transport close by for these shipments," Megan offered.

"That would be better than me calling the airlines," Wade responded.

"The amount of this sample material going back to Atlanta will be more than they ever expected from me," Megan explained as she moved around the table to help her fellow technicians open the next round of petri dishes.

"So after this specimen material is shipped where do we go from here?" Wade asked.

"We're going to be taking a break in a minute. Let's talk then," Megan responded.

"Sure. Is there anything I can do?" Wade asked loudly enough so that everyone could hear as he stood over the table of delicate high-level procedures he didn't understand.

"Just watch carefully and make sure we don't make any mistakes," Megan replied as the other women chuckled. Wade didn't respond to her comment, already feeling that he was less useful than a doorstop.

A break soon came and Megan guided Wade's arm to a pair of chairs off to the empty side of the room. The technicians grabbed water bottles and grouped in a cluster remaining on the other side of the room.

"I forgot to ask you, whatever happened to Dr. Kemp?" Megan asked.

"We have him in custody. He's at a safe house with his family. Why do you ask?" Wade replied.

"In the end Dr. Kemp turned out to be one of the good guys. He secretly showed us a method using a chemical inhibitor in the formula to cause a delay in the production of shadow cells in the children's bodies." She paused for a moment thinking of the consequences to Dr. Kemp's help.

"He could have easily gotten himself killed for doing that. He risked his life to slow everything down here and I didn't want to see him taken out and shot. That guy really tried to help," Megan explained.

"He's fine. He will probably have to answer some questions with the authorities but I think he will come out fine," Wade replied.

Megan paused, looking deeply into Wade eyes. Her intense stare was making him feel nervous.

"Look, we both have a lot of questions to ask each other and I'm not sure I can deal with that right now. I'm just going to need some time. I hope you understand that," Megan explained, showing the stress on her face.

"We have all the time in the world now. Stop thinking I'm trying to rush you. I'm not. I just know I lost something special in my life and I wasn't sure I would ever have the chance again to tell you that I love you," Wade responded, surprising himself as much as Megan.

"I love you too. That has never been the issue. I've learned so much about myself over these past few months. It's all a big blur right now. I have to sort everything out now that the mission is over. The last thing I need is to put more pressure on myself right now. I've also learned a lot about you during this process," Megan responded holding his arm a little tighter.

"About me?" Wade exclaimed.

"Yes. I thought I knew you. I convinced myself I did, but I was wrong. You are much more than the person I thought I knew," Megan replied, pausing for a moment.

"It gets very complicated. If it's okay with you let's not talk about all this right now," Megan replied

"Sure," Wade responded as her fellow workers waved her back into action resuming the tedious extraction process.

Wade thought to himself, *this break is over.*

As Megan turned to walk back to the table Wade caught her arm. "There's someone I want you to meet. His name is Don Carlos. He and his family played a major part helping these children get free. I need to thank him before I leave the country and I want you to meet him," Wade explained quickly adding, "You don't have to worry, we won't blow our cover."

"When do you want to meet with him?" Megan asked, surprised.

"He's invited me to dinner tonight at 7:00 p.m. I'd like you to join me," Wade replied

"Pick me up at the orphanage at 6:30 p.m., I'll be ready. You can fill in the details on the way," Megan replied smiling.

"I'll be there at 6:30 sharp," Wade replied as he turned to leave the room in a flash of baby blue, waving to the technicians before closing the door behind him.

On the way to the Don Carlos estate Megan and Wade briefed each other on their cover stories.

As the large front door open Don Carlos was waiting in the foyer with open arms. After brief introductions they moved to the library for refreshments.

"So tell me how you came to meet this beautiful young lady," Don Carlos asked.

"I heard about all the commotion at the orphanage and medical clinic with the Army today and stopped by just out of curiosity. Standing outside in her laboratory garments was this American medical technician. We introduced ourselves and started talking. I thought you might like to meet her," Wade explained.

"I am certainly honored to have the pleasure. How did you happen to come to our small town from the U.S?" Don Carlos asked.

"I was just finishing a graduate research project in biochemistry and read this ad for medical technicians. I was intrigued by the lure of international travel and was fortunate enough to be hired by Dr. Kemp at the clinic," Megan explained.

"Well, I hope Argentina has not disappointed you with all this military activity," Don Carlos replied.

"No. Not at all. It's been a wonderful experience. I don't really know anything about the military activities," Megan exclaimed.

"Those activities will soon pass like everything else unpleasant that sometimes passes through Argentina," Don Carlos replied.

"Don Carlos is very modest but I would like him to tell you about the substantial role he played in helping the children at the orphanage," Wade commented.

Pointing to Wade, Don Carlos commented, "You see it is not me but this man who is responsible for bringing the children's problem to my attention. If it were not for his poor wife's barren condition he would not have been looking into the possibility of adoption. That is how everything got started." Don Carlos explained to Megan emphasizing Wade's important role.

The butler knocked and opened the door to tell Don Carlos and guests that dinner was being served.

"Perhaps over dinner Don Carlos will tell you how through his connections with the church he has stepped in and helped the children," Wade stated.

"I can't wait to hear this story," Megan replied.

"I will be happy to tell you the story," Don Carlos replied, gesturing his guests through the door and into the dining room where they were served an elegant five-course meal. Over the wonderful meal Megan heard the details of how the children were saved and what Don Carlos was doing to ensure the children's future safety. After the meal they retired to the library only to be interrupted again by the butler.

"Sir, you have a call from Father Francis. He says it is important," the butler exclaimed.

After thinking about it for a moment Don Carlos said, "Will you please excuse me? This is my evening call from the priest about the children." Don Carlos explained in an apologetic tone.

"By all means, please take the call," Wade stated. "We will go out on the patio. It is a beautiful evening."

Wade walked with Megan to the French doors and opened them leading to the stone patio overlooking the estate. The view was breathtaking. There were miles of plowed fields before them shimmering by moonlight and a beautiful starlit sky above. A small chill was in the evening air. Wade sensed Megan's slight shiver and put his arm around her shoulders. They stood speechless taking in the view before Megan spoke.

"Your barren wife in Canada? I'm sure she can't wait to have children," Megan commented.

Wade smiled. "I had to get in the orphanage somehow," he replied.

"And all this agricultural experience, where does that come from?" Megan asked.

"I've grown my share of plants," Wade replied.

Her face turned to a more serious comment as she inched closer to Wade "You said at dinner you were leaving tomorrow. Did you mean it?" Megan asked.

"Yes, I have unfinished business in Buenos Aires before I leave the country," Wade replied and followed with a question. "What about you?" he asked.

"I spoke with my handler last evening. We have an extraction plan to get me back to the States. They want me to stay undercover for a while after I return to make sure there are no tracers," Megan replied.

"I assume you're not going back to Washington. How will I find you?" he asked, worried that she would soon disappear again.

"I don't know where I'm going to be yet, but the last time I checked they haven't moved Greenstone, Alabama from where it used to be. Don't worry, I'll find you," Megan replied.

Epilogue

Shortly after Wade left Argentina the Buenos Aires newspapers reported that Manuel Ocholo and four bodyguards were missing after a robbery at his large palatial city estate. Missing from his home was an extremely valuable collection of 8th and 9th century religious artifacts and artwork valued in the millions of dollars.

The article suggested that Ocholo's disappearance may have been connected with friction among rival organized crime bosses in the city over drugs and territory. The article went on to say that a major crime investigation was already underway by a joint government agency taskforce. Cited in the article were the names of individuals already arrested and believed to be part of Ocholo's organization. The investigative reporter also suggested that with Ocholo's organization in decline this would be an ideal time for the government to step in quickly before other crime bosses took over his syndicate. Also taken were some historical German studies believed to be connected with early medical treatments.

Intelligence rumors persisted that the original German shadow cell technology was never sold to international third parties buyers. Instead a harmless biochemical formulation claiming to have the same properties as the German original formulation was sold to international buyers as part of a sting operation. The technology was sold by an unknown intelligence organization working on behalf of the United States Government.

The international buyers of the child weapons were said to have been arrested on the spot and are now serving long sentences at several U.S. high security prisons. Ocholo was never seen or heard from in Argentina or anywhere else in the world. Stories circulating around the U.S. intelligence community say that Ocholo was taken to another country for intensive interrogation which he did not survive. However, those rumors could not be confirmed.

Three years after the shadow cell mission Sister Sara Torrez left her duties at the orphanage to live in a home for retired nuns in Buenos Aires. She passed away peacefully in her sleep knowing that her children were safe.

Don Carlos continued with his aid to the orphanage and children and was instrumental in finding a new benefactor for the children. Through fundraising efforts by him the old orphanage was rehabilitated and put back into service supported by a collection of agricultural farms in and around the city of Realta.

Two years after the arrest of Captain Ruso, legal documents signed by Manuel Ocholo assigning the orphanage and medical clinic to the Catholic Church appeared as part of legal pleadings in Argentina high court. The pleadings were made by Roberto Gallos, Esq., Don Carlos' attorney. Handwriting expert testimony confirmed that the signatures of Ocholo were authentic and signed with an engraved pen known to be in Ocholo's possession at the time. The high court approved the assignment without opposition.

Samples of stem cell specimens and protein compounds related to the shadow cell child experiments arrived safely by military transport to Dr. Isaac Palmer for Project 461-C at the U.S. Army Medical Research Institute of Infectious Diseases in Fredrick, Maryland and were used to not only develop a long-term permanent inhibitor to prevent shadow cells from performing carrier functions, but for the project's research leading to curative treatments and vaccines for other serious childhood diseases.

Five years after the shadow cell mission Don Carlos died of a massive heart attack while inspecting one of his agricultural fields. His estate was passed on to his two sons who continue to run the estate today in the Don Carlos tradition.

Wade and Megan did not see each other for some time after that night on the patio of the Don Carlos estate. Friends have reported seeing them walking on the beach in Destin, Florida holding hands. Their current whereabouts and agency affiliation are unknown.

ABOUT THE AUTHOR

Award winning author, Joseph D'Antoni is also a true practicing forensic and economic expert having spent many years testifying in court cases throughout the world. His clients have included the FBI, Department of Justice and various Intelligence Agencies as well as some of the largest law firms in this country.

He holds an undergraduate, masters and doctorate degree and has taught at three major universities. Performing technical analysis and writing legal reports were a regular part of his daily work for many years before exploring popular fiction writing. Inspired by actual case histories he successfully straddles two very different worlds of the courtroom and the suspenseful, fictional world of covert intelligence operatives.

D'Antoni was born and raised in New Orleans, Louisiana and is now living in Southern California. His fictional writing started late in his forty plus year career as a forensic expert. His first book, *Silent Sanction* is about a main character Wade Hanna, who grew up in a difficult home environment in the depths of a Louisiana swamp to eventually become a covert intelligence agent.

The author recently received the acclaimed Irwin Award for the Best Literary Series of 2015. Currently, his writing supplements an active career as a forensic economic expert. The beauty of having been in the forensic field for such a long time is he won't run out of interesting stories for new novels anytime soon. In addition to being a writer in the spotlight he is also a highly acclaimed fine art photographer and artist. His acclaimed photography book, *Louisiana Reflections* is a beautiful example of his artistic accomplishments.

Also by JOSEPH D'ANTONI

LOUISIANA REFLECTIONS

Award winning hard bound fine art book with pristine fine art photographic images of New Orleans and Cajun Country taken before hurricane Katrina.

SILENT SANCTION

The first novel in the Wade Hanna covert intelligence series. A journey through Hanna's formative years in New Orleans as an unwilling mob undercover agent for the NOPD. Seeking refuge from mob retribution Wade finds solace in the deep swamp. He soon joins the Navy submarine service where they confront a Soviet submarine during the Cuban Missile Crisis. As the Vietnam War heats up Wade joins the intelligence service and begins his dangerous career as an international spy.

INVISIBLE MARKINGS
UNDERSEA VOICES

Two short stories provide insight and supplement to the saga of Wade Hanna's ventures in Silent Sanction.

LETHAL AUTHORITY

The second novel in the series finds Wade Hanna at the murder scene of a Special Forces sniper. The initial homicide investigation quickly changes from suicide as the cause of death to a carefully executed murder only made to look like a self-inflicted bullet wound. Hanna follows the lead to the jungles of Belize where he discovers a terrorist plot and the primary murder suspect. Out-gunned and understaffed Wade finds the sinister activities are closer to home and his agency than he ever thought possible.

ROGUE ASSET

A fugitive MI-6 agent has gone rogue by supplying Russian arms to rebels in a West African nation. Wade Hanna accepts the deadly Tangier assignment to stop the arms before they arrive.
His fellow agent and lover, Megan, remains in the dark about his disappearance. Unwelcomed uncertainties greet Wade when he finds his separation from Megan may be permanent at the hands of others he can no longer trust.

Made in the USA
Middletown, DE
05 December 2016